MEMORIAL

FOR

THE

DEAD

By

KATHERINE
PATHAK

THE GARANSAY PRESS

Cover design © Catacol Bay Images, all rights reserved, 2014

Imogen & Hugh Croft Mysteries:

Aoife's Chariot

The Only Survivor

Lawful Death

Full Beam (short story)

The Woman Who Vanished

Memorial for the Dead

This is a work of fiction. Names, characters, businesses, places, events and incidents are either the products of the author's imagination or used in a fictitious manner. Any resemblance to actual persons, living or dead, or actual events is purely coincidental.
All rights reserved. No part of this publication may be reproduced in any form or by any means - graphic, electronic, or mechanical, including photocopying, recording, taping or information storage and retrieval systems - without the prior permission in writing of the author and publishers. Nor be otherwise circulated in any form of binding or cover other than that in which it is published and without a similar condition including this condition being imposed on the subsequent purchaser.

The moral right of the author has been asserted.

© Katherine Pathak all rights reserved, 2014

≈

The Garansay Press

Prologue

February 1943

It was nearly dark as the S.S Minerva, pride of the Ronaldson Line, arrived at its rendezvous point just off the rocky coast of Mull. The liner joined the small convoy of destroyers that would accompany it across the turbulent waters of the north Atlantic.

Captain Douglas Cairns would have loved to be able to report good weather conditions to his passengers and crew, but he could not. A strong easterly wind was battering the ship with rain and spray on its starboard side. Despite the enormous size of his vessel, the Captain predicted they would be in for a rough voyage before reaching their final destination in Saint John, New Brunswick.

Cairns was transporting nearly a thousand troops and several hundred civilians on board the Minerva that particular trip. Although the convoy system had made the route infinitely safer than it was at the very start of the war, Cairns still made a point of crossing himself as the ship proceeded away from the shelter of the Western Isles, surging into the vast emptiness of the Atlantic Ocean.

Regardless of the fading light, Cairns had to keep his vessel blacked out, relying almost entirely on his instruments to maintain the course to Canada. Of serious concern to all shipping which followed this particular route to the Americas, were the Rockall Banks, where a small yet precipitous islet loomed out of the crashing waves and could catch an inexperienced crew unawares. This treacherous outcrop had sunk hundreds of unsuspecting boats over the centuries. Captain Cairns had learnt to steer a passage well to the south of this perilous landmark.

In the encroaching darkness, he began to feel unsure of his previous calculations. Just to be certain, he radioed to the accompanying gunships and suggested they suspend their defensive zig-zag manoeuvres until he was confident the entire convoy was well clear of the rocks.

Ploughing a direct route through the high waves, the Minerva picked up speed. From his elevated position within the wheelhouse, Cairns stared out into the black night. The Captain could see almost nothing except his own ageing, careworn features reflected back at him in the glass.

Without warning, the ship listed violently to the left, causing the men on the bridge to reach out and grip the nearest fixed object in order to remain on their feet.

'What is happening?' Cairns immediately demanded, looking to his First Officer for answers.

Bracing himself against the desk, the younger man picked up the receiver of a telephone, attached to one of the supporting pillars, and quickly dialled a number. After a brief exchange with someone in the Engine Room, he reported back. 'We've been hit by a torpedo, Sir, on our port side. Damage is severe. Water is filling the lower decks. The Chief Engineer recommends we abandon ship.'

'Launch the lifeboats!' Cairns ordered.

His crew sprang abruptly into action, beginning the well-rehearsed evacuation procedures without a second's delay.

The torpedo from the German U-boat had succeeded in gouging a hole in the hull of the Minerva which measured about 10 feet wide. The weather conditions on that evening were not on the crew's side. Rough seas meant the huge vessel was sinking fast. Cairns made sure his civilian passengers got into the lifeboats first. A number were picked up almost immediately by the nearby destroyers. Several Scottish and Scandinavian fishing boats answered the Minerva's distress call and came out to assist. The Captain knew very well that the submarine which had hit them would have dived deep into the ocean by this time, avoiding detection now that their task of sinking a liner carrying British troops had been successfully achieved.

Cairns was the last living soul to leave the stricken Minerva. As the only remaining lifeboat powered back towards the Scottish coast, Cairns looked over his shoulder, peering into the impenetrable darkness. Just then, a gap formed in the thick, leaden clouds and the moon lit up the ocean for a fleeting moment. When it did so, the Captain suddenly saw the silhouette of Rockall, jutting tall and proud from out of the pounding surf, only a few hundred yards away from the spot where the Minerva was rapidly disappearing into the churning waves.

It was the first time the seasoned mariner had set eyes on the unusual formation and he was struck by how much the rock appeared to resemble a jagged gravestone. Cairns thought to himself in this instant how the uneven monolith stood as a permanent memorial to the dead - a natural monument to commemorate those poor people who had lost their lives out there in the lonely waters of the Atlantic; finding their final resting place in the depths of this immense and merciless sea.

†

Chapter One

Portnacreagan, Appin. Scotland.

Present Day

Allan Nichols leapt up onto a bench, pointing an expensive-looking camera towards the group of people who were gathered below. 'Let's get a shot with Castle Stalker in the background,' he called over.

The group issued forth a collective groan. But they dutifully got into position for yet another photograph.

'We don't want to release a calendar of Scotland's greatest landmarks, Al. We just want a few decent pics of the bride and groom for the family album!' his brother-in-law shouted back impatiently, from somewhere on the back line.

'Simmer down, my good man. They'll be plenty of time for you to get your hands around a tumbler of single malt. I'm very nearly done.'

Hugh Croft laughed good-naturedly at the rebuke, slipping an arm around his wife's waist and smiling broadly as Allan finally took the shot.

Ten minutes later, the modest wedding party were settled comfortably at a large table in the bar of the Ramsey Hotel, with all but the very youngest nursing a glass of Scotch whisky. Allan raised his dram in a toast. 'To Mike and Julia!' He pronounced. 'It's been a fabulous day, and I think you will all join with me in wishing them many more years of happiness together.'

The assembled family and friends let out a hearty cheer and several glasses were clinked in approval.

Allan's older brother, Michael, pushed back his

stool and stood to address the guests. 'Thank you Allan,' he responded, his voice thick with emotion. 'I can't really express how overjoyed I am to have you all here to celebrate my marriage to Julia Alexandra Thomson.' The grey-haired, elegant man in his late fifties clasped his wife's hand before continuing, 'as you are aware, the road which has led us to this point has not been an easy one. We have both lost the person we believed would be our partner for life. But out of that terrible despair and sorrow, has come hope and joy. Julia and I were drawn together just when we had resigned ourselves to spending the remainder of our lives alone. I have found a love which is incredibly special, because it entered my life at a time when I had not sought it.' Michael paused for a moment to clear his throat. 'Yet, I find that now I have this wonderful woman in my life, it would not be possible to carry on without her.' Julia rose from her seat and spontaneously threw her arms around her husband's neck, placing a tender kiss on his lips. Any further attempt by the groom to press on with his speech was completely drowned out in a hail of merry applause, cat-calls and whistles.

As the evening drew to a close, Michael's younger sister, Imogen, and her husband, Hugh, sat quietly together in the corner of a cosy booth. Imogen was leaning heavily against her companion, resting her weary head on his shoulder. 'It's been a great setting for the wedding,' she commented, whilst suppressing a yawn. 'I don't know why we've never been to this part of Scotland before.'

'It's because we always go to Garansay. Certainly before your mum died, we wouldn't have considered staying anywhere else,' Hugh supplied.

'That's true. But I suppose we've got more freedom now, especially with the kids growing up and moving away. They never wanted to holiday somewhere different. If we were in Scotland, we had to be on Garansay.'

'It worked out pretty well for all of us. We're surrounded by the loch and the mountains here and it's extremely beautiful. But the scenery on Garansay is much the same, just on a slightly smaller scale.' Hugh polished off the last dregs of his whisky.

'Julia's family seem very pleasant,' Imogen added, in a change of tack.

'I hope her parents haven't felt overwhelmed by Michael's clan. There's an awful lot more of us than there are of them.'

'It was good of the local minister to allow Julia's dad to perform the service. He looked so proud of his daughter. It brought a tear to my eye.'

'Was that the church where Rob had been a minister before he retired?'

'No, Julia's mum was telling me that their Kirk was further up the coast from here, in a village opposite Shuna Island.'

'Was that where Julia grew up? It must have been quite a remote existence, especially as an only child.'

'There's a small town there, apparently, with a handful of shops and a school. It's less isolated than Kilduggan Farm. You can drive from there to Oban in less than two hours.' Imogen yawned openly now, making no further attempt to hide her exhaustion.

'Let's gather up the kids and get them into their rooms, before Allan has a chance to buy Ewan and Ian another pint.'

'Good idea,' she replied, 'we don't want to end up making a show of ourselves in front of the newest branch of the family. I get the distinct impression that the Thomsons aren't particularly big drinkers.'

Chapter Two

When Imogen Croft rose from her bed the following morning, she moved straight across to the window, where a small seat had been created within the recess. Pulling back the curtain, she silently took in the impressive view.

Portnacreagan lay on the shores of Loch Laich, which was a branch of the larger Loch Linnhe. Imogen was looking straight across at Castle Stalker, which sat on a small island in the centre of the bay. Today, in the sunshine, the façade of this stony fortress was being reflected in the tranquil waters. Behind it, in the far distance, were the mountains of Kingairloch. Although she had never been to this place before, Imogen felt as if she knew it well, the famous image before her having adorned every Scottish calendar worthy of the name.

After a quick shower, the couple made their way down to breakfast in the hotel's lounge, which looked out across the town's main golf course. This spacious room was quiet and half empty. Hugh had given their three offspring a wake-up call about twenty minutes ago, but there was no sign of them yet. Imogen spotted Julia's parents, sitting at a table by one of the tall windows. She gave her husband a nudge with her elbow, indicating they should really go and join them.

Robert and Jacquie Thomson were a neatly dressed and reserved couple, whom Imogen would place in their late sixties or early seventies. Jacquie seemed a very self-composed person and Imogen could tell it was from her mother that Julia had inherited her considerable poise. When Imogen and Hugh reached their table, Robert stood to greet them. 'Good morning,' he declared rather formally. 'Please sit with us.'

'Thank you. I trust you both slept well?' Imogen took the seat next to Jacquie.

'Oh yes, we were tired after all the excitement of yesterday. Your brother insisted we have a glass of whisky to celebrate. Rob and I don't usually drink, so we went off like a light as soon as our heads hit the pillow!'

'Sorry about Allan. He gets a little carried away when extending the hospitality,' Hugh explained. 'I don't think we'll be seeing him or any of the younger folk for a good while yet.'

'Everyone over-indulges at weddings, Hugh,' Rob added in good humour. 'It's all part of the fun.'

'It was a lovely ceremony, Rob. How long has it been since you last took a service?' Imogen helped herself to a cup of tea from the pot.

'I've been retired from the Church for six years. But I still do a certain amount of preaching now and again. Some of the more remote congregations struggle to find a permanent minister. I'm happy to help out when I can.'

As they continued their conversation, more people began to enter the dining room. Julia had only a small number of guests from her side of the family attending the wedding. These included an uncle and aunt who lived in Fort William and another uncle from Canada. It was this group of relatives who were making their way towards Rob and Jacquie's table. This time, however, the couple didn't appear quite so pleased to see them.

Julia's father rose once again to make the introductions, but Imogen noticed his posture had stiffened. 'Imogen and Hugh, this is my sister Jeanette, and her husband, Donald. And this is my cousin, Harry, who has travelled all the way from

New Brunswick in Canada to join us for Julia and Mike's union.'

They made the appropriate noises and Hugh pulled across a few extra chairs. Imogen felt compelled to examine Harry's appearance for a moment or two. Although he was probably not more than a couple of years younger than Rob's sister, he looked to be from a totally different generation. His skin was tanned and healthy looking. His thick head of hair had no doubt received some kind of professional colour treatment, but the effect was extremely natural, making him seem much younger than his years. The man was tall and athletic, possessing an easy and friendly manner.

Whilst Harry was telling Hugh and Imogen about his journey to Scotland, Rob and Jacquie unexpectedly got to their feet. They abruptly took their leave of the group and, just as rapidly, strode purposefully out of the dining room.

Imogen could not hide the surprised expression which had formed on her face.

'Don't worry,' Harry quickly explained. 'It's got nothing to do with you or your husband.' The man chuckled heartily. 'My lovely niece is keen to maintain a good relationship with her uncles and cousins on the Canadian side of the family, but, as you just saw, her father isn't quite so enthusiastic.'

Imogen still appeared totally bemused so he added, 'it's a very long story, Mrs. Croft, but if you're staying on here for a few days, I'll be sure to take the time to explain it to you.'

Chapter Three

By lunchtime, the majority of the wedding party had finally surfaced. Michael and Julia said goodbye to their guests about an hour ago. They successfully fielded an affectionate outpouring of good-wishes before climbing into an awaiting taxi, bound for Glasgow Airport. The couple were honeymooning for a week in New York.

As the Crofts made their way towards the lounge bar, Hugh suggested that after they'd eaten, the family should take a brisk walk along the shore.

'I don't believe that Bridie is dressed appropriately for a walk,' Ian teased, ruffling his younger sister's light-brown hair.

'Are you really going to wear that outfit for the *entire* weekend?' Ewan chipped in.

Neither young man had managed to drag on anything more presentable than a sweatshirt and jogging pants.

'I *am* wearing a jumper over the top,' Bridie swiftly countered, used to her brothers' joshing. The teenager then carefully smoothed out the pink chiffon, knee-length skirt of the vintage-style dress she wore for yesterday's celebrations.

Imogen slipped an arm around her daughter's shoulders. 'I think you look gorgeous, darling. I'd like to see you in that beautiful dress every day of the week.' She smiled indulgently, 'you might just need to stick on a pair of wellies, though, if you're going to have a walk on the beach later.'

'We can't do it anyway. Uncle Allan's challenged us to a game of pool this afternoon,' Ewan explained, striding off ahead to bag them a table with comfortable chairs.

Hugh could not hide his disappointment.

As Imogen glanced towards the bar, she added in a hushed tone, 'I'm afraid your uncle may have made himself alternative plans.'

Allan Nichols was leaning casually against the counter, with his back facing the room. Beside him was a tall and slender woman, her blond hair resting just above her shoulders.

'That was bloody quick work!' Hugh blurted out in disbelief. 'The man's only been up and dressed for about half an hour.'

Imogen laughed. 'It's *Penny*, darling, don't you recognise her? She must have travelled all the way from London to meet him. I think it's rather sweet.'

Hugh grunted. 'I still can't believe those two are seriously contemplating a relationship. They've got absolutely nothing in common.'

Imogen leant over and whispered in her husband's ear, 'not jealous are you?'

'Don't be ridiculous!' he replied, a little too loudly, causing the pair to turn around, curious to see where the noise was coming from.

'Hugh! Imogen! Come and have a drink.' Allan pulled out a couple of stools whilst Bridie and Ian dashed away to commandeer the sofa by the window.

Penny greeted her old friends with a continental-style kiss on both cheeks. 'Lovely to see you. I'm not gate-crashing your family get-together, I promise. I've got to consult with a client in Glasgow tomorrow afternoon. Allan and I are going to have dinner here this evening.'

Hugh immediately wondered where that meant she would be spending the night, but he certainly did not ask.

'Have you been to Scotland before, Penny?' Imogen enquired.

'Yes, but it was many years ago. My parents took my brother and me to Aviemore for the skiing. It was great. I'd not been out to the west coast before, though. I'm hoping to find a friendly local who can show me around.' Penny smiled mischievously and laid a hand on Allan's knee.

Hugh cleared his throat. 'Are we eating today?' he demanded, 'because *some* of us have been up and about since the crack of dawn.'

There was a soft breeze blowing across the rocky shoreline as the Crofts took their afternoon stroll along the beach. It was the height of summer, but thick layers of cloud were preventing the temperature from rising to any significant level. The resulting conditions were pleasant, but not exactly warm. Hugh and Imogen paused for a moment to gaze across the Sound at the gently undulating profile of Shuna Island.

'I'm not really jealous of Allan getting it together with Penny, you know,' Hugh said rather awkwardly, as he slotted his arm through his wife's.

'I do realise that,' she replied quietly, smiling to herself.

'I'm just concerned about what her motives might be. I hope she isn't taking him for a ride, or using the fling to get closer to me.' Hugh kept his eyes steadily directed towards the perfectly still waters of the loch.

'I think it's genuine. They enjoy each other's company. They've had dinner together in London a few times and the arrangement seems to suit them both. I don't believe that either of them is looking for a serious relationship right now. They have busy jobs and value their independence. It's the perfect set-up for Allan at this point in his life.'

Hugh nodded thoughtfully, as he silently observed

Bridie and the boys jogging down the beach to join them.

'Can we go back to the hotel now?' Ewan asked breathlessly. 'I said I'd ring Chloe before dinner.'

'Ian wants to use the gym and I'd like to go in the pool,' Bridie put in.

'Fine, you are dismissed,' Imogen said good-humouredly, with a light flick of her hand. 'We'll meet you in the dining room at 7.30, okay?'

'Yeah, Mum!' came the unanimous reply. The couple stood and watched their offspring tear off along the shore, heading purposefully towards the town.

When they turned round to continue their walk, Imogen and Hugh saw a small group of people up ahead. As they got closer, Imogen identified them as Julia's aunt and uncles.

Jeanette recognised them straight away. 'Hello Imogen, Hugh. It's a great day for a walk, isn't it? Not too hot. We saw your children earlier, climbing on the rocks, so we knew you would be around here somewhere.' The woman was kitted out in cotton trousers, sturdy boots and a robust looking fleece. Imogen imagined that she and Donald must do a fair amount of hiking. Again, she was immediately struck by the contrasting figure that their cousin, Harry, presented. He too was dressed casually, but his sweater and chinos looked like they had designer labels and he held himself with an indefinable air of confidence.

'Good afternoon,' he said, in his sing-song Canadian accent. 'Perhaps we might meet you guys for dinner in the hotel later on?'

'Yes, of course,' Hugh replied politely. 'We're going to carry on up to the headland first, but we'll certainly return in plenty of time for a meal.'

'Great,' Harry declared, displaying a set of

strikingly white teeth. It's a date, then.'

Chapter Four

Hugh spotted Rob and Jacquie, sitting themselves down at a table for two in a far corner of the dining room. They must have slipped in quietly a few minutes ago, he decided.

As if Harry King could tell what his dinner companion was thinking, he said, 'please don't take offence. Julia's parents are good people. But my being here is difficult for them.' The man dug into his venison cutlet.

'How come?' Imogen asked bluntly, temporarily setting her knife and fork down on the side of the plate.

'Well, if Jean and Don don't mind hearing the story over again, then I can explain the situation to you.'

Jean nodded her head in an easy manner. 'We don't mind in the least. It doesn't actually relate to us directly, you see. I suspect it would make things easier if someone from Mike's family were told the background. It could avoid potential awkwardness at future family gatherings.'

Imogen was really intrigued now.

Relaxing back into his chair, Harry carefully folded his arms across his chest. 'The fact that some of Rob's family ended up living in Canada wasn't exactly planned, shall we say.' He took a long sip from his glass of red wine. 'Rob's father, Alexander Thomson, known as 'Sandy', married a local girl, Margie McBain, in 1941. They lived in a little village called Dallanaich, which is a couple of miles up the coast from here. Young Sandy Thomson was training to be a minister in the Church of Scotland. He wasn't far off receiving his Ordination. He was also the Headmaster of the local primary school, and the only one in the town with a proper teaching qualification. This was why he hadn't been called up to fight in the war.'

'So, Rob's father was a churchman, just like him?' Imogen added.

'Yes,' Harry continued, 'the minister of Dallanaich, Mackenzie Cowan, had taken Sandy under his wing. In early 1943, Cowan was asked to address a convention of the Reformed churches, which was taking place in New York City. They planned to discuss their position on the war. Cowan must have viewed this as a great chance for Sandy to meet with some of the big wheels in the church hierarchy, because he asked the young man to accompany him there.'

'It was a dangerous time to be crossing the Atlantic,' Hugh said with feeling. 'Dozens of passenger liners were sunk before Bletchley Park cracked the German codes.'

'Absolutely right,' Harry agreed, warming to his story now he knew his audience were clued up on the subject. 'It was February 1943. Alexander Thomson was about to set off for Canada, from where he and Cowan would make their way to New York City. I expect Sandy saw it as the opportunity of a lifetime. However, his young wife, Margie, was six months pregnant at the time. There's no record of what she felt about the whole thing.'

'But if Sandy hadn't been the only qualified schoolteacher in the town, he would have had to fight in the war like all the other young men. Whichever way you look at it, *he* was one of the lucky ones,' Donald said.

'Well, their trip certainly didn't start out in a way that could be described as lucky,' Harry explained dryly. 'Mackenzie Cowan and Sandy Thomson booked their passage on board the S.S. Minerva, which sailed out of Greenock, heading for Saint John, New Brunswick, in February '43.'

'I've heard of it,' Hugh chipped in, but remained quiet, allowing Harry to finish the tale.

'Then you will be aware, Hugh, that the Minerva was hit by an enemy torpedo as it was navigating past the Rockall Banks in the northern Atlantic at roughly half past midnight on the 23rd February. A full-scale evacuation of the ship took place. The weather wasn't good and the Minerva was sinking rapidly. But the Captain was very experienced and he acted fast. Half of the passengers and crew made it off the stricken vessel and onto the lifeboats. A few more were picked up out of the water by the fishing boats who had responded to the ship's Mayday. Sadly, a couple of hundred didn't survive. The damage to the hull of the Minerva was severe. A number of the lower decks were flooded within minutes of the attack. The people down there just didn't stand a chance.'

'And Sandy? What happened to him?' Imogen leant forward, resting her elbows on the table.

'Margie Thomson received a telegram a few days later. It informed her that her husband and Mackenzie Cowan had gone down with the ship. Their cabin was on one of the decks which would have suffered a direct hit from the torpedo. There didn't seem to be much doubt they had perished.'

'Poor woman,' Hugh muttered.

'Oh, Margie did okay for herself,' said Jean, taking up the story. 'Her wee bairn, whom she called Robert, was born at the end of August and Mum doted on him. Three years later, a local man by the name of Alistair McClelland, who'd been away fighting in North Africa during the war years, asked Margie to marry him. He took Robert on as his own son. Then, my brother, John, was born in 1948 and

I came along in '51. We had a very happy childhood.'

Imogen's mind was ticking away. 'So how did the Canadian branch of the family come about?'

'Thirty years after the sinking of the Minerva, in the early seventies, a man who had lived all of his life in Dallanaich, went on holiday with his wife to Ontario. This chap was called Kenneth Garvie. One day, he took a train into Toronto, so he could cash some travellers' cheques. As he walked down a busy street in the financial sector, who should happen to walk past him but Sandy Thomson, although, by then, he was known as Alex King.' Harry paused here for dramatic effect.

'How on earth did this Garvie chap recognise him after all that time?' Hugh marvelled.

'Kenneth claimed that my father looked no different, just a few grey hairs and a couple of wrinkles. Both of them stopped dead in the middle of the sidewalk. Neither said a word for about five whole minutes. Then Ken says, 'hello Sandy, how are you?" Harry laughed. 'The two men went off into the nearest bar. I sure wish I could have been a fly on the wall for that conversation!'

'How old were you when this happened?' Imogen asked; her meal sitting half-eaten in front of her.

'I'd just gone off to college, so I'd be in my early twenties. My brother, Jim, was still a teenager. My Dad had a *lot* of explaining to do. But first, he gave Kenneth Garvie his account of the events.

Apparently, Mackenzie Cowan certainly had been drowned when the Minerva went down. The clergyman was fast asleep in their cabin when Sandy had last set eyes on him. But my father was sea-sick and just couldn't settle. The liner was rolling about in the waves, so he'd gone up on deck for some fresh air. Sandy was sheltering by the entrance to the ship's galley when the torpedo struck. He tried to go back down for Mackenzie, but the crew stopped him. He was bundled pretty fast into a lifeboat. Dad was a civilian, you see, and they took priority.'

'So how did he end up in Canada, when the liner never actually got there?' Imogen looked puzzled.

'This is the part that none of us is terribly proud of. Dad was taken back to port by the Danish fishing trawler that picked them up. He said it was totally chaotic in Gourock that night. Survivors were being transported to different places all the way up and down the west coast of Scotland. The fishermen never took a record of his name, they couldn't even speak English. Sandy suddenly realised the significance of what had occurred. If he didn't inform anyone that he was still alive, no one would ever know. It dawned on my father that he could go anywhere in the world and start a new life completely from scratch. The war was raging in Europe and it was a good time for someone to disappear. Sandy pretended to be a wounded soldier. He worked the bars in the city for a few months, cash in hand, and saved his money. As soon as he had enough, he booked himself onto another ship out of Glasgow. He still had his passport. He'd kept it stuffed in his back pocket so he didn't lose it. At no point did anyone cross check his name with the passenger list of the Minerva. Dad said they were more concerned with rooting out German spies than worrying about men they already believed were dead. As you pointed out, Hugh, the Atlantic had become a little safer by this stage and he finally reached his destination in Saint John, New Brunswick, Canada at the end of December 1943. From this point onwards, Sandy Thomson was no more and *my* father, Alex King, had been born.'

Chapter Five

Imogen, Hugh and Harry retired to take their coffees in the residents' lounge. Jean and Donald decided to join Rob and Jacquie for an after dinner drink in the bar. Jean didn't want her older brother to feel they were leaving him out. The Crofts' children went straight upstairs to bed when they'd finished their meals, the excitement of the previous day finally catching up with them.

'I know these things did happen, but I still find the story absolutely extraordinary.' Imogen helped herself to a mint chocolate from the bowl on the table, suddenly hungry as a result of not finishing her main course.

'Even after practising as a psychologist for all these years, it does amaze me how some people yearn to completely re-invent themselves. They would happily erase all evidence of their past and in many instances, never even think of it again.' Hugh reclined in the armchair, resting a coffee cup in his lap.

'I believe that in my father's case, it had something to do with his religious calling. Sandy had felt constrained by the hierarchy of the established Church in Scotland. He was even having second thoughts about being ordained into the ministry when they set off on that ill-fated trip to New York. When he did ultimately reach Canada, towards the start of 1944, Sandy referred to himself as Alexander King. In due course, he joined an independent religious community in northern Ontario and became a preacher there, teaching the local children part-time too. The group were pacifists and the Canadian government never pursued any attempt to get the menfolk involved in the war effort. My mother, Eleanor Kinslett, had been born into this remote community. Alex married her in '49.'

'But wasn't your father already married to Margie?' Imogen asked cautiously.

Harry managed a thin smile. 'My parents had a wedding ceremony within their own church, Mrs. Croft. It meant a great deal to them, but Alex never registered the new marriage with the Canadian authorities. My father wasn't a bigamist.'

Imogen immediately wondered what Margie's situation was - marrying Jean's dad when her own husband was still alive. But she said nothing.

'I was born in 1952 and my brother, Jim, in '54. Throughout our childhood we believed our father had grown up in the suburbs of Ottawa, with Scottish parents who were long since dead. He could even speak a reasonable amount of French, which he said he'd learnt at school. It might seem incredible, but we never had the slightest clue that Alex had this whole other existence he had kept a secret from us. Like Jean said, we all had a great family life.'

'But Robert doesn't feel as well disposed towards the set up as the rest of you,' Hugh stated.

Harry's expression darkened. 'Sadly, it's not the same for Rob, is it? He always believed his biological father was a kind of hero. Sandy was a young schoolteacher who had bravely set out to cross the Atlantic in order to spread the word of God, tragically losing his life in the process. He even kept his real father's surname. Then, in the seventies, he suddenly discovers that his dad is actually alive and well. Rob had to come to terms with the fact his father chose to leave him and his mum - that he never even came back home for the birth of his baby boy. Believe me, I have every sympathy for Rob. Jim and I can understand why he's so angry with our dad, but we still wish he'd get over it and welcome us into his life. Dad is long gone now and we shouldn't have to pay for his mistakes forever.'

'Was Julia the one who got in contact with you, then?' Imogen gently enquired.

Harry's face brightened. 'Ever since dad told us the full story of his youth here in Scotland, back when he bumped into Kenneth Garvie that day in Toronto, our family have been in regular touch with the McClellands. Firstly, dad wrote a letter to Margie, explaining everything and begging for her forgiveness. Kenneth took the letter back home with him. Of course, Margie had a new life by then and two more kids. There wasn't much for her to forgive. But dad really wanted to start having some kind of relationship with his first born son. Robert refused. He was thirty years old and a highly dedicated minister, not long ordained into the church. Rob took the news of his father's abandonment of him and his mother very badly. Dad developed heart problems in his later years and he couldn't travel much. I think they spoke on the phone maybe a couple of times, but I know that Dad and Rob never saw each other before he passed away in the early eighties.'

'It's terribly sad,' Imogen said.

'I wrote to Rob and Jacquie once a year. My wife, Connie, told me to keep the lines of communication open. It turned out to be good advice. Although he never replied to my letters, Rob kept them and, when Julia was old enough, he showed my letters to her, explaining that she had relatives in Canada. Rob gave her the option to make contact with us. We got our first correspondence from Julia in the summer of 1996.' Harry's eyes glistened with unshed tears. 'I've still got it at home, kept nice and safe. It was one of the most wonderful moments of my life when I received it.' Harry cleared his throat. 'We wrote to one another quite regularly after that. Julia started coming over to visit us about ten years ago. I attended her first wedding - to poor Callum. My girls, Sally and Christa, absolutely adore their cousin. Connie and I will meet up with Mike and Julia whilst they're in New York. Connie can't wait to be introduced to your brother. We were both so upset when Julia lost her first husband. Jim had wanted to come here for the wedding too, but he and his partner are in the middle of a big project at work. They're both producers for a major T.V network in the States.'

Imogen was surprised to discover she felt quite emotional. It just seemed incredible to her that blood-ties could mean so much to people. Harry continued to write to his half-brother for over twenty years, even when he received no reply. Then, finally, his efforts had paid off and he gained a lovely new relationship with his niece. Imogen suddenly experienced a rush of sadness for Julia's father. He was caught between two clans – the McClellands and the Kings - and to neither did he fully belong. Rob was always a Thomson, and the chances of that little family being allowed to exist had disappeared along with the S.S. Minerva, lost to the murky depths of the dark and pitiless sea.

Chapter Six

Whilst Hugh accompanied the youngsters down to breakfast the following morning, Imogen decided to take the car for a short drive up the coast to the village of Dallanaich. They were planning to leave for their next port of call on the Isle of Garansay, shortly after lunch, so this would be her only chance to have a look at the place where Julia and her father had grown up.

Imogen drove the car along the shore road, past the reference point created by the contours of Shuna Island and onto the more open, eastern bank of Loch Linnhe. Dallanaich was a small settlement positioned at the mouth of the Salachan Burn. The views of the mountains across the water from there were truly spectacular. It was a very clear day and Imogen stopped for a coffee in a tearoom which boasted an impressive outlook on the tiny islet of Balnagowan. The village had a couple of shops and maybe a few dozen houses, many of which were spread out across the glen. Imogen imagined there must be a reasonable number of farms around the area too.

A diminutive but rotund lady, with carefully sculpted silver-grey hair and a stripy apron tied about her ample middle, presented Imogen with her drink. 'Is there a church in Dallanaich?' she asked.

'Not in the village itself,' the woman replied, pointing northwards towards Cuil Bay. 'The chapel is about half a mile up that way. They still hold services there, but not every week. Most locals drive down to Portnacreagan, if they want to worship regularly, that is. We haven't got a full-time minister any longer.'

Imogen smiled and nodded her head. 'When did you lose your minister?'

'Och, it was a good few years ago now. Reverend Thomson comes back to deliver the occasional sermon, but only because he grew up around here. He was baptised in that wee chapel and hates to think of it rotting away like it is. It would cost thousands to restore it properly,' the woman lowered her voice a fraction. 'It's just not worth it, in my humble opinion. Not when our young folk haven't got decent homes to live in. The money could be better spent elsewhere. Not that I'd tell the Reverend that, mind you.' She chuckled.

When Imogen finished her coffee, she took the car a little further along the road, parking in front of the crumbling church building. It was constructed from a dark stone which had become badly weather-beaten. The structure was rather small and perched right on the very edge of the shoreline. Imogen couldn't imagine any more than thirty or forty people fitting inside it at one time. The doors were padlocked shut and the windows barred. The place looked extremely uninviting.

As she drove back through Dallanaich, Imogen noticed there was a modern village school and a modest development of brand new bungalows to the east of the town. In spite of this, she could still gain a sense of what the community might have looked like during the war years. There certainly didn't appear to have been a great deal of change in the town during the intervening decades.

When Imogen returned to the hotel, Hugh and the kids were gathered around a smart new BMW, which was in the process of exiting the car park. She pulled up at the kerbside, climbing out to see what was going on.

'Here she is!' Hugh exclaimed, beckoning his wife over. 'Penny and Allan are just leaving. They wanted to say goodbye to you before they went.'

It was Penny who was sitting in the driving seat. Imogen assumed this was a hire car. Her clients in Glasgow must have been footing the bill.

Allan leant forward, eyeing his younger sister suspiciously. 'What have you been up to this morning? No, on second thoughts, don't answer that,' he laughed. 'Just try to stay out of trouble if that's possible. And we'll see you back in London.'

Penny blew her friends an affectionate kiss and they sped away along the seafront, beeping the horn as the high performance car turned the bend, before promptly disappearing out of sight.

'You were a long time, darling,' Hugh said quizzically, without any hint of a rebuke. 'I brought all of our cases down into the lobby, ready to go in the boot. Let's grab a bite to eat and then we can head off ourselves.'

*

Chapter Seven

When travelling to the Isle of Garansay from the north of Scotland, it was possible to take a ferry from the little port of Claonaig, on the Kintyre peninsula. This boat deposited its passengers at the small harbour in Port na Mara Bay. From there it was a short car journey along the coastal road to Lower Kilduggan Farm, where Imogen and her brothers spent their childhood.

Imogen's eldest brother, Michael Nichols, was a semi-retired Glasgow-based architect. He had devoted the last few years to renovating the old farmhouse at Lower Kilduggan. The three siblings inherited the property and the small amount of land encircling it, after their mother died. Imogen's father had passed away in the mid-seventies, when she was only a little girl. It was Michael who spent the most time at the farm now. He and Julia came across to Garansay most weekends and at other times Michael's daughter, Sarah, and her husband had use of it. Imogen and Hugh lived on the east coast of Essex, where Hugh was a professor of psychology at the university in Colchester. Allan worked for a bank in the City of London and had a flat in Highgate, so it wasn't quite so easy for them to make the trip up to Garansay as regularly.

The Crofts' estate car had to negotiate a steep stony track to reach the farm. They parked to the left of the large Victorian building. Imogen immediately surveyed the front garden.

'The Lavatera has gone completely mad. We'll need to get someone from Kilross to come over and tidy the outside space up a bit.' She sighed heavily.

'I'll cut it back whilst we're here if you like -

although, I actually think it's very pretty.' Hugh paused to appreciate the profusion of pink flowers cascading down the wall of the house. 'The place looks homely and lived in now. You have to admit it never appeared that way when your mother was alive. I'd even go as far as to suggest it was downright unwelcoming.'

Imogen said nothing but she was inclined to agree. Michael's landscaping of the plots at the front and back had transformed this 19th Century, one-time boarding house, into an attractive home. When she was growing up, Kilduggan Farm was a busy, working establishment. Her parents were constantly on the go. Even after she had retired, Isabel never dedicated any time or money to 'doing the place up'. It simply wasn't in her nature. She would have considered it unnecessary and frivolous.

'Do you know what the gardens remind me of now?' Hugh suddenly said, 'the house that Mike and Miriam lived in, just after they got married. Do you remember it? It was in Bearsden, I think.'

'Yes I do.' Imogen let her mind drift back to the unassuming modern detached property her brother and his family had shared some twenty five years ago. 'I wouldn't mention that to Julia, though. I'm sure it wasn't intentional.'

'No, I don't expect it was,' Hugh replied thoughtfully.

The kids hauled their bags and cases up the twisting staircase, while Imogen deposited the cool bag on the kitchen table. She was surprised to see a vase sitting on the draining board. It was filled with several enormous white peonies, which had clearly been cut when in full bloom. There was a card resting against them.

'Colin has left us some flowers!' Imogen called out to Hugh, who was carrying the rest of their luggage into the hallway.

'That was kind of him. Does he still have a key then?'

'Yes, he keeps an eye on the place when Mike and Julia are in Glasgow.' Imogen concentrated on unpacking the essential supplies they brought from Portnacreagan, placing them in the empty fridge.

Colin Walmsley was the same age as Imogen and he owned the farm which bordered Lower Kilduggan. She had known him since childhood. He had been a good friend to her family over the years. Colin was a successful businessman, based mainly on Garansay, where he had a stake in a number of local ventures. Imogen had always considered her neighbour to be a fair man, who would put the interests of his community before the pursuit of profit.

Hugh came into the kitchen and poured out two glasses of water from the tap. 'It was a shame about Kitty,' he stated.

'I think her mind had deteriorated rather badly towards the end. Colin said it was a blessing the situation didn't drag on for too long.' Imogen took a sip of the cool liquid, immediately identifying the peaty, slightly metallic taste that tainted the water there. It was a sign that not so very long ago, the content of the tap was flowing freely in the burn. She knew it would do her no harm.

'I always got the impression Colin absolutely doted on his mother.'

'Yes, he did. But he wouldn't have wanted her to suffer. Kitty had that indefinable, almost childlike quality. I can imagine the poor lady became desperately confused as her condition got worse. It's not an easy thing to witness in a loved one.'

'No, it certainly isn't.'

It was early the following day when Imogen strolled

out to stand by the stone wall at the end of the front garden, with a mug of coffee in her hand, silently admiring the view. The sky was crystal clear. The waters of the Kilbrannan Sound, which separated western Garansay from Kintyre, were absolutely still and glistening in the light. Despite the morning chill, she felt a warm glow of contentment radiate throughout her body.

Just then, a loud noise fractured her peaceful solitude. It seemed to have been caused by the spluttering engine of a small motorbike, which was making its way along the coastal road from the north of the island. Because of the lack of any noticeable breeze, Imogen was able to listen to the bike approach from several miles away.

The noise suddenly stopped. Imogen assumed the rider would not attempt to get the little vehicle up the steep gravel track which led to the farm. It turned out she was right. A few minutes later, a young man in tatty leathers, carrying a helmet under his arm, emerged on foot along the overgrown lane. He broke into a broad smile when he caught sight of her.

'Hi, Mrs. Croft!' He called out.

'Hello, Murray,' she replied, 'how wonderful to see you again.'

Imogen led their unexpected visitor into the kitchen and placed a kettle of water onto the hob.

'How was the wedding?' He asked eagerly, sitting himself down at the table.

'It was lovely.' She took the chair opposite. 'Julia's dad performed the service. We all had drinks and a buffet in the hotel bar afterwards. It was just a modest celebration, but it was exactly how the couple had wanted it.'

The lad immediately looked forlorn. Murray White became friendly with Imogen's brother, Michael, after his boat was sunk in a terrible storm in the Kilbrannan Sound. Murray lost his grandfather that night. Michael had become something of a father-figure to the boy ever since. His own dad was lost at sea when Murray was just a baby. His mum was very young at the time and she inevitably re-married. Murray had never quite found a role for himself within his mother's new family and was pretty much living full-time with his grandad when the boat accident occurred.

'I'm really sorry I missed it. But Colin and I had this important booking, with a group of ten American tourists coming over for a sailing fortnight. We're hoping it might help to open up the U.S. market for us. I just couldn't afford to cancel it.'

'Michael and Julia completely understood, I promise. They're both rooting for the business to do well. Sarah and Ross send you their love, too.'

Murray's handsome face broke into another grin. 'I will give Sarah a call tonight.'

'So, how is the sailing school going? Are you getting much trade?' Imogen enquired before jumping up to make the coffees.

'We're fully booked for the summer season,' he explained proudly. 'Colin and I have come up with some plans for how to generate more interest too. We want to introduce a few new events for Garansay to get involved with. We think it will be good for trade across the island. In fact, it's one of the reasons I came over this morning - other than to catch up with you all, of course.'

'Sounds intriguing,' Imogen said with interest, placing a couple of brimming mugs on the chipped surface of the table.

'Actually, Mrs. Croft, I was rather hoping I might be able to have a word with Ian - if he's up yet, that is,' Murray replied cryptically, before taking a slow and careful sip from his scalding hot drink.

Chapter Eight

Hugh found some old secateurs in one of the sheds. He was using them to cut back the heavily bowed branches of the Lavatera.

Imogen emerged from the house to deliver him a cold drink. 'That looks *much* better,' she stated firmly.

'For now maybe, but I'm probably just encouraging more growth.' Hugh put down the shears and wiped the sweat away from his forehead. 'What are the kids up to?'

'I told Ewan they could take the car over to Murray's place. He said they've no classes today so he'd take them out on the water. That's okay isn't it?'

'Of course. It will give Ian and Murray a chance to talk properly. I think it's a great idea to have a round island yacht race on Garansay. I can't believe nobody's organised one before.'

'Yes, but I can't help thinking it's all happening a bit fast. Murray and Colin have set a date for the end of September. It only gives them a couple of months.'

'But you said they've got a major sponsor already. Now all Murray needs to do is ramp up the publicity. He'll have to encourage plenty of high profile yachtsmen and women to take part in the event. I must say the idea is pretty inspired. Regardless of who wins the race, it will bring visitors flocking to the island, just at a time of the year when the tourist season has begun to dwindle.'

'We shouldn't be surprised by the ingenuity of the plan. Murray has already shown us how *resourceful* he can be.' Hugh shot her a disapproving look, which his wife completely ignored. 'Well, Ian's certainly keen to get a crew together. The competition will take place before his university term begins again, so it shouldn't be a problem. Murray said they're happy to start small and build from there. Apparently, the original Isle of Wight race had just 25 boats competing in it - now there are well over fifteen hundred each year.'

'You can't fault the lad's ambition. He's certainly worked very hard to make something of his sailing school business. I bet Mike's really proud of him.'

'Yes, and Murray hasn't had the best start in life, either. He is obviously an extremely bright boy but he didn't get the chance to continue with his education beyond sixteen - largely because his mother wanted him out of the house, working to support himself.' Imogen took a healthy gulp from her glass of water.

'Sometimes it's the lack of a safety net which drives people to get ahead. Our three are just too comfortable. They know full-well that Mum and Dad or Gran and Grandad will always bail them out if things go wrong. It probably means they'll never possess the ruthless desire needed to reach the very top of their chosen professions.'

'As long as they have a career that challenges them and pays the bills, does it really matter? I'd rather the kids were happy and healthy than millionaires.'

Hugh chuckled. 'Of course, I quite agree. In fact, the drive to succeed can often mask underlying psychological issues. It doesn't always go hand-in-hand with a thriving home life, for instance. Actually, it has always struck me as interesting that Colin never married.'

'He's had a few girlfriends in his time – Julia, for one.' Imogen smiled. 'But I just don't think Colin is the marrying type. Some folk simply aren't. Now his mother has passed away, things might change, although I still wouldn't bet on it.'

'He's definitely a great guy, but ultimately, I think it's work that makes Colin tick. Perhaps he's simply witnessed too closely the damage that relationships can do and he doesn't want any part of it.'

Imogen considered this suggestion for a moment. 'You might very well have a point there,' she concluded.

They heard the sound of the front door being slammed shut. Ewan, Ian and Bridie were making their way across the courtyard to where the car was parked. Ewan held up a bunch of keys. 'We're off now, okay?' He called over, shaking the set vigorously, as if to provide a jangly rhythm to accompany his words.

'Keep an eye on Bridie!' Hugh automatically hollered back.

'I'll be fine, Dad. We've all got our phones.'

'Have a great time,' Imogen interjected. 'Just check in with us every couple of hours, that's all we ask.'

The youngsters grunted their assent, jumping into the family car and disappearing down the steep, dusty track.

Chapter Nine

The skies over New York City were a perfectly clear blue. Michael and Julia Nichols were seated on a bench opposite the statue of George Washington in Union Square. It was late morning and the temperature in the city was gradually climbing. The pair had been sightseeing for the past few hours and now began to feel the pace.

Michael was twenty years older than his new wife, but the age gap was not immediately obvious. Julia was a slim and graceful woman in her late thirties. She wore her shoulder-length hair in a feathered style. It was still naturally dark in colour. Michael was tall and lean. His demeanour had an understated elegance to it. Apart from having gone entirely grey, he looked much the same as he did at forty.

Julia rested her head against Michael's shoulder. 'I'm just going to close my eyes for a moment, darling. Keep a look out for Harry and Connie, will you?'

'Of course, you rest for a while,' he replied, slipping an arm around her narrow waist.

No one was more surprised than Michael Nichols that he had got himself married for a second time, and to someone so comparatively young. Just two years ago, Michael was utterly content to remain single for the remainder of his days. He had his memories of the life he shared with Miriam, and that had seemed to be enough. It was only when Julia took on the role of his clerical assistant, whilst he was working from the farmhouse on Garansay for three days a week that his feelings began to change. Initially, Michael had simply found her very easy to work with. She was intelligent, practical-minded and good company. After a few months, Michael discovered he was missing her whenever he went back at his flat in Glasgow. He started to wonder if she felt the same way too.

One particular week, Michael had a series of important meetings in the city and he gave Julia some time off. He knew he would have to stay away from Garansay for longer than usual. When she did finally arrive at Lower Kilduggan Farm for work one morning, after this brief period of separation, Michael could immediately see in her eyes that she had missed him as desperately as he had her. Michael had automatically stepped forward and taken Julia's hands. Tears began to escape down her pale cheeks. They spent the rest of the day sitting in the two armchairs by the bay window, drinking endless cups of coffee, and discussing, in both elation and fear, what on earth they would do now they knew they were in love with one another.

Michael smiled at the memory.

Julia shifted about next to him. He pulled her closer. A few minutes later, he shook her arm gently. 'Darling, I think that's your uncle over there.'

She slowly opened her eyes, finding the sudden vividness of the sun-drenched, bustling city took her by surprise. 'Yes, it's definitely Harry.'

They stood up and gestured towards Julia's uncle and aunt, who swiftly made their way over. Connie put down a Bloomingdales shopping bag, pulling her niece into a warm embrace. 'Congratulations! I'm so sorry I couldn't come over for the wedding,' she gushed.

'Oh, don't worry about that. It's wonderful you're both here now. Connie, this is my husband, Michael.' Julia stepped back.

'I'm very pleased to meet you, Mrs. King.' He

politely reached out his hand.

'My, what a very handsome and distinguished gentleman you've hooked yourself, Julia.' The petit blond woman in a summer dress and heels ignored the offer of a handshake and hugged him tightly instead.

'You'll have to make allowances for my wife, Mike. Connie's had to put up with me for the last thirty years, so she gets a little carried away whenever a *real* gent comes onto the scene.'

They all laughed good-naturedly.

'Now,' Harry continued, 'let's find one of those world renowned restaurants they claim to have in this town, so we can grab ourselves a bite to eat.'

The two couples enjoyed a short stroll down Fifth Avenue into Greenwich Village, where Harry had ear-marked an Asian-fusion restaurant for lunch that his guidebook raved about. The place turned out to be very busy, but a table was quickly cleared for them out in a tiny, shaded courtyard garden at the rear.

'Wow, now I really feel like I'm in New York,' said Connie, ordering a round of martini cocktails and pouring ice cold water into their empty glasses. 'I can just picture Woody Allen and Diane Keaton having a heated, existential discussion at that little table over there in the corner.'

'The city has such a creative buzz,' Julia added, taking a sip of the refreshing liquid. 'Do you visit here very often?'

Harry chuckled. 'This is the first time we've ever been. Christa drove us to the airport in Halifax and the flight took less than two hours. Now we know it's this easy, we'll certainly have to do it again sometime.'

'How are the girls?' Julia enquired.

'Sally's expecting her second little one. They know

it's another boy. He's due at Christmas time.'

'Oh, how wonderful!' Julia exclaimed.

'Yes, we're overjoyed, of course. But Harry wishes she and Patrick would get married.' Connie sighed.

'I can just imagine what my old Dad would have made of it.' Harry tasted his martini, with a sombre expression on his face.

'What *would* he have thought?' Julia couldn't help but ask, always intrigued by any mention of her grandfather.

'Dad was extremely dedicated to the teachings of our church. Having children outside of marriage was very much a no-no.'

Knowing a little about the story of how Sandy Thomson ended up living in Canada, Michael couldn't prevent himself from raising an eyebrow at this statement.

'I can see what you're thinking, Mike. That my father was a hypocrite to hold those views, what with him not being legally married to my mother and all. But in the eyes of our church they *had* been married. God had blessed their union.' Harry smiled as the waitress arrived with the food.

Michael said nothing. He concentrated on the plate of spicy Thai noodles which had been placed before him. The meal was delicious, but he wasn't really enjoying it. Instead, he was silently mulling over Harry's words. Michael hadn't actually considered the issue of the Kings' illegal marriage. He had been thinking about that poor young family back in Scotland – Margie Thomson and her baby. If Sandy truly believed it immoral to have a child outside of wedlock, then how on earth did he square the fact that he'd left behind his first wife and son, allowing them to believe he was dead and barely giving them a moment's thought for the next thirty years?

Chapter Ten

In the evening, they had gone to see a Broadway show with Connie and Harry, before parting for their respective hotels. Michael and Julia were staying at The Liberty in Greenwich Village, where they seemed to be a short walk from most of the main attractions of the city.

Julia woke first, slipping quietly out of the crisp Egyptian cotton sheets and taking a look out of the window. She breathed in the atmosphere. Even this early in the morning, the narrow streets were buzzing with life. Julia had never holidayed in the United States before. She got close once, when visiting the Canadian side of the Niagara Falls. Julia and her first husband, Callum, had always intended to come. But he had worked very long hours when they were newly married and hardly ever took time off. Callum was planning for a future that never came. He died of a heart attack at just 43 years old. Julia had been utterly shattered by his death. It was so completely unexpected. Julia's parents were an enormous support to her when it happened, but Harry and Connie had been great, too. She would always be thankful to them for that.

Michael had woken now and moved across the room to stand behind her. 'What would you like to do today, darling?'

Julia leant into his warm body. 'Let's not have breakfast here at the hotel. I fancy a wander around the village. Maybe we could get some pancakes and a coffee somewhere.'

'Sounds like a good idea,' Michael pressed his face into her soft, silky hair, depositing a kiss on the base of her neck. 'Are we seeing your uncle and aunt later?'

‘No, they’re going up the Chrysler Building and then having a look at some of the tourist stuff we’ve already done. I don’t think they want to be considered guilty of gate-crashing our honeymoon.’

Michael chuckled. ‘Whilst we’re stateside, it’s a perfect opportunity for you to spend time with them. If they want to meet up again, I really don’t mind.’

Julia turned to face him, hooking her arms around his waist. ‘Are you really this perfect, or will you suddenly transform into a bullying tyrant as soon as we get back home?’

Michael laughed, ‘I could be a tyrant right now if you wanted me to.’ He roughly pulled her close, in an act of mock aggression. But the gesture seemed so contrived they both immediately collapsed in a fit of giggles.

‘I don’t think you’re capable of being ungentlemanly, even when you try,’ Julia said with affection. ‘It just isn’t in your nature, Michael Nichols.’

After strolling through Greenwich Village, the couple ended up taking the subway to the Upper West Side, where they entered the huge Cathedral Church of St John the Divine. They ambled along the nave, past the beautiful hanging tapestries that lined both sides, coming to a stop beneath the Great Rose Window. ‘It’s breathtaking,’ Julia said in a whisper. ‘I’m finding it hard to imagine we’re still in the centre of New York.’

It was cool within the church, so they spent an hour or so examining the incredible sculptures and paintings. The theme of the art on show reflected the often turbulent history of the city itself. The statues appeared to Michael not to be offering hope in the midst of darkness, but instead, to be auguries of disaster and human suffering.

Michael was not a religious man, although he respected the fact that Julia's family were so closely involved with the church. So he didn't share with his wife just how unsettled the place was making him feel.

'Isn't it strange to think that my grandfather was heading here with the minister of Dallanaich, when their ship was sunk in the Atlantic,' Julia suddenly said.

'They weren't coming to this particular cathedral, were they?'

'Oh no. By all accounts, Sandy Thomson wasn't very keen on this kind of frippery and ceremonial. He and Reverend Cowan were planning to attend a convention of the *Presbyterian* Church. I don't know where in the city it was being held, though.'

'I'm sure I could find out - if you wanted me to?'

They both stopped walking and looked at one other.

'According to my map, the National Archives aren't far from here. If you remind me of the dates again, I'll go and check it out.' Michael smiled and took Julia's hand. 'Why don't you give Harry a call on his mobile, see where he and Connie are right now? If they're close by, then you could meet them for a drink. I'll catch up with you back at the hotel later.'

Chapter Eleven

If he were being honest, Michael would have to admit that he didn't really enjoy sightseeing. He never had. Of course, the architecture of different cities interested him and he would often make sketches of the buildings which particularly grabbed his attention. This only resulted in him becoming more restless to return home to his own designs. Michael thought that perhaps he wasn't the travelling type. It might have been because his own family hardly ever took a holiday whilst they were growing up. Lower Kilduggan was very much a working establishment. Even during school breaks he was required to help his father on the farm. Maybe, he had never properly learnt how to leave his professional life behind during these kinds of trips. Michael hoped it wouldn't cause future problems for him and Julia, as his wife certainly seemed to enjoy visiting new places.

Michael had been directed by the archivist at the National Records Office to make a short trip to the very heart of the Midtown district. Here, amongst the skyscrapers and the sidewalks packed full of theatregoers, was the oldest Presbyterian Church in the city. Tucked down a narrow side alley, the imposing building was set within a small churchyard. The noticeboard in the vestibule was covered in posters for upcoming concerts and events. Michael assumed the church still possessed an active congregation.

He twisted the heavy handle that secured the thick wooden door. The temperature dropped noticeably as he stepped inside, but he found the simplicity of the church's interior strangely welcoming. The noise made by Michael's entrance must have alerted the minister to his presence, because a middle aged man in cords and a white shirt secured at the top with a dog collar, strode down the aisle to meet him.

'You must be Mr. Nichols,' he called out warmly. As he got nearer, Michael assessed that the chap was probably in his late forties. 'Irene called to tell me you were coming.'

They shook hands.

'I'm Reverend John MacMillan. We keep our records in an office down in the crypt. Please follow me.'

Upon closer examination, Michael could see the church really needed some money spending on it. The pews were tatty and the cushions threadbare and scuffed. They descended a set of uneven stone steps into a basement area, which was clearly used for storage. There was a small side room full of filing cabinets and cardboard boxes. Reverend MacMillan gestured towards a pair of wooden seats placed in front of a desk which was strewn with dusty papers. 'Please sit down, Mr. Nichols. Now, what is it that I can help you with?'

Michael fished a folded piece of paper out of his pocket. 'My wife's father is a minister in the Church of Scotland,' he explained. 'And her grandfather was closely involved in the Reformed Church movement.'

MacMillan nodded patiently.

'Her grandfather's name was Alexander Thomson, and he set out in February 1943 with his local clergyman, Reverend Cowan, to attend a convention of the Presbyterian Churches which was due to take place here in New York a few weeks later. Tragically, their liner was torpedoed in the Atlantic and Cowan was drowned. Thomson survived but never made it to New York City. He ended up in Canada instead, where he eventually settled down. But I wondered if you had any information about this convention. My wife would be very interested to know.'

'Is your wife Canadian then?' the man asked innocently.

'No, she's actually Scottish. It's a long story Reverend.'

'Okay, well we don't need to go into that.' He smiled kindly and went across to the filing cabinet. Using a small key which was hanging on a larger ring, he unlocked the middle drawer. 'My grandfather was involved in the Battle of the Atlantic, you know. He was part of the U.S. convoy system. Wasn't the threat from U-boats pretty much eradicated by '43?' he enquired, whilst sifting through the files.

'Yes, by the end of '43 it was over. But the Atlantic was still extremely dangerous in the early months of that year.'

'Here we are,' he said, sitting back in the chair with a stack of papers in his hands. 'March 23rd, 1943, is the date the convention took place. The venue was the West Avenue Reform Club, which sounds very grand but was more like a town hall, really. I know it isn't there any longer. You can take a look at the list of attendees if you'd like?'

Michael gratefully received the sheet of paper and skimmed through the text. The list provided the details of clergymen from all parts of the world, with a small number hailing from Europe. 'Is there any mention of what was discussed at the meeting?'

'I'm afraid not. If somebody did record the minutes, the document has long since disappeared. I do know there was much debate at the time about what role the Presbyterian Church should take in the war effort. Our leaders were concerned about how the Church in Germany had given in so easily to Hitler. They didn't want to be perceived as collaborators. At the same time, there was a reluctance to justify the prolonging of violence and suffering. The Christian instinct is usually to turn the other cheek.' The Reverend smiled ruefully, 'if you ignore the Crusades, of course.'

'Can I have a copy of this?' Michael asked.

'Sure, I've got a scanner in the vestry.' He led Michael out of the musty room and up into the main body of the church. 'I expect those chaps are all deceased by now,' he added thoughtfully. 'Senior Churchmen are always old, even these days.'

When Michael was furnished with his print, he thanked Reverend MacMillan sincerely. Stepping into the warmth of the city street, Michael immediately reached for his mobile phone, determined to find out where Julia was, so that he could share the information with her as quickly as possible.

Chapter Twelve

Harry and Connie were staying at the Piazza Hotel on Fifth Avenue. Julia was having afternoon tea with them there. It was only a ten minute walk from where Michael was now. Armed with a tourist map, he made his way in their direction.

The lobby lay behind a glass frontage. Well-heeled guests were continuously coming and going through a large set of revolving doors. Michael knew the Piazza was one of the most prestigious establishments in the city. He concluded that Harry's real estate business back in New Brunswick must be flourishing.

He found the threesome at a table in the huge mezzanine restaurant, which had imposing views of the towering Seagram Building. Harry stood up as Michael approached, pulling out one of the chairs, which had been moulded out of some type of orange-tinted plastic. An assortment of dainty cakes and sandwiches were laid out artistically on a circular glass dish before them.

'Hello darling,' Julia said excitedly. 'Isn't this impressive?'

'Yes, it certainly is,' Michael replied, as Connie poured him a cup of tea.

'We fly home in the morning,' Harry added with a note of bitterness to his tone, 'if we stay here one more night I'll be bankrupt!'

'Don't exaggerate Harry - it isn't something we do very often. This is a special occasion.' Connie placed an arm around Julia and gave her a squeeze.

The younger woman turned towards her husband. 'How did you get on at the National Archives?'

Michael sensed Harry's posture stiffen. He immediately wondered whether it would be very tactful to discuss the matter right now.

'I was advised to take a look at the Church records instead,' he replied cautiously.

'What's all this about?' Connie enquired lightly.

'You know the reason Sandy set out for America in the first place was to attend some kind of Church conference? Well, Michael said there might be a record of it somewhere. I was curious to find out if it ever actually went ahead, what with all the disruption of the war. Mike said he'd see if he could dig the information up whilst we're in New York.' Julia took a nibble from a tiny triangular cucumber sandwich.

'And did he?' Harry asked in a level voice.

Michael cleared his throat. 'It took place here in the March of 1943. As we were already aware, neither Sandy nor Mackenzie Cowan attended. There was a different representative from the west of Scotland, instead.' Michael referred to the piece of paper in his pocket, 'the Rev. Stewart McLeod of Ganavan, Oban. Perhaps he had been a last minute replacement.'

'Maybe he was,' Harry said quietly, holding the china tea-cup to his lips.

'I didn't think you'd be able to tell us so much,' Julia gushed, her eyes shining brightly. 'I feel closer to my grandfather just being here in this city. I mean, I do realize he and Cowan never reached New York, but it's such an important part of the story. Do you think Rev. McLeod is still alive? I actually know Ganavan quite well. Callum and I lived very near to the town after we got married.'

Michael reached across and gently touched her hand. 'I really wouldn't have thought so. He must be long dead by now, darling.'

Harry placed his cup back into the saucer with a clatter. 'I'm not sure what connection you believe this man has to my dad,' he said, sounding put out.

'If you really want to discover what your grandfather was all about, then you need to come back to Canada. Sandy Thomson had no time for the conventions of the old Church after he settled in Ontario. Alex King was devoted to the religious movement my mother had grown up in. You certainly won't find any answers from this McLeod chap - alive or not.'

Michael had never seen Julia's uncle appear so ruffled.

'That's perfectly true I'm afraid, my dear. Our faith is very different from that practised by your father - with all due respect to him and his beliefs, of course.' Connie smiled kindly.

'But Sandy was *brought up* in the Church of Scotland. He had trained to be ordained as a minister before leaving the country. It *must* have had some kind of impact on his later life.'

Michael wished his wife would pick up on the charged atmosphere around the table and let the whole issue drop. But she seemed determined to push on.

'Didn't you notice *anything* in your dad's behaviour which harked back to his Scottish heritage? His background may have influenced the types of books he read, or the sorts of films he chose to watch?'

Michael was really concerned they may actually end up in a full blown argument. But when Harry replied, his voice had noticeably softened. 'Now you mention it, Dad always enjoyed that series of mystery novels set in the Highlands of Scotland. Who was the author, again? Oh yes, Catriona Gregory - that's it.'

Julia's face lit up. 'I've read all of her books too! How wonderful to think Sandy was a fan.' Michael noticed how she settled back comfortably into her seat, appearing totally satisfied with the meagre scrap of information she had just been thrown.

'You know, Harry is absolutely right,' Connie suddenly declared, clasping Julia's hand tightly. 'The two of you *should* come to New Brunswick for a visit. Can't you spend a week or so with us before you fly back home? You'd need to change your visas, but it's a very straightforward process. I'm sure we could get your flights changed. We've got loads of room at our place since the girls moved out. I'd love it *so* much. What do you say? Is there really anything you desperately need to get back for?'

Chapter Thirteen

The west coast of Scotland had experienced several days of persistent rain. The Crofts had been forced to stay in and around the farmhouse. The youngsters didn't appear too concerned. They were generally happy to immerse themselves in the amusements provided by their tablet computers and mp3s. Ian was the only one becoming restless. He had been keen to help Murray with his preparations for the sailing regatta later in the summer, and was becoming increasingly frustrated by the weather.

'It looks a bit better out there today,' Ian announced, sweeping into the kitchen and helping himself to a cup of coffee from the pot.

A covering of steel grey cloud hung ominously over the Kilbrannan Sound, but the rain was holding off for the time being.

'Yes,' Imogen conceded, peering out of the window, 'the wind has definitely let up. Do you want me to drive you over to the Cove this morning?'

'Great, Mum.' The tall young man leant across and gave her a kiss on the cheek. Imogen automatically beamed at this rare gesture of affection from her middle child.

Murray's sailing school and guest house was set in a pretty little cove, about two miles north of the Kilduggan Shore. With Colin Walmsley's investment, Murray was able to have a timber-framed, chalet-style building constructed, overlooking the bay. They named the place, Cove Lodge. The guests enjoyed professional sailing instruction during the daytime and then retired to the comfortable, modern chalet in the evening, where they had a meal cooked for them by a chef whom Colin employed for the season.

The business was doing well. This was only the second summer they had been up and running. They were already getting bookings for the following year, mainly from happy visitors, keen to return again.

As Imogen turned the bend at the headland, where the coastal road meandered towards Murray's property, she could tell something was amiss. There were three police cars parked up along the grass verge at the top of the beach. She could barely manoeuvre her wide estate car past them.

'What's going on?' Ian said in puzzlement, gazing at the group of men gathered in a kind of human circle down on the sand.

Imogen abruptly came to a stop, sensing she shouldn't proceed any further. 'Ian, just stay here for a second, will you? I'm going to see what's happening.'

Her son nodded in agreement, for once, not putting forward any objection. Imogen grabbed her mac from the back seat and pulled it on as she walked towards the main house. The rain had begun to come on again and a brisk breeze was blowing in off the Sound. Before she reached the front door, Imogen spotted a man striding towards her across the stony shoreline. As he grew nearer, she saw it was Colin.

'Imogen!' he called out, a smile briefly flickering across his otherwise grimly set features. 'Please come into the house for a moment.'

She dutifully followed him inside. 'What's the matter, Colin?'

He gestured for her to sit down on a long, wooden bench in the centre of the huge, open-plan kitchen. Imogen noted how well the man looked. He was deeply sun-tanned and was obviously kept very fit by his many business ventures. Colin's only concession to the ageing process was that his sandy blond hair had become streaked with grey.

'We experienced an unusually high tide last night, along with heavy rainfall for several hours. Our next group isn't due to arrive until later today, so Murray was sleeping here at the house on his own. As the tide went out this morning, Murray went down onto the shore, intending to clear away any debris that might have been washed up.' He paused, placing his hand on her shoulder. 'Murray found a body.'

'Hell. Is that what the policemen are gathered around, down there on the beach?'

Colin nodded sombrely.

'Shit, I hope Ian stays in the car,' Imogen stood up, ready to go out and check on him.

Before she left, Colin added falteringly, 'he's not been long dead. A few days or a week at most, they think. But the problem is that Murray recognised him – the body, I mean.'

Imogen looked confused.

'It was one of our guests – he was a member of the last party who were staying here.' He put a hand up to interrupt her as she started to speak, 'and don't ask me how the hell he wound up dead, because neither of us has the slightest idea.' He sighed and then said bleakly, 'this could be the end for our business, Imogen.'

It could mean far more than that, Imogen thought to herself, but did not say. Instead, she gently squeezed his hand. 'I'll leave you to get this sorted out. You know where we are if you *or* Murray need us. I'm really sorry this has happened Colin.'

Chapter Fourteen

Returning from the hallway, Imogen found Hugh reading the paper. He was sitting comfortably in an armchair, by the bay window, in the front sitting room of Kilduggan Farm. Hugh placed the broadsheet down as she entered. 'What's the latest news?'

'Strathclyde Police have been there all day. They've only just airlifted the body to the mainland. The detective in charge has sealed off the entire area for the time being.'

'It's not Inspector Zanco, is it?' Hugh asked with alarm.

'No, it's a woman, I believe.'

'Good. I don't think it would have been particularly favourable for Murray if Zanco had been leading the investigation.'

'That's very true. Colin says he's done a deal with the Glenrannoch Hotel. The manager there has a couple of chalets free this week, so he is going to take Murray's guests - the ones who are coming today on the six o'clock ferry. Colin will pay for them to have sailing tuition in Kilross for the duration of their stay on Garansay. It isn't ideal, but it's the best they can do for the moment.'

'What about the longer term?'

Imogen shrugged her shoulders. 'I've got no idea.' She sat down in the chair opposite her husband. 'Colin says the man's name was Gordon Parker. He came from Norfolk, Virginia and was 42 years old. Gordon was one of the ten strong party of American tourists who spent a fortnight at Cove Lodge. They left last Saturday.'

'Then how come nobody noticed he was missing?'

Hugh enquired.

'Apparently, this chap possessed some kind of Scottish ancestry. He'd never visited the country before, so he was meant to be leaving a few days early to tour part of the Highlands – the area where his great grandparents had originated from. Murray didn't see him in the final few days of their stay. The lad assumed he'd already gone on to continue his travels. The rest of the party were behaving completely as normal. It was another fellow who settled up the bill, so Murray didn't realise anything was wrong.'

'It could be a case of crossed wires. Everyone in the holiday party believed that Parker had left for the Highlands, when in fact he'd ended up in the Sound. Perhaps he'd headed out for an early morning swim and got into trouble. Or maybe he was washed off a rock during an evening stroll – the weather's been pretty volatile the last few days. Was he clothed when they discovered him?'

'Yes, and the body was badly bashed about. It must have been circling around that little cove in the swirling currents, getting increasingly pulverized. It was fortunate he was washed up at all, otherwise there wouldn't have been much of him left to identify.'

Hugh made a face. 'Did he have any family back home in Virginia?'

'He had a wife and two children, according to Colin. That fact shouldn't make it worse, but somehow it does.'

'Why weren't they with him on holiday?'

'The group were all members of a sailing club, based somewhere along Chesapeake Bay. The trip was supposed to improve their sailing skills. Some of them were couples, but others were travelling alone. Murray told Colin that Gordon Parker had mentioned fairly early on how his wife isn't much interested in boats.'

'Should we tell Michael what's happened?'

Imogen was silent for a moment. 'He and Julia have decided to extend their visit for another week. They're going to stay with Harry King and his family in Canada. If I let Mike know what's going on here, he'll want to come back straight away to see how Murray is. I don't think I could do that to poor Julia, it is their honeymoon, after all.'

'I think you're right. If we wait for a few days, this whole episode may have sorted itself out – death by misadventure and all that - best not to act too hastily.'

'Exactly,' Imogen replied with feeling. She turned to gaze out of the window. The thick cloud had cleared and blue sky had begun to prevail. It looked as if they would finally have a calm night. Imogen's thoughts drifted to the poor family of Gordon Parker, who would have to be told - perhaps right at this very moment - that the man they said goodbye to, just a few weeks ago, would never be returning home.

Chapter Fifteen

Murray looked tired and pre-occupied when they met him and Colin on the seafront in Kilross. Benn Ardroch, the largest mountain on Garansay, towered over the little port town. On a clear day like this one, when there was no cloud cover to obscure the great peaks, it appeared even more magisterial.

'Thanks for ringing this morning, Imogen. It was very kind of you to invite us out.' Colin gave her a wide smile and shook Hugh by the hand.

'I just thought the youngsters would enjoy a walk to the castle along the shore. It might help to take your minds off things.'

'I'll let Rusty out of the car then,' Colin commented, turning back to open the boot of his 4x4. An energetic Irish Setter bounded straight out, before coming to rest by his master's side.

'Can I hold Rusty's lead, Mr. Walmsley?' Bridie immediately asked, carefully stroking the animal's silky fur.

'Aye, go ahead - as long as your parents don't mind. You'll have to hold on to him tight if another dog comes near. He's still very young and impetuous.'

'Sure, I know what to do thanks,' she replied with confidence.

Murray and Ian quickly began an in-depth discussion, striding off along the beach in front of the group.

'It's good for the lad to keep himself occupied,' Colin said to Hugh and Imogen, as they followed on behind. 'He's been getting pretty uptight about the death at Cove Lodge. Murray is convinced it will ruin the business.'

'What do *you* think?' Hugh enquired.
Colin furrowed his brow. 'The police still haven't told us when we can start taking guests again. The case is being run from Glasgow by a D.I. Bevan. I met her briefly at the Lodge. She seems efficient enough. But she was asking a lot of questions about our safety procedures and how we make sure our guests are properly accounted for when they come in and out of the water. Bevan warned me that Parker's family might very well take out a lawsuit against us. The U.S. is more litigious than we are over here.'
'That would be awful,' Imogen remarked gravely.
'Aye, and totally unfair. Gordon went out with Murray and one of our other sailing instructors on the Wednesday afternoon. He came back safe and sound. The man was alive and well when the party ate their evening meal. Murray saw him at breakfast on Thursday, but there are no recorded sightings of him after that point. We aren't responsible for what the guests get up to in their spare time. The Lodge and its facilities have passed the inspection requirements. We've got all the necessary certificates.'
'Then it will get sorted out, eventually,' Hugh added.
'It probably will. The only problem is that it places a seed of doubt in people's minds. They're left with the impression that our operation is unsafe.'
'With time, the whole episode will blow over,' Imogen offered. 'There are accidental deaths around this coastline every year. The locals are certainly used to it.'
'Aye, that's right enough,' Colin conceded.
'Do the police have any idea how he ended up in the water?'
'The *post mortem* didn't tell them much. His body was badly battered by the rocks. They analysed his

stomach contents and decided he'd died not long after he'd eaten breakfast on Thursday. Bevan's theory is that he'd planned to take a walk out to the headland before getting on the ferry. A wave could have caught him off balance and swept him into the sea. The wind was pretty fierce on that day.'

'Hang on,' Imogen suddenly interrupted, 'where was his luggage then?'

Colin smiled at his friend's investigative instincts. 'They'd been sent on ahead to the ferry terminal at Kilross. Parker asked a cab company to pick up his suitcase and soft bag first thing on the Thursday morning. The cab dropped them off at the left luggage office. Bevan said they'd been sitting in a locker, unclaimed, until his body was found a few days later. They never turned up his mobile phone. Bevan thinks it might have been in his pocket - or even in his hand when he went into the water. It simply got washed away.'

'Why did Parker do that – send his stuff on ahead without him, I mean? Why didn't he just travel in the cab along with the bags?' Imogen demanded.

'These people have a lot of money, Imogen. They don't do things in the way that we would. I expect he wanted to be able to travel to Kilross without the burden of carrying his luggage. He'd probably paid someone at the ferry terminal to take his bags onto the boat for him as well, once he'd arrived.'

But Imogen wasn't satisfied with this. 'It sounds to me like he'd booked a cab to take him *and* his luggage to the boat on Thursday morning, straight after breakfast. Then, just before the taxi arrived, when it was too late to cancel it, something came up that he felt he had to stick around for. I've no idea what. So Parker tells the cab driver to take his bags for him and that he'll follow along later. He may even have said he'd call again, in an hour or so.' Imogen looked directly at Colin. 'Has the taxi driver been interviewed? He may very well have been the last person to see Parker alive.'

Colin shrugged his shoulders. 'I've no idea.'

Hugh addressed his wife. 'So, what might have caused Parker to hang about at Cove Lodge? He would probably have missed his ferry as a result. Do you think he was meeting somebody?'

'I'd need more information to be able to tell you that.'

'Bevan said that she and one of her officers were flying out to the States today to interview all of the people who were in the sailing party along with Gordon Parker. Bevan said she would be speaking to the widow, too.' Colin explained.

'I expect she wants to know why his wife hadn't reported the fact she'd had no contact with her husband between the time he went into the sea and the time when his body was discovered, three days later.'

Colin smiled. 'I don't know why you never joined the police force, Imogen. I expect Bevan could really do with your input on this case.'

Nothing more was said. Instead, they turned their attention towards the route ahead. Murray and Ian had reached the entrance to the castle. The young men waited dutifully by the stone gateway, whilst the rest of the group slowly caught them up.

Chapter Sixteen

The Kings owned a traditional Victorian house in the New Brunswick town of Fredericton. The area in which they lived was located in eastern Canada and, along with Nova Scotia and Prince Edward Island, it was fringed by the Atlantic Ocean.

Harry picked Michael and Julia up from the airport in Halifax, Nova Scotia, early that morning. It was then another hour and a half's drive back to their place in Fredericton. As soon as they landed, Michael felt that this was more his kind of holiday destination. He noted how the landscape was lush, green and mountainous. The whole region seemed to him to possess a kind of old-fashioned charm.

The Kings had given their guests a lovely double room which looked directly out onto farmland. The décor was surprisingly plain and understated. Somehow, Michael was expecting Harry's house to be more flashy. He wasn't totally sure why.

Connie had cooked them a simple supper. They gathered around the table in their modest, country-style kitchen to eat it.

'How were your last few days in New York?' Harry asked.

'Very good, thank you,' Julia replied. 'The city was becoming too hot for us, so we took a trip out to Coney Island.'

'Oh yes, these big cities can get a bit much after a while,' Connie commented, placing down a pot of chicken stew and taking a seat.

'You certainly have a great deal of open space here,' Michael added. 'The countryside is beautiful.'

'I always think it's like a cross between Scotland and Cornwall,' Harry explained, 'what with the hills and the pretty fishing villages.'

'I'd have to take your word for it,' Connie said cheerfully. 'I've never been to the U.K.'

'You must come and visit us on Garansay,' Michael immediately responded. 'We have plenty of room at the farmhouse.'

Connie smiled. 'You're very kind.'

'She's unlikely to take you up on the offer, Mike. Connie doesn't like to fly. She has to psyche herself up for a short-haul. I can't see her managing a flight any longer than a couple of hours.'

'I had a friend at university with the same problem,' Julia said. 'She did a few courses, you know – the ones that the main airlines run. It really worked wonders for her.'

'It doesn't bother me terribly, Julia. To be honest, I was brought up to believe that God didn't plan for us to travel in that way. Oh, I know it is all part and parcel of the modern world. But I still like to adhere to some aspects of my parents' way of life.' Connie got up to make the coffees.

'Have you ever heard of the Acadians?' Harry directed this question towards Michael.

'No, I haven't.'

'They started out as a group of 500 French Settlers, who colonised the Annapolis Valley in Nova Scotia in the 1600s. They took on the name *Acadie*. Their aim was to create an ideal pastoral society. They maintained a traditional farming lifestyle for decades and their community flourished. However, after the French were defeated by the British at the end of the Seven Years War in the 1760s, the Acadians were expelled from Canada. Many went to the U.S., but when the British and French made peace a decade later, the Acadians gradually began to return. Connie's family were descendants of the Acadians. They lived a simple rural life in a farmstead near

Campbellton.'

'Yes, I think I do recall reading something about them,' Michael said. 'Didn't the original Acadian refugees who fled to Louisiana become the Cajuns of today?'

'That's right. Despite the simplicity of their churches, the community was both French-speaking and Catholic.'

Connie poured coffee into a set of china cups. 'My folks spoke a little French, but I barely know any. It was the lifestyle which made our set-up different. I recall my grandparents driving around in a horse and trap. This was well into the 1950s.'

'How fascinating,' Julia said. 'What about the community that your mother was born into, Harry, were they similar to the Acadians?'

He took a sip of coffee. 'Whilst you're here, we'll take you to visit the Acadian Village near Bathurst. They've got the place set up pretty much as it would have been after the first settlers arrived. In answer to your question, my experience was a little different from Connie's. Jim and I grew up in Ontario, on the northern shores of Lake Superior. The religious group your grandfather joined wasn't really like the Acadians, although they certainly promoted a simple existence. I suppose, the closest comparison would be to the Mennonites. We believed in living our lives in the way the Bible had taught us. My father refused to take an oath of allegiance to anyone other than God. By the time he had reached Canada, Alex had completely rejected the hierarchy advocated by the established Church in Scotland.'

Julia considered this for a few moments, enjoying the taste of her Canadian coffee. 'The Mennonites became known as the Amish when they settled in the U.S.A., is that right?'

'Yes, that's correct. Members of the sect then

moved into Ontario in the early 1800s,' Harry clarified. 'Our beliefs could be seen as an offshoot of their ideas, but in many ways we were quite different.'

As they lay in bed together, later that night, Julia rested her head on Michael's shoulder and said, 'the life my family lived here in Canada is so dissimilar to the upbringing I had. My dad has always been critical of these independent religious sects. He feels the way they cut themselves off from mainstream society is unhealthy.'

'I get the sense that the community Sandy joined, when he created a new life for himself here in Canada, was convenient to him. Arriving in Ontario must have been like entering a new world. It's frontier territory. The northern part of the region is almost completely uninhabitable. To join a sect which had deliberately set itself apart from the usual laws and practices of Canadian society might have suited him.'

Julia sat herself up. 'Because he was living a lie, you mean, and had left a wife and child behind in Scotland. So being a part of this group meant he was less likely to be discovered.'

Michael nodded.

'That makes it sound as if his faith had nothing to do with the choice. It sounds as if actually, he was trying to *hide* himself within this community, which was perfect for Sandy's purpose, as it was so remote and isolated from mainstream society. It seems a little extreme, doesn't it? Why didn't he simply file for a divorce from Margie? She met Alistair McClelland only a couple of years later, I'm sure she would have been happy to agree to it. Sandy certainly wouldn't have been the first man to ever have walked out on a wife and child.'

'No,' Michael answered quietly, 'which makes me wonder if there was something else. There could have been *another* reason why he had to leave Scotland in such a hurry, a reason that was far worse than abandoning a young family.'

Julia said nothing at all. She slowly lowered herself back down to rest against her husband's chest, her eyes wide open and her mind ticking away, knowing that her chances of getting to sleep tonight had all but disappeared.

Chapter Seventeen

Detective Inspector Danielle Bevan arrived at Dulles International Airport late the previous night. They transferred onto an internal flight heading to Norfolk, Virginia in the early hours of the morning. When she and Detective Constable Andy Calder grabbed some breakfast at their hotel, they had barely managed to get any sleep at all.

'We'll speak with the widow first,' Bevan stated, sipping from a huge mug of strong coffee. 'You ask the questions, Andy. I'll observe her reactions. We want to know why she hadn't clocked on he was missing for three whole days. I'm also interested in the reason he was holidaying alone. Maybe there were problems in the marriage.'

'Do we really think the death is suspicious, then?'

'I'm keeping an open mind. His body was so mangled there's no chance of being able to tell whether or not he was attacked *before* he went into the water.'

'But we do know that drowning was the cause of death.'

'Yes,' she replied steadily, 'it's just this issue with the luggage that I'm not comfortable with. Something about it doesn't sit right. The taxi driver said it was a last minute decision to send the bags on ahead. So, if Parker suddenly decided not to leave, what was he hanging around at the Cove for?'

After they picked up the hire car, Bevan let Calder do the driving. She wanted to be free to think. Danielle Bevan had reached the rank of Detective Inspector just before her thirty-fifth birthday. Some of her colleagues had found this fact difficult to swallow, especially as she looked even younger. Danielle had a tall, slender frame and wore her dark brown hair in a closely cropped style, which gave her pretty face an elfin-like appearance. Danielle had found that the secret to her career success was twofold; she didn't have a family, and she didn't drink. This seemed to make Bevan at least twenty percent more efficient at her job than the majority of her fellow officers.

Andy Calder was a case in point. Danielle liked him a lot and believed he was an excellent policeman. But he'd got married a year ago and his wife was now expecting their first child. Since his wedding, Andy seemed to have put on at least two stone. He was always the first to suggest a trip to the pub after a shift and although he'd not yet reached the age of thirty-four, he looked a good decade older than Bevan. In fact, when they worked together, he was often mistaken for the senior officer. Bevan knew it wasn't sexism. She was quite confident she would make the same assumption herself, if she didn't know any better.

The Parkers' residence was positioned on a wide, leafy street, where each detached property was set back from the road within a sizeable plot of land. There was an estate car parked in the driveway which Bevan would estimate as being no more than two years old. 'Parker's I.T. consultancy business must have been doing well,' she commented, as they climbed out of the car.

'Maybe the wife works too,' Calder added, leading the way along the path to the front porch.

Gabriella Parker directed them into a small and cosy sitting room at the rear of the house. Bevan decided there must be another, bigger lounge, somewhere else on the ground floor of the property. She wondered why they hadn't been invited in there.

The woman spent at least ten minutes preparing them a tray of coffees and when she returned to the room, she had an expression of grim forbearance on her face.

'We are very sorry for your loss, Mrs. Parker.' Bevan maintained steady eye-contact.

She nodded, sitting down heavily on a chair in front of them. Gabriella Parker was a thin woman, aged in her early forties. Her long, blondish hair was pulled away from her face in a ponytail. She didn't appear to be wearing any make-up. 'I've sent the boys to my parents' today. They wanted to go. My folks will take them out someplace.'

'We need to ask you a few questions, Mrs. Parker.' Andy took the lead now, shifting forward in his seat. 'We know that your husband died at some point between 9am and 12.30pm on Thursday 29th July. But we are still unsure as to why his absence after this time, before his body was discovered on the Sunday, wasn't picked up by anyone. Were you accustomed to having regular contact with your husband whilst he was away?'

'Call me Gabby,' she stated quietly. 'You want to know why I never reported him missing. You don't understand how I couldn't have realised something had happened to him for those three days before he was found.' The woman looked up, catching the eye of both detectives.

'When had you last spoken to him, Gabby?' Bevan prompted.

'When he left here for the airport, three weeks ago. After that, we only communicated by e-mail. I was angry with him, you see. It's the summer vacation and I was cross that he'd organised a sailing holiday, leaving me to look after the boys. I have my own retail business online and I work from home. I always felt that Gordon didn't properly appreciate the fact I wasn't on-call for round the clock child-care.' Tears had begun to stream down her face. 'I specifically asked him not to travel to Scotland. But he insisted he was going. It made me wonder if there was a woman involved, someone from the Sailing Club, maybe.'

'Were you thinking of anybody in particular?' Calder asked, writing it all down in his notebook.

'No,' Gabby sighed heavily and shook her head. 'I've met them all before and it never struck me that Gordon was overly friendly with any specific individual. Most of the women were married, although I expect that doesn't mean much. It was just that he was so *determined* to take this trip. Usually, if I wasn't happy about something, then we would talk it out, reach a compromise. But I just couldn't get through to him on this. Now he's dead. Why the hell didn't he listen to me?'

'Do you have a copy of the last e-mail you received from your husband?' Bevan asked.

'I've got all of his messages saved. I'll print them out for you. The last one arrived on the Wednesday evening. He was telling me about the sailing they'd done that day and how much he was looking forward to his visit to the Highlands. But do you know what's really awful? I was so upset with him, and resentful that he was having such a good time without me, that I never even replied.'

Chapter Eighteen

The Virginia State authorities had been very cooperative. Bevan was given permission to interview all of the witnesses involved in the case. The local police accepted that it was unfortunate the holiday party had already returned home before the body of Gordon Parker was discovered on Garansay. Otherwise, they would most certainly have been questioned whilst still on Scottish soil. Bevan was keen to tread softly, as she would need to work alongside her American counterparts if this turned into a full-blown murder investigation further down the line.

There were nine people who needed to be interviewed, so Bevan and Calder were splitting the list between them. Most of the individuals lived within a few miles of each other in the Virginia Beach area of Chesapeake Bay. It was a Saturday morning, the sun was blazing down, and for once, Bevan wished she wasn't on the job, but was able to take a few hours out to explore the region instead. She had never been to America before and this part of the Atlantic coastline struck her as particularly impressive.

The first house call Bevan made was to a married couple, who lived in the suburbs of Virginia Beach. As soon as Mrs. Morgan opened her front door to the detective, she immediately looked guilty. They sat on sun-loungers in a large patio area, shaded by a maple tree. The lady required no prompting to begin telling Bevan everything she knew.

'We feel absolutely terrible,' she declared. 'John and I were good friends with Gordon. We'd chatted to him at breakfast on the day we thought he'd left. But it didn't occur to us to find out if he'd reached the hotel safely. We simply said we'd see him back in the States.' Liz and John Morgan looked a little older than the Parkers. D.I. Bevan simply could not picture this lady as Gordon's lover.

'And you didn't see Mr. Parker again on that day? Walking along the beach, or up on the headland, perhaps?'

'No, we did not. We said goodbye to Gordon at breakfast.' It was John Morgan who spoke this time. 'Then, we pottered around Cove Lodge until lunchtime. Liz did some washing, I think.'

'Where in the Highlands did Gordon Parker say that he was heading off to?'

'The place had a funny name, didn't it, John? Drumna - something or other.'

'Drumnadrochit?' Bevan suggested.

'Yes, that's it!'

'We haven't managed to locate any hotels or B&Bs in the Highlands who were expecting Gordon to arrive that evening. There was no documentation relating to a booking in his luggage either.'

'That is odd,' John Morgan said. 'Gordon was a very organised sort of guy. He wouldn't have simply turned up in a town without knowing where he was going to stay.'

'What was Mr. Parker's mood like during the sailing holiday? Did he appear worried or pre-occupied at all?'

Liz glanced across at her husband and then stared down at her lap. 'He wasn't his usual self. When I asked if anything was wrong, during the first week, he told me that he and his wife had argued before he went away. Gordon said he hated upsetting her, but he really needed to take the trip. I said, why couldn't Gabby have come along too. Gordon replied that she didn't like sailing and besides, they couldn't ask

Gabby's parents to have the boys for so long.'

'You suggest that Gordon wasn't himself on the holiday. But was it more than that, could he have been described as depressed?'

'You're asking if we think he took his own life,' John responded levelly, 'I would say definitely not. He and Gabby had a pretty good relationship. The fact they had argued was out of character for them both. I'm sure they would have resolved the problem when he got back home to the U.S. But having said that, Gordon was one of the most sensible and able sailors I've ever shared a boat with. He understood the dangers of the sea. We've been out in the open Atlantic together many times, occasionally in very rough conditions. So I cannot picture Gordon getting himself swept off a rock and drowning. I know these things do happen, but not to experienced sea-farers like him. I'm just not prepared to accept it.'

When they met up later at the hotel, hot and exhausted, Bevan and Calder compared notes over a burger and fries in the near-empty lounge bar.

'What were your impressions?' Bevan asked carefully, setting down her half-finished glass of coke.

'None of the women I spoke to seemed to be a candidate for Gordon's lover. They all had their husbands with them on the trip for starters. Only one other bloke was single,' Calder flicked through his pad. 'Mark Johnson, 47 years old, divorced. Didn't know Parker particularly well, but thought he was a very good sailor, says he respected him. Nobody claimed to have seen Parker after breakfast on the Thursday morning. They all assumed he'd left on the ferry like he'd told them he was going to.'

'I didn't come across any potential love-interest on

my side either. But one couple told me something interesting. The Morgans were adamant that Gordon Parker was far too sensible and experienced a sailor to get himself washed out to sea. The husband didn't seem to be suggesting it was suicide either. He was hinting that someone else must have been involved.'

'Did he provide you with any suspects?' Calder ordered another beer.

'No. They both said that Parker was out of sorts during the holiday, he told them it was because of the argument he had with his wife. According to them, Gordon Parker was headed to Drumnadrochit after leaving Garansay.'

'At least that narrows down our search area for hotels.'

'*If* he was telling them the truth. I've got a feeling wherever Parker was going, the details were on his smartphone, now somewhere at the bottom of the Kilbrannan Sound.'

'Not unless whoever killed him pocketed it.'

'The techies couldn't get any kind of signal from the phone, so wherever it ended up, it's now been destroyed.'

'Parker was an I.T. expert, right? There wasn't any other device in his luggage was there - a laptop or a tablet computer or anything like that?' The barmaid handed him a fresh bottle. Calder took a lengthy swig, knowing they had already been over all this back at the briefing room in Glasgow.

'Nothing. His wife says he used the smartphone for everything when he travelled. We've got permission to seize his computer and laptop from the house. The Virginia Police are going to process it for us.'

'Is there anything more we can do from here?'

'I want to share what we've got with the local detectives, see if any of the sailing party have got previous convictions. Somehow, I doubt it.' Bevan pushed away her empty plate. 'I was inclined to believe them, when the witnesses said they hadn't seen him since the Thursday morning. I don't think we'll find Parker's murderer here. I want to go back to Garansay, take another look around that Cove and speak with the owners again. Parker met up with someone the day he died, I'm certain of that, but I don't believe it was one of the sailing group.'

'So it *was* murder then?'

'Oh yes, I'm pretty sure of it now – aren't you?'

Chapter Nineteen

The still waters of the Kilbrannan Sound were sparkling in the morning sunshine. A soft breeze was gently disturbing its turquoise-blue surface, making the conditions perfect for a sail.

Murray White was preparing to take out the *Iona*, which was his largest yacht. At 40 feet in length, this sailing boat could comfortably take a crew of four or five. Murray used her when teaching his more advanced clients. The *Iona* was a step above the more typical, weekender yachts their visitors were used to. She certainly wasn't cheap, but the investment had been worth it. His sailing school could now challenge any other that currently operated on Garansay - or anywhere else along the west coast for that matter.

But over the last 24 hours, Murray had two more bookings for Cove Lodge cancelled. News certainly travelled fast. The police had permitted them to start receiving guests once again, but as soon as the Assistant Chief Constable of Police Scotland announced on television that the death of Gordon Parker was being treated as murder, the phone calls and e-mails started to trickle in. Murray had felt obliged to return every single deposit. He could understand people's reticence to come and stay here, not while the case was still being investigated, anyway.

Murray was brushing down the deck when the Crofts arrived. He heard their car pull onto the gravelled area outside the lodge. Murray was glad that Imogen and Hugh were here. He hadn't always got on well with Michael's younger sister, but he hoped all that was behind them. He had to admit he needed her support right now.

Bridie was the first to reach the jetty. She pounded along the wooden slats in her canvas pumps, stopping when she got to the stern of the boat. 'Can I come aboard?' She called out eagerly, smiling broadly at her friend.

'Sure,' Murray replied, offering his hand and guiding her carefully onto the deck. He immediately noticed the blood rush to her pale cheeks, making her pretty face appear flushed and healthy. Murray was perfectly aware Bridie Croft had a crush on him. He knew that his blond hair, piercing blue eyes and tanned physique attracted attention from girls. Even the older women who came to stay at Cove Lodge become giggly and flirtatious whenever it was he who led a sailing course. His assistant at the school, Mackie Shaw, didn't have the same effect on their female guests, although Murray sensed he would really like to.

The others followed on close behind. Imogen had brought along a large and heavy-looking cool box, which Murray took from her and placed down in the galley. Hugh asked the young Skipper what he would like him to do and quickly got on with the job of untying the yacht from its mooring.

The wind was only very slight and they needed to rely on the outboard engine to power them into the middle of the Sound before there was enough of a breeze to lift the sails. Imogen deeply inhaled the cool sea air. There was not much for her to do, with Murray, Hugh and Ian on board, all of whom were experienced yachtsmen. The hills of Garansay and Kintyre flanked them on both sides. The view of Ben Mhor was so clear that you could see the smooth contours of the slate grey rocks on its surface, reflected in the sun.

Once they were scudding comfortably through the

centre of the channel, heading towards Port na Mara Bay with the wind behind them, Murray left Ian in charge and moved across to sit beside Imogen.

'The police are coming back to interview me again tomorrow,' he said. 'But there isn't any more I can tell them.'

'How's business?'

'I've had two more cancellations this week. Hopefully, the whole thing will blow over when they find out what happened to the man.' Murray continued to gaze out to sea, his handsome face expressionless.

'So the police think Parker met up with someone on the morning he was killed. Did you or Mackie see anyone hanging around the Cove on that day – or in the days leading up to Parker's death?' Imogen asked.

The young man shook his head. 'I really don't recall seeing anyone out of the ordinary. We're pretty isolated out there. Occasionally, walkers will come across the shore. They're usually heading towards the King's Caves. I don't always take much notice of them, especially in the summer months.'

'What about the English couple who you bought the jetty from? Their holiday cottage is down by the roadside. Have they been staying on Garansay recently? They could have seen something,' Imogen suddenly enquired.

'Actually, I'm not sure. Their parking space is beyond the headland, so I don't always know if they're at the house or not. Part of the agreement when they sold us the land was that we wouldn't bother them. But I'm sure the police will have already checked that out.'

'They probably knocked at the door, but if the couple had already left the island, like the American tourists had done, perhaps they didn't pursue it any further. Have you got contact details for them?'

'Aye, I have. It was quite a complicated process to purchase the land. I've communicated with them quite a lot over the last two years. Would you like their phone number and address?'

'That won't be necessary, but I think you should provide the police with their details. If they spotted something unusual that week, it might help to put you and Colin in the clear.'

Murray nodded and then manoeuvred along to the bow of the boat, noticing it was time to help Ian and Hugh bring the *Iona* into port. They planned to have lunch at the Gilstone Hotel, before sailing back to Kilduggan via the north-end of the island. Imogen looked across at the little fishing village. Its row of white-washed stone cottages was shining brightly in the sunlight as their boat slowly approached the tiny harbour.

Michael and Julia were due to return at the weekend. Imogen hoped she had done the right thing by not telling them about the body that washed up on the beach at Cove Lodge. She and Hugh had expected the whole matter to have been resolved by the time they got back from Canada. Sadly, this hadn't proved to be the case. Instead, Murray had found himself caught up in the centre of a murder inquiry, and Imogen sensed her older brother wasn't going to like it one little bit.

Chapter Twenty

The more she considered it, the more determined Julia became to visit the place where Sandy Thomson had begun his new life. She and Michael hired a car and spent a day driving through eastern Quebec, reaching Montreal by evening and staying the night in a modern hotel on the banks of the St Lawrence River.

'Thanks for agreeing to take this trip,' Julia said quietly, as they strolled arm-in-arm through the old city, early the next morning.

'Whilst we're here in Canada, it's an opportunity to see something of the country. It would be silly not to take a tour around,' Michael commented. In fact, he was quite relieved to get away from the Kings for a few days and spend some time with his new wife, although he didn't tell Julia that.

'Harry said he and Uncle Jim had grown up in a place called York Bay, which is on the northern shores of Lake Superior. I'd love to be able to visit it.'

'Why don't we drive there today? We can stay in a hotel in the area tonight and head off towards Toronto the following day. Then, we can easily take in the Niagara Falls before we travel back to New Brunswick. We can't really come out all this way without seeing the most famous attraction in the region.'

Julia squeezed his arm tight. 'That's a great idea. Let's get back to our room right now. We might as well make a prompt start.'

'It looks more like a sea than a lake,' Julia said, in awe of the powerful waves which were crashing against a series of rocks, projected in jagged clusters from a long shoreline that ran parallel to the road.

'Lake Superior covers over 31,000 square miles,' Michael stated, having been poring over the guidebook at their last rest-stop. 'Apart from a couple of fresh-water ports, there's nothing along this northern coastline but dense forest and untamed wilderness.'

'There's the sign for York Bay,' Julia pronounced, directing Michael to take a sharp left turn which led them along a twisting, narrow track flanked by towering fir trees. The centre of the town consisted of a single u-shaped street which followed the contours of a small, stone-built harbour. They found a parking space along the waterfront and strolled towards what looked like a row of shops.

'It's very quiet,' Julia said. 'I hope there's somewhere open. It is miles back to civilization.'

A general store sat half-way along the street and it appeared to be open for business, although there weren't many products out on display. A middle-aged woman was serving behind the counter. Julia gave her a wide smile. 'Good afternoon,' she said. 'Could you tell me if there's a place in town we could get a drink and something to eat?'

The woman eyed her suspiciously. 'There's a hotel opposite the harbour. Is that what you mean?'

'Yes, that would be perfect, thank you. Is it open now, do you know?'

'Are you English?' She leant her ample weight onto the counter-top, appearing suddenly interested.

'Scottish,' Julia corrected. 'A branch of my family lived near here after the war. I wanted to come and visit, whilst we were in the area.'

'What was their name?' She tilted her head to one side. The hint of a smile flickered across her thin lips.

'Alex and Eleanor King. Their two boys were called

Harry and James.'

'I knew them,' the woman said flatly. 'I was at school with Jim King. Nice guy.'

'He's my uncle,' Julia explained.

'Don't go down to the hotel,' she said sharply. 'Come out the back and I'll fix you both a coffee.'

The woman didn't give them a chance to reply but quickly disappeared through a doorway at the rear of the shop. Julia and Michael could do nothing except obediently follow. The room she led them into was not at all as Julia had expected. Just beyond the stock room was a huge open-plan conservatory with a newly fitted kitchenette at one end and a sofa and chairs at the other.

She gestured towards the seating area. 'Sit yourselves down. My name is Mariella Wilson. Jim might remember me. We were quite good friends for a while.' The woman busied herself filling an impressive-looking coffee-maker.

'I'm Julia Nichols and this is my husband, Michael. I'll certainly mention to Jim that we spoke with you.'

'Is he okay these days?' Mariella asked with genuine concern.

'Oh yes, Jim and his partner live in Chicago. They're both producers for a cable T.V. network.'

Mariella carried over the drinks. 'I'm really pleased to hear that. York Bay wasn't the most tolerant of places to grow up in, as I'm sure you can imagine. The whole family left under something of a cloud, when Jim was only in his late teens. I always hoped he would get in touch with me, but he never did. It was a real shame.'

Julia looked puzzled, she wondered if the news of her grandfather's double-life had somehow reached here. Perhaps the shame had forced them to leave. 'What do you mean?'

Mariella settled comfortably into one of the soft

chairs, rested her generous bosom on her crossed arms and sighed. 'Jim's dad was a preacher. He held services out of the old chapel on the edge of town. We have a special spiritual tradition here, it goes back decades. I'm not even sure if Mr. King was part of any kind of established faith, you know?'

Julia nodded.

'Back in those days, the church was packed with folk every Sunday. My parents went too. Mr. King was a very charismatic man and most of York Bay followed his teachings. But it *was* the 1970s and us kids made the mistake of believing that times had moved on. Jim told his closest friends that he was gay when he turned 18. Gradually, the word filtered out. Finally, his parents got to hear about it.'

'I thought Alex and Eleanor were okay about Jim's sexuality?' Julia was shocked.

'Oh, they were fine with it. Jim says he thought his parents always knew anyway. No, it was the pious folk of York Bay who didn't take too kindly to the news. The congregation started to boycott Mr. King's services. Even my mum and dad stayed away. The Church relied on the generous donations from its congregation in order to keep running. After a few months it was clear that Alex King couldn't stay here any longer. Harry was already at college by this time, but Eleanor and Jim had to leave town along with Mr. King. They went out east, I heard.'

'They moved to Ottawa first and then settled in New Brunswick, a few years later.' Julia mulled things over for a moment. 'Harry has never said anything about this to me - the poor family.'

'Well,' said Mariella, leaning forward conspiratorially, 'feel sorry for Jim, by all means, but as far as the rest of the family goes, it was a case of the chickens coming home to roost. Alex King had been preaching about 'family values' and railing against 'ungodly relationships' for decades, so he couldn't then be surprised when his followers refused to accept a leader who had a gay son.'

Julia was reduced to silence by this revelation.

'What's strange, is that this is the second time I've heard the Kings mentioned in the space of only a month. Before that, I'd not had cause to think of them in nearly forty years.'

'Who else has been talking about the Kings?' Michael asked, sensing that Julia's mind was temporarily pre-occupied.

'Sam at the Hotel said a man was in the bar asking about the family about four weeks ago.'

'Did he say what this man looked like?' Michael probed.

'He was well dressed, a city type, Sam thought. But the guy was local – a Canadian, I mean. He came into the shop afterwards and bought some batteries. We don't get very many visitors from out of town, so it tends to stick in your mind when we do.' She peered closely at Michael. 'I'd say he was about your age.'

Mariella stretched across to a cabinet beside her and retrieved a pen and paper. 'Here,' she said, scribbling something down. 'This is my address and phone number. Give it to Jim when you next see him. I'd like him to know that I never felt the same way my parents did. His Dad might've brainwashed the rest of the town, but there were still some of us left who had a mind of our own.'

Chapter Twenty One

Julia and Michael found a pleasant guest house on the shores of Lake Huron to spend the night. They were both tired after all the driving they'd done over the past couple of days. After having an early dinner in a local Italian restaurant they went straight back to their modest room, which had a lovely view across the still waters of the lake.

Julia kicked off her shoes and lay down on the bed. 'I suppose it's pretty obvious when you think about it. It was bound to be difficult for the leader of an independent religious group to have a son who was gay.'

'Not necessarily,' Michael replied, sitting on the eiderdown next to her. 'Most denominations of the Church are fairly tolerant about same-sex relationships these days. The United Reformed Church has just agreed to perform the marriage ceremony for same-sex couples. It sounds like it was your grandfather himself who had stoked up the prejudice amongst his congregation. Harry did say his father was a die-hard traditionalist.'

Julia shuffled back, so that her upper body was supported by two plumped up pillows. 'But that is what seems strange. Harry and Connie always told me how great Alex and Eleanor were about Jim coming out. Apparently, they were both really close to Jim's partner, Steve.'

'It's like Harry with his daughter. He'd really prefer it if she was married to the father of her children, but he still loves Sally just the same and he's probably never told *her* that. We might have our strongly-held beliefs about how life should be, but when it's our own family involved it changes things.

Hugh has always maintained that it's not what people *say* that counts, but what they *do*.'

'Yes, I can see all that. It's just I suppose I must have built up an idealized picture of my grandfather in my mind, because I'd imagined him as a kind and tolerant person. But actually, I don't really think he was. Perhaps my dad's been right all along. Alex King really wasn't worth forgiving.'

Michael laid his hand on Julia's arm. 'Can we be *absolutely* certain that Alex King was Rob's father? Is there any evidence that Harry and Jim's dad *was* Sandy Thomson other than the fact Kenneth Garvie recognised him on a street in Toronto thirty years later?'

'Have I never told you?'

Michael looked puzzled.

'Harry, Jim and I took a D.N.A. test in the late nineties. It was Harry's idea. He wanted to prove to Dad that we really were related. The results were totally conclusive; Jim and Harry are definitely my uncles and, therefore, Dad's half-brothers. There isn't any doubt about that.'

'So Margie *was* carrying Sandy's child when he left on the ship in 1943.'

Julia furrowed her brow. 'Did you think she might not have been?'

'Well, it *was* another possibility I'd considered. If Sandy had suspected Margie was expecting another man's baby, it would have given him a reason to abscond.'

'But Margie wasn't like that,' Julia said flatly.

Michael didn't contradict her, but simply smiled and clasped her hand. 'Darling, I really don't think we should mention to Harry and Connie what Mariella told us in York Bay. He has never talked to you about it before. I think he might be angry if he finds out we went snooping around behind his back.'

'I agree. It's their family business, not mine. I don't know why he never confided in me about it because I would have understood, but that isn't my concern. I haven't got the right to know everything about them.'

Michael wasn't so sure that was true. Alex King had abandoned Julia's father and grandmother without ever giving them so much as a penny in support. Michael discovered himself feeling that Julia deserved to know every last detail about Alexander King and his family. And suddenly, he was gripped by a determination to assist her in finding it out.

Chapter Twenty Two

When Detective Inspector Dani Bevan first encountered the business partners who ran Cove Lodge Sailing School, she thought they were father and son. It quickly became clear they were not, but the similarities between the pair remained marked.

Colin Walmsley was tall, broad shouldered and obviously physically fit. He had blue eyes and sandy-blond hair which was rapidly turning to a kind of ash-grey. Murray White was also very fair. His piercing blue eyes were the first thing Bevan noticed about him, along with the fact that the young man was strikingly handsome.

As the Detective Inspector drove towards the west coast of Garansay, in order to interview the two men again, Andy Calder briefed her on what he had discovered since they returned from America.

'Did you realise Ma'am, that Murray White was the kid who tried to claim that dead lad's trust fund a couple of years back?'

Bevan took her eyes off the road momentarily, turning towards her companion. 'Shit. I thought his name rang a bell. Did he serve any prison time?'

'No, according to the report, a chap called Michael Nichols paid back the money he'd spent and the dead boy's grandmother refused to press charges. She was the chief beneficiary of the estate.'

'Murray's got a fan club then. Who says that good looks don't pay?'

Andy chuckled. 'He started up the business here not long after that. Colin Walmsley is the main investor. Murray is really just his employee. He manages the place and runs the sailing courses.'

'Have we got anything on Walmsley?'

'No convictions or criminal record. His finances are healthy. The farm he runs is very profitable. This venture is just a side-line for him. Early signs show it was starting to do well. This murder is bad news for both of them.'

'So, neither White nor Walmsley have any motive for wanting Gordon Parker dead. And murder is a big step up from small-time fraud.'

'I agree,' Andy said, as his boss swung the car into the driveway of Cove Lodge.

Bevan had arranged to meet the men here. Colin Walmsley looked apprehensive as he led the police officers into an impressive kitchen-diner. Murray was sitting at a long refectory table with an impassive expression on his face.

'Can I offer you a drink?' Colin asked.

'Two coffees please; white, no sugar,' Andy quickly responded. It had been at least half an hour since he had his refreshments on the ferry.

'I wanted to update you both on where we are with our inquiries,' Bevan began. 'We understand the adverse publicity hasn't been good for your business, but when someone has been murdered, I'm afraid the investigation has to take priority.'

Colin nodded, but Murray stayed silent, his countenance remaining unchanged.

'We now believe Parker met up with a man or woman on the morning he was killed. It is crucial that we identify this person. I know we've asked you before, but can you recall *anybody* hanging around the Cove on that morning?'

Murray snapped out of his reverie, as he recalled the conversation he had with Imogen. The lad told Bevan about the English couple who had a holiday cottage at the headland, he gave her their details and suggested they may have seen something, but returned home before the police made their house-to-house inquiries.

'Thank you Murray, that's very helpful,' Bevan stated.

Colin and Murray went over the events of the previous week again, whilst the detectives sipped their coffees. After hearing them out for ten minutes or so, Andy Calder directed a question to Murray. 'You were with the group most often for that fortnight. Did you get a sense of how they all got on? I mean, you would have been well-placed to notice if there were any tensions or rivalries between the men. I know a little bit about sailing, and I'm aware of how competitive it can be.'

Murray smiled ruefully. 'I've always tried to avoid that element of the sport myself, but I certainly know what you mean. In the case of this group, I thought they were all extremely polite. I've found Americans usually are – if that's not a stereotype?' The lad started to shift about awkwardly, suddenly looking embarrassed. 'The only thing I did notice, was that one of the ladies, Mrs. Moore, she could be quite flirtatious - with me, I mean.' He glanced at Colin. 'I did absolutely nothing to encourage her, I swear. I could tell her husband was getting annoyed about it.'

'What did you do?' Andy enquired levelly.

'I made sure the Moores always went out on the boat with Mackie and not me. That seemed to sort the issue out. I didn't have very much to do with her after that. The situation didn't affect Mr. Parker, though. His wife wasn't even on the trip with him.'

Bevan wrote something down in her notepad. 'Is Mackie Shaw around the Cove today? We'd like to have another word with him, too.'

'He'll be in the boat shed,' Murray replied. 'I've asked him to do some maintenance work on the yachts - so he isn't twiddling his thumbs, what with us having no guests at all.’

Chapter Twenty Three

Bevan would have placed Mackie Shaw somewhere in his early thirties. When she and Andy located him, the man was busily scrubbing the fibre-glass hull of an impressive looking yacht, which was placed on a stand in the centre of the boat shed. He glanced up as they entered, but then carried on with his task.

'Mr. Shaw?' Andy called over, raising his warrant card. 'We'd like to have a word with you.'

The man carefully put down the soft-bristled brush and wiped his hands on a cloth. 'I don't think there's anything more I can help you with,' he said.

'Mr. White told us he had some bother with a lady who was in the American party. Mrs. Moore, her name was. He moved the woman and her husband into your group. Did you notice if there were any issues between the couple?'

Shaw looked puzzled. 'I didn't know there was a problem in the first place. As groups go, that one was probably the easiest. We've had far more demanding clients than them to deal with.'

Bevan examined his appearance closely. Shaw had a mop of curly brown hair and a tanned face. He was tall and loose-limbed. She would say he was reasonably attractive, but certainly not in the league of Murray White.

'What do you recall about Gordon Parker, Mr. Shaw?' Andy asked.

'He was in Murray's group - I didn't have much to do with him. Quiet chap, I thought, but that's really all I can tell you.'

'Did you see Mr. Parker on the Thursday of last

week at all?'

'No. I wasn't due to start work until the afternoon, that's when we had another training session. I arrived here at 1.30pm and took my group out on the water at 2pm. Murray can confirm that.' Shaw paused for a moment, as a thought seemed to strike him. 'Did this Moore woman have the hots for Murray?' He grinned unpleasantly. 'Our female clients go mad for him. I expect her husband didn't react very well to it.'

'Has Murray ever acted on the attention he receives from women? It must be very tempting,' Andy said casually.

Shaw laughed. 'You obviously don't know my boss all that well. I've never seen Murray take any notice of the attractive women we've had staying here.' When Andy raised his eyebrows at this, the man quickly clarified, 'oh, I don't mean he's gay. It's just he's not interested in that kind of stuff. He's a bit *other-worldly* is Murray, if you know what I mean by that.'

'I think I do,' Bevan added. 'Whereas, you would describe yourself more as the *worldly* type, would you, Mackie?'

The man couldn't prevent a lecherous smile from spreading itself across his face. 'Aye, perhaps I would. But I'm not gonna get much of a look-in with golden boy around the place now, am I?'

Bevan smiled sweetly at this observation and with a nod to Calder, the two police officers made their way back to where the car was parked.

'You interviewed the Moores when we were in the United States,' Bevan said, as they drove over the Glenrannoch Road towards Kilross. 'What did you make of them?'

Andy flicked back through his notebook. 'Gillian

Moore is 44, and her husband, Clifford, has just turned 50. They've got two college age kids, she's a housewife and he works for a bank in Richmond. To be honest, they seemed totally normal to me. I never had the wife down as a potential lover for Gordon Parker. If I remember rightly, she was slim, with dyed blond hair. Nice-looking, I suppose, in a mumsy kind of way.'

'What is Clifford Moore like - did he strike you as the jealous type?

'He's a big bloke, certainly, although most of his girth is made up of belly fat. He was friendly and cooperative with me, but then I wasn't trying to get it on with his wife. It might be a different story then.'

Bevan sighed. 'I can't see how all this fits in with Parker's death. It's probably a blind alley. The only idea that crossed my mind was whether Parker had been attracted to Murray as well. He may have mistaken the young man's lack of interest in women for something else.'

Andy shifted himself around in the passenger seat so that he was facing his superior. 'So, Parker starts coming on to Murray, pestering him, maybe. They arrange to meet on the morning that Parker is due to leave. Perhaps they take a walk along the rocks, up at the headland.'

'Parker starts to get heavy with Murray, who doesn't want things to progress in that way. The lad's a bit 'other-worldly', like Shaw said, and he didn't see it coming.'

'So Murray has to fight him off. He punches Parker, who topples back into the water. Murray panics and leaves him there, hoping the body will wash out to sea. Do you buy it, Ma'am?'

'We've no evidence that Gordon Parker was gay. Besides, I know he's a bit odd, but I can't see Murray White leaving the guy for dead. If it were Mackie

Shaw, yes, but with Murray, I just can't picture it.'

'Also, why would he tip us off about the English couple who may have seen something, if it was *him* who was out on the cliffs with Parker the day he died?'

'It might be a dead end. He could be wasting our time because he knows they were nowhere near the place on the morning of the murder. When we get back to Pitt Street, I want you to check out the details Murray gave us. Let's see what this couple have got to say. I'll give Mrs. Parker a call. I'd like to know if the problems in their marriage were caused by something more deep-seated than we first thought.'

Chapter Twenty Four

Hugh offered to help Michael and Julia shift their luggage upstairs to the main bedroom of Kilduggan Farm. The couple looked tired after their journey, but Hugh knew they must tell them as soon as possible about the murder at Cove Lodge - they'd delayed it for long enough as it was.

Imogen cooked a family dinner. After they'd eaten and settled into the armchairs by the fire in the sitting room with their coffees, she informed her brother and sister-in-law of what had been going on.

'How is Murray taking it?' Michael immediately asked, with obvious concern.

'Well, you know what Murray's like, he doesn't give much away, but I think he's fine. They've got concerns with regards to the business, but he's not too upset about finding the body.' Imogen took a deep breath, 'look, I'm really sorry about not telling you sooner, we didn't want to ruin your honeymoon.'

'It's okay,' Michael said gently, 'I understand.'

'We've been keeping an eye on him, I promise.'

Julia leant forward and placed her hand on Imogen's arm. 'I'm sure you have. Do the police have a suspect?'

'It's hard to know what they're thinking, actually. Two detectives have already questioned Murray and Colin a couple of times. They must be struggling to pin down any kind of motive for the killing, unless they know something about this Parker chap that we don't.'

They remained quiet for a few moments. Then Julia broke the silence by telling Imogen and Hugh what she and Michael discovered about her grandfather whilst they were in Canada.

'Your Uncle Harry told us some of the story at the wedding. It's incredible your grandad was able to create this whole new life and identity, although I know it does happen. The whole thing must have been really tough on your dad, Julia.'

'Yes, I think it was particularly upsetting for him when Alex King turned up alive and well in Canada. I was only a baby when it happened. My mum said that dad was very angry and upset about it. Margie, my grandmother, was quite philosophical. She'd had a great marriage with Alistair, and two more children, John and Jean. Mum said they'd been a little worried about the legality of their marriage – what with Sandy having still been alive all along – but the solicitor said Margie was officially informed, after the liner went down in 1943, that Sandy was dead (she still had the letter). He'd effectively abandoned her, so they simply renewed their wedding vows and that was that.'

'Did the solicitor say that any kind of criminal charges could be brought against Alex King?' Hugh enquired.

'There was so much upheaval after the war. I suppose my grandfather could be deemed an illegal immigrant of some sort, but he'd always worked whilst he was living in Canada and he paid his taxes. His partner and children were Canadian citizens. I suppose it didn't seem worth pursuing.'

'It was clever of him,' Imogen suddenly added, 'not to try and marry Eleanor Kinslett legally. If he had, then Alex King would certainly have been guilty of a criminal offence. It was smart of him to find a religious community to join. It meant he remained on the fringes of society. I wonder if he consciously planned it that way.'

'The thought did cross our minds too,' Michael chipped in.

'I can't deny that my grandad did some terrible and immoral things. But Jim and Harry aren't responsible for their father's mistakes. I really wish Dad could find it in his heart to let them into his life, they are his *brothers*, after all.' Julia sighed heavily, looking worn out.

'Jim and Harry are only Rob's brothers in blood. They weren't brought up together like Rob, John and Jeanette. I know that genetic ties mean an enormous amount to some people, but for me, the folk who raise you and are there for you throughout your childhood, in good times and bad, are the ones who truly matter. I believe that is what your dad must feel too.'

Julia nodded, she knew her husband was talking sense and he was speaking also of his own experience. She didn't have the strength or the inclination to disagree. But Julia still longed for her father to stop clinging onto the anger he so clearly harboured for the Kings. She wished he could put into practice his own religious teachings and finally find the strength to forgive them.

Chapter Twenty Five

Imogen was up early the following morning. Standing at the kitchen window, watching the sun rising slowly over Carradale in the distance, she heard a movement behind her. Imogen turned to see Michael, opening the fridge door and bringing out a carton of milk and a plastic bag full of coffee beans.

'Do you want a cup?' He said, shaking the packet for emphasis.

'Yes, please.'

'Julia's still fast asleep. We were warned the jet lag is worse after the return journey from the States.'

'How are *you* feeling, Michael?'

'Oh, I'm okay. I wanted to get over to the Cove and see Murray first thing. He must think I've totally abandoned him as it is.' Michael busied himself at the coffee-machine.

'I expect he would have been mortified if you'd cut short your honeymoon on his account. The lad is more robust than you give him credit for.' Imogen laid a hand on Michael's shoulder, to soften the impact of her words.

'I expect you're right. I just feel responsible for him, that's all.'

'I know you do.' Imogen reached into the freezer for the croissants and brioche rolls she kept stored in there. Then she lit the range cooker, so she could pop them in to gradually warm up. Hopefully, they would be ready by the time the rest of the house was awake.

'This body washing up at Cove Lodge,' she stated, sitting down at the table to drink her coffee, 'it's just a stroke of really bad luck for Murray and Colin. But once the police have got a culprit, it will all blow over. Colin says he's very impressed with the investigating officer. He thinks she's sympathetic, intuitive and extremely on-the-ball.' Imogen chuckled self-consciously, 'he actually said she reminded him a bit of me.'

'Which is incredibly high praise coming from Colin,' Michael said with a grin.

Imogen ignored the comment, swiftly changing the subject instead. 'So, you found out quite a lot about Alex King whilst you were in Canada, then?'

Michael lowered his voice, 'Julia wasn't paying attention at the time, but the woman we met in York Bay said someone *else* had been asking questions about the Kings recently too.'

'That's odd after all these years.'

'I know, it does seem strange and somehow, the more we found out about how well Sandy Thomson had orchestrated his disappearance from the UK, the more I started to suspect that maybe he was fleeing something more serious than just his responsibilities to Margie.' He cradled the coffee cup in his hands.

'I thought the same. Julia's grandad was certainly very adept at keeping himself under the radar. He was obviously a con-man, because he took on a new identity and gained a fair amount of money from the donations made to this independent church he was a part of. Perhaps he'd been involved in something similar when he was still living in Dallanaich and that's why he had to disappear.'

'Julia would say that Alex King only ever took a reasonable wage from the Church. The rest went into the upkeep of the building, the heating bills and all those kinds of expenses. She doesn't think there was anything underhand about it. All the money Harry has made comes from his own property business. I don't think there was much of an inheritance left after Alex died.'

'I'd still be interested to find out what Sandy Thomson's life had been like in Scotland, before he embarked for Canada. There must be some evidence remaining of his existence in Dallanaich.'

'It was an incredibly long time ago. Are you sure there'll be any trace of him left?'

'People remember things, Mike. It's only a couple of generations back and these small communities recall stuff better than most. If I tread carefully, I expect I'll be able to dig something up, and don't worry, I'll do my very best to be discreet.'

Michael returned from Cove Lodge by mid-afternoon. Julia was up and dressed but she still looked groggy. Imogen jogged down the staircase, with her mobile phone gripped tightly in her hand.

'That was Allan,' she called out, to anyone who happened to be listening.

'Is everything OK with him?' Michael shouted back.

Imogen strode into the sitting room and stood in the doorway. 'He's fine, but Suz has broken her ankle. She fell down the cellar steps at work, apparently.'

Julia shifted herself up higher on the sofa. 'Is she able to manage?'

'Well, Al says that Owen is with her and Alice is coming over every day after she's finished at the office, to fix the dinner and stuff. But I thought I might go up and see her, as we're so close. It would be nice if one of the Nichols could show her some support.'

'I agree,' Michael added, 'you can take my car.'

Suz was Allan's ex-wife. They separated nearly a decade ago. Both of them had new partners, but Suz was the mother of Allan's two grown up children and Imogen remained close to her. They had shared many holidays together whilst their children were young, often on Garansay. Suz now lived in Fort William, in the Western Highlands. The Crofts didn't get a chance to visit her that often, so Imogen found herself pleased to have a reason to go and see her sister-in-law once again.

Hugh came up behind his wife and placed his arms around her waist. 'What's all this?' He asked pleasantly.

'I'm going to drive up to see Suz for a couple of days. Her leg's in plaster and she can't get about. You'll be okay here with the kids won't you? I haven't seen her for ages. It'll be good to have a chance to catch up. Michael's lending me his car, so you'll barely even notice that I've gone.'

Chapter Twenty Six

Dani Bevan knew that she would have to make Detective Chief Inspector before she got her own office. Within the floor of the Pitt Street Headquarters which was devoted to serious crime, Dani shared a desk with her Sergeant, Phil Boag.

'Any news yet from the Virginia Police?' Phil asked, not removing his eyes from the screen in front of him.

'They're threatening to send someone over to *assist* me with my enquiries, which I could do with like a hole in the head.'

Phil's face crinkled into a grin. He was aged in his late forties, but was naturally trim and still good-looking. Phil's wife was the Headmistress of one of the huge comprehensives in the city. She was constantly on T.V., being interviewed about how she had turned the place around. Dani sensed that Phil was comfortable to let his career take a backseat to hers.

'They've just e-mailed me the contents of Gordon Parker's computer hard-drive. Apparently, there's no evidence he's accessed gay porn sites, but he's glanced at a couple of hetero ones – fairly mainstream stuff, according to the Yanks. His wife was adamant her husband was not and never had been attracted to other men. Do you fancy having a trawl through it all for me?'

'Sure, send it over.'

'I'd say that's our theory about Murray White being the attacker pretty much discredited. If Parker was a gay man trapped in a sexless marriage, he would certainly have been accessing pornography of some sort.' Dani sighed, taking a sip from a cardboard cup filled with milky instant coffee.

'Unless he was viewing it on a different device – his phone, perhaps?' Phil offered.

'The Detective in Virginia says Parker's Google history covers his mobile phone too. The guy had made absolutely no attempt to hide what he'd been up to online, which makes me think he was a reasonably straight shooter. But I'd be really interested to know who he'd been communicating with before he came to Scotland and in the days and hours leading up to his death.'

'Aye, will do,' Phil replied, in a matter-of-fact way. Unlike many of her colleagues, Dani's Sergeant didn't have any problem with taking instructions from a woman.

Andy Calder was reading carefully through the notes he made during his phone conversation with the Thorpes of Grange-over-Sands, Cumbria. The couple *had* been staying at their holiday home on Garansay over the last few weeks, but they returned to the Lake District two days before Gordon Parker was killed. However, Richard Thorpe still had something interesting to tell him. Andy pushed back his wheelie chair and strode over to Dani Bevan's work station.

'Have you got a minute, Ma'am?'

'Of course, pull up a seat.'

'The Thorpes left their cottage on the Tuesday afternoon. They don't tend to have much to do with Murray's sailing school when they're staying at the house, but the couple *had* noticed there was a large party at Cove Lodge during that particular fortnight.'

'Had the group made themselves conspicuous in some way then?' Bevan enquired.

'Not all of them,' Calder said cryptically. 'Richard Thorpe was out walking their dog on the previous Sunday evening, along the headland behind the cottage, when he passed two men. Apparently, they were both American, he could tell, because their voices were slightly raised. Thorpe wasn't sure if it was an altercation or not, but they were certainly in deep discussion. The two men didn't even acknowledge him when he called out good evening to them as he went by. Thorpe knew the tide was about to come in and he nearly warned them to be careful, but somehow he sensed he shouldn't intervene in their conversation. Thorpe suggested the atmosphere between them was extremely tense.'

'Could he provide a description of either man?' Bevan spun around in her chair, looking suddenly interested.

'He said one of the men was a little younger than the other, but they were both over forty. What's interesting, Ma'am, is that Thorpe described the older one as tallish and really quite overweight, with his girth being predominantly spread about his middle. It immediately made me think of Clifford Moore, because I'd used the almost exact same words to describe him, too.'

'What time is it in the States?' Bevan asked levelly. 'Let's try and get the Virginia Police on the phone. I'd like to have another word with Mr. and Mrs. Moore.'

Chapter Twenty Seven

Suzanne Hunter's three-bedroom house was situated in a modern estate on the outskirts of Fort William. In the near distance lay the Grampian Mountains, whose dark silhouettes, contrasting sharply against the bright blue sky, gave the only indication that this modest home was just a stone's throw from the remote, untamed landscape of the Scottish Highlands.

Imogen filled the kettle and then took a few minutes to find her way around Suz's narrow, well-appointed kitchen. Owen had already left for work and Alice wasn't due to call round until her lunch break at half past one.

'What would you like for breakfast?' She called into the living room, where her sister-in-law was sitting on the sofa with her plaster encased leg supported on a padded footstool.

'Just some toast and tea would be great, thanks. There's jam in the fridge and a jar of marmalade in the door if you fancy that, Im.'

'Great, found them. It won't be long.'

Imogen busied herself preparing a tray with plates of buttered toast and jam which she carried into the living room and placed on the coffee table. She then fetched two mugs, brimming with strong, sweet tea.

'Just how I like it,' Suz grinned, taking a steaming mug and resting it on the cushion beside her. Although she was dressed in a plain sweater and jogging pants, Imogen's one time sister-in-law still looked gorgeous. Suz possessed a naturally athletic build and a bob of curly, honey-blonde hair perfectly complemented her pretty, even features. Imogen was always surprised that Suz hadn't settled down with a new man sooner. She and Owen had only been together for about 12 months, yet the divorce from Allan came through almost a decade ago. Before that, this highly attractive woman had seemed reasonably content to remain on her own, focusing all of her attention instead on Alice and Robin.

'So, how is Allan doing?' She immediately asked, obviously taking advantage of the fact that her boyfriend was not there, to enquire about her ex-husband.

'He's much better than he was a few months back. Did you know he was seeing Penny Mills? She's the lawyer who went to school with Hugh.'

Suz nodded. 'Yes, Allan told me, but he said it wasn't anything serious yet. I was sorry to hear that Abigail had gone to New York. She was such a sweet girl. The kids always liked her.'

'To be honest with you, I don't think Allan really wants to settle down again. Abigail is free now to meet someone else. She's still got plenty of time to get married and have a family. Speaking of which, are you and Owen considering tying the knot?'

Owen Williams ran a local building firm. He moved up to Fort William from Cardiff about two years ago. Suz met him when he came into the café in the city centre where she worked. He became a regular customer and asked her out to dinner a year ago, they'd been together ever since.

She crinkled up her face. 'He's a lovely guy and we're enjoying being together, but I like the fact he's got his own flat to go back to. Maybe I'm just like Allan, and deep down, I believe we only really do it once.'

'I would be tempted to agree with you, but look at Michael and Julia. They seem to be so very much in love.' Imogen sat back and sipped slowly from her mug of tea.

'Oh, I wouldn't begrudge Mike his happiness for one moment. We all know what he and Sarah went through when Miriam died. But he's exactly the kind of guy who *would* find true love twice. Mike's such a pure and decent sort of chap - do you know what I mean? Meanwhile, back on planet Earth with the rest of us mere mortals, the ending isn't always quite so much like a Disney fairytale. Sorry, that sounded rude.'

Imogen laughed. 'Not at all, I understand completely. Sometimes I find it pretty hard to live up to Michael's exacting standards. Allan can be an easier person to be with, simply because he gets things wrong. Although, I do realise his mistakes have hurt people along the way.' She laid her hand lightly on Suz's arm.

'Don't worry, I've made plenty of those myself,' she swiftly replied, without any hint of self-pity. 'I'm glad you're here. I've missed our chats.'

Imogen smiled, feeling a lump forming in her throat, she gulped down some more tea before adding, 'you know I was telling you about Julia's grandfather last night, and how he went off to Canada to start a new life?'

Suz nodded, fishing a packet of cigarettes out of her pocket and popping one into her mouth. 'Do you mind?'

Imogen shook her head. 'Not at all. Well, the family came from Dallanaich. Julia wants to know some more about his life in Scotland, before he left her grandmother, so I thought I might take a drive down there to see what I could find out.'

'It's a tiny place,' Suz commented, blowing smoke up towards the ceiling. 'You'll probably unearth the odd person that remembers him. These small communities tend to revolve around a few local families. There's always the incomers of course, but

Dallanaich isn't one of those picturesque seaside towns that attract the wealthy English settlers. There must be some folk who live there and commute to Fort William for work - it *has* got stunning views across Loch Linnhe. But the settlement itself is fairly run-down.'

'When I drove through it, I did notice there was a new development of houses on the outskirts of the town. Perhaps in a few years it will be quite different from how it is now.'

'Aye, you're probably right,' Suz said philosophically, stubbing her cigarette out in an ash tray on the coffee table. 'My mum and dad lived a few miles from there, just beyond the Glenduror Forest in Ballachulish. It's absolutely gorgeous around that area. Dad had a great aunt who lived in Dallanaich. We used to go and see her there before she died in the mid-seventies. There was always an atmosphere about the place I didn't much like. Oh, it was probably because I only ever saw the inside of my aunty's pokey wee flat, which smelt of boiled cabbage and had a T.V. set constantly blaring out in one of the only two rooms it possessed. I can't quite put my finger on it, but there was something about the town itself. It just had a vibe I didn't take to as a child. After Aunty Ailsa was gone, we never ever went back.'

Chapter Twenty Eight

Michael's high performance German sports car proved tricky for Imogen to handle. It wasn't so bad on the main roads from Glasgow to Fort William, but on the winding track which followed the eastern shoreline of Loch Linnhe, the vehicle seemed to possess a mind of its own. Eventually, she learnt to allow the car to lead her and not vice-versa. This appeared to make the going much smoother.

Although it was a sunny day, Dallanaich didn't seem any more inviting now than when Imogen was last there. The repeated lines of little cottages and bungalows created an uninterrupted vista of grey pebble-dashing. The only splash of colour was being provided by the yellow and red insignia of a Quick-Stop shop, positioned on a corner of the deathly quiet main street.

Imogen had done some digging before arriving here. She was interested to know if there were any Thomsons still living in the town. To find this out didn't require the deployment of any sophisticated research methods. She simply went to the main library in Fort William and flicked through the appropriate phone book. Imogen already knew that Sandy's parents were deceased at the time he left the country, but she was curious to know if he might have any other relatives who were still alive. After highlighting a handful of possibilities in the directory, Imogen went back to Suz's place and did some ringing around.

Imogen spoke to a very helpful young man called David Thomson. It turned out he had lived in Dallanaich all his life and was the grandson of Sandy Thomson's cousin, Archie. David's grandfather passed away several years ago but the man gave Imogen the address of his elderly aunty, Valerie Black, whom he believed was a second cousin of Sandy Thomson and his older sister, Annie. David told Imogen to drop in on her at 10a.m. He would inform Val she was coming.

When she pressed on the doorbell of the little terraced house, at ten minutes past ten, it was a tall and handsome man, most likely in his early thirties, who swiftly opened the door to her.

'David?' She enquired warily.

'Hi, Mrs. Croft, please come in. Aunty Val is in the living room. I'll make you both a coffee and then dash off, if you don't mind. I need to get back to work. My wife told me to hang around and check I hadn't given Val's address to an axe-murderer.' He laughed good-naturedly, disappearing into a galley kitchen at the end of the dingy corridor.

Imogen peered through a doorway to the left of the hall. It led into a pleasant front room with a large window facing the street. Val Black was sitting in a huge armchair just beneath the window. She was expertly wielding two enormous knitting needles, which were feverishly clicking away at the head of an elaborate trail of wool. The woman barely glanced up as Imogen entered.

'For my granddaughter,' she immediately declared, with as much import as if there were lives depending upon its completion.

'It looks very complicated.' Imogen sat herself down on the sofa opposite.

'Och, I've conquered more difficult patterns than this in my time.' She finally raised her eyes from the task and studied her guest through a pair of small, round glasses. Val smiled, 'have you got children yourself?'

'Two boys and a girl. All three are nearly grown-up now, though.'

'You don't seem old enough,' she said matter-of-factly, as David entered the room with the drinks.

'I agree. If you don't mind me saying, Mrs. Croft, you look like a modern-day Snow White. My three year old daughter's mad on her at the moment. She plays with the doll constantly. You should think about doing panto – I think you'd make a packet.'

Imogen chuckled, 'I've not been told that in a very long time. Frankly, I'm flattered.'

David placed the cups on the coffee table. 'I really must go now, Val.' He turned towards Imogen again, 'please tell Julia to drop round and see us. She was a few years ahead of me at school but I remember her well. We should definitely try to keep in touch.'

After they heard the front door being firmly shut behind him, Imogen said, 'did David tell you that I was interested in finding out about Sandy Thomson?'

'Aye, he did.' She placed the pile of knitting on the arm of her chair and reached for a mug. 'Does Reverend Thomson know you're here?'

Imogen felt suddenly uncomfortable. 'No, he doesn't. But Julia is really eager to find out as much as she can about her grandfather.'

Val sighed. 'When Rob was growing up, his mother wasn't keen on him having much to do with us Thomsons. She tried to make the boy feel like he was a McClelland, which I can totally understand. Margie didn't want Rob to dwell on his dead father. Then, after it became clear that Sandy had been alive all along, well, we became *persona non grata* for quite a few years. It was almost as if Rob thought we'd helped to keep the secret from him, which of course we had not. Sandy abandoned *us* as much as he did his wee bairn.'

'What relation were you to Sandy and his sister?'

'Our mothers were first cousins, so we weren't

particularly close. I was born in 1926. I must have been 17 years old when Sandy set sail on the Minerva. He was in his early thirties, I think. The family was greatly affected when we learnt of his death. It was a tragedy for us all, not just Margie.' Val shook her head at the memory.

'What about his sister, Annie, what became of her?' Imogen leant forward in the seat.

'Annie had left Dallanaich with her fiancé, before Sandy was declared missing. She married a man who was a good few years older than her, if I remember rightly. She had a very strident personality. My mother always referred to her as a 'bluestocking'. The husband died a couple of decades later. She continued to live on in their big old house up in the Highlands somewhere. There were no children from the marriage and Annie never came back to Dallanaich after Sandy's ship went down. As far as I'm aware, she had very little contact with Rob either. Goodness, Annie would be over a hundred now, if she were alive. Doesn't that make you think?' Val looked wistful.

'Did Alex King ever make contact with you from Canada?' Imogen asked this carefully, hoping she wouldn't cause offence.

'After Kenny Garvie sprung him, d'you mean?' Val laughed. She sipped thoughtfully from her mug, looking genuinely amused. 'I don't think he would have dared, not when he'd left his relatives believing he was dead. The man clearly didn't want us in his life. That much was obvious. I for one made no effort to contact *him.*'

'Can you tell me much about Sandy's existence in Dallanaich *before* he went missing?'

Val seemed caught off guard by the question. She took a few moments to consider it. 'He was quite a bit older than me, but this is a small community and we all knew one another fairly well. Sandy was a quiet and unassuming man. He appeared to be completely dedicated to the local school and the Church. Reverend Cowan had allowed him to take a number of services in preparation for his ordination. Sandy was a very good speaker. I preferred him to old Cowan, if I'm honest with you. I suppose everybody says this, but he seemed like the last person on earth who would have walked out on Margie and the baby. He was an honourable person. He really cared about the youngsters he taught. Sandy was a man of God…' Val's words trailed off as a sob forced its way up into her throat. Tears began to fill her watchful, grey eyes.

Imogen leant forward and took the lady's hand. 'I'm so sorry to have upset you.'

'I don't know why I *am* so upset. It's just when you asked what he had been like *before* the ship went down, it stirred up these old memories and *feelings*. When we found out about Alex King being alive and having been living in Canada for all that time, it's hard to explain, but the whole situation was almost comical. I was busy with my own family and I suppose I just thought 'to hell with him'. But when you encouraged me, just then, to think about the *old* Sandy and those early years of the war, when we were so young, it properly struck me, as if it had happened only yesterday.' Val blinked back the tears and looked defiant. 'My cousin was a decent man, Mrs. Croft, that's what I recall, and what's more, we all loved him.'

Chapter Twenty Nine

D.I. Bevan hadn't expected to be back on Garansay so soon. She'd dropped Andy Calder off with her colleagues at the Kilross Police Station an hour ago, but Dani wanted to pay a visit to Colin Walmsley, at Loch Crannox Farm, before she returned there herself.

The farm sat half-way up the hillside, a couple of miles west of Cove Lodge. It was a large operation. The impressive stone farmhouse being situated in the centre of a courtyard filled with huge barns and office pre-fabs. She parked up alongside one of the outhouses and made her way towards a single-storey building which appeared to house the reception area.

As Bevan reached the entrance, she noticed Walmsley striding towards her across the gravel courtyard and paused to watch him approach. Bevan knew that Colin Walmsley was 43 years old and unmarried. On the first occasion she met him, a few hours after Gordon Parker's body was washed up on the shore, Bevan had felt the immediate jolt of physical attraction. Walmsley wasn't her usual type, with his unconsciously rugged, outdoorsy look. Bevan would normally find herself drawn to the smart-suited paper-pushers who tended to populate metropolitan Glasgow these days. But Colin quickly struck her as having a lot more about him than the average Highland hill-farmer.

'Has something happened?' Colin demanded, as he grew closer.

'Can we have a word in private?' Bevan asked, her tone indicating it would be wise for him to agree.

The man led her through the side door of the

farmhouse into a large and pleasant, if somewhat old-fashioned, kitchen. Colin automatically filled a kettle and placed it on the stove. 'Has there been a new development, Detective Inspector?' He made this enquiry warily, pulling out a chair for her at the table.

Bevan decided to loosen up her approach a little. She was only there to gather background information, after all. The Detective sat down and provided Colin with a reassuring smile, resolving to let him in on what they had discovered. 'Did you spend much time with Mr. and Mrs. Moore, when the American party was staying at Cove Lodge, Mr. Walmsley?'

'I chatted to them for ten minutes when they were paying their bill. Was Mrs. Moore the lady who Murray had a problem with?'

'Yes, that's correct. We followed up Mr. White's suggestion that we speak with the couple who own the holiday cottage at the headland. It turned out they had some significant information for us.'

Colin took the seat opposite Bevan and gave her his full attention.

'Richard Thorpe saw a man matching Mr. Moore's description arguing with another man on the headland the Sunday before last. The Virginia State Police brought Clifford Moore in for questioning yesterday. It seems he had not told us everything.'

The kettle started to whistle and Colin got up to prepare their coffees. 'Please carry on,' he said, 'I'm still listening.'

'After Murray White moved Gillian Moore into the other sailing group, Clifford Moore suspected that his wife had struck up some kind of relationship - or flirtation - or what have you, with Mackie Shaw.'

Colin stopped what he was doing and turned to face Bevan. 'Was he positive about this?'

'Clifford says he spotted them exchanging significant looks during the lessons. Then, one evening in the first week, when his wife told him she was going for a stroll along the beach, Moore followed her. According to him, Gillian met up with Shaw down by the rocks at the tip of the headland. He said they began kissing and cuddling.'

Colin placed the mugs down heavily on the tabletop. A few drops of the dark liquid spilt onto the plastic cover. 'Bloody idiot!' he rasped angrily.

'Has Shaw done anything like this before?' Bevan looked searchingly at Colin's face.

'Not that I'm aware of. Murray would have told me if he'd suspected it. I trust my manager completely.'

'Do you know much about Mackie Shaw's background?'

Colin shook his head. 'He's been with us for two years now. Mackie's family hail from Kilross, I believe. He was engaged to be married a while back, but it got called off for some reason. I did know he had an eye for the ladies, but I had no idea he was going to try it on with our clients. I'm going to have to let him go after this.'

'It may be more serious than that.'

Colin furrowed his brow, sitting down and clasping the hot mug between his palms.

'Moore spent a couple of days stewing about what he had witnessed. He knew his wife was discontented, but he hadn't been aware of any other men being involved until now. Moore decided to share his burden with a good friend he had made on the trip, Gordon Parker. They agreed to meet at the headland on the Sunday evening at the end of the first week to discuss the problem.'

'Was that who Richard Thorpe saw arguing?'

'Yes, it was Clifford Moore and Gordon Parker. However, Clifford maintains that it wasn't an argument. He says he was baring his soul to Parker and asking for his help. Moore had decided to confront Mackie Shaw and tell him to back off, but the more he'd worked himself up to do it, the more he feared he'd lose his cool with Shaw and possibly even go for him. Instead, Moore had decided to ask Parker to approach Mackie on his behalf. At first, Parker had been reluctant to get involved, but Moore pleaded with him. This exchange is what Thorpe witnessed and mistook for a row. Eventually, Parker agreed to arrange to meet Shaw and have it out with him.' Bevan paused here and drank from her cup, allowing the implication of her words to sink in.

'You think Parker met with Mackie Shaw on the Thursday morning that he was due to leave Garansay. Parker confronted Mackie with what he knew and there was an altercation, the result of which left Parker dead at the bottom of the Kilbrannan Sound.' Colin whistled through his teeth. 'I know Mackie's a jack-the-lad, but is he really capable of murder?'

'I was hoping you might be able to answer that particular question. In the heat of the moment, the lad feels cornered, he knows full well that if you or Murray find out he's been knocking off one of the guests he'll be out of a job. Or, perhaps it wasn't that calculated at all, Parker simply wound Mackie up, interfering in an affair which was not of his concern - Shaw hit out at the man and Parker fell backwards into the water. What do you think?'

Colin sighed heavily. 'I think it's just possible Mackie lost his temper and struck Parker, somehow landing him in the sea. Why the hell didn't Clifford Moore mention all of this earlier?'

'Because he didn't want to reveal his wife's affair *and* I suspect he knows that it's partly his fault Parker is dead. Moore probably didn't want his family to find that out.'

Colin sat back in the chair, folding his arms across his broad chest. 'What a bloody mess,' he declared.

Chapter Thirty

Mackie Shaw didn't look as self-assured as the last time Bevan had encountered him. His shoulders were hunched up so tightly, that the collar of Shaw's shirt was skirting the base of his earlobes. Tiny beads of sweat were forming across his sun-kissed forehead.

Bevan observed the man's posture closely, on a television monitor which was wired up to the camera in Interview Room 3. She watched as D.C. Andy Calder casually entered through the door, sitting himself opposite Shaw and the duty solicitor.

Calder ran through the initial formalities in an even, droning monotone, which seemed to be doing nothing to settle Mackie's frayed nerves.

Finally, Andy was ready to begin. 'Do you know why you're here, Mr. Shaw?'

'It's got something to do with Gordon Parker,' he mumbled.

'That's correct. How well did you know Mr. Parker, Mackie?'

'I hardly knew him at all,' he replied, almost sulkily. 'I told you before. He was in Murray's group.' Mackie kept his head down low, apparently examining the current state of his finger-nails.

'What about Mrs. Gillian Moore. Did you know her any better?'

Mackie flinched at the mention of her name. Bevan noted that unlike many of the criminals she'd seen interviewed during her career, Shaw was pretty awful at this.

'Well?' Calder leant in closer.

'I was seeing her,' Mackie murmured.

'Could you repeat that more clearly please - for the

benefit of the tape?'

'After the Moores moved into my teaching group, I began a friendship with Gillian Moore.' Shaw forced himself to look up at Calder. 'It was just a fling, I swear.'

'Could you describe the nature of that relationship, Mackie?'

'We had sex a couple of times, down by the rocks.'

'Were you aware that Clifford Moore saw you with his wife?'

'Not at the time, but I found out later.'

'How did you find out?'

Mackie Shaw sighed deeply and tilted his head back so that he was looking straight up at the polystyrene tiles on the ceiling. 'Gordon Parker told me.'

'Now we're getting somewhere,' Bevan muttered to herself.

'When, exactly, did Parker discuss this with you?'

Shaw flicked his head back again, so that his heavy brown eyes were level with Calder's. 'It was on the Wednesday evening before he died. After dinner, Parker saw me packing some stuff away in the boat shed and he followed me in there.'

'It was late for you to still be at the Lodge, wasn't it?'

'I'd done a long afternoon session, because there had been a temporary break in the weather. There was a lot of clearing up to do. It's not as if I've got anyone to rush back home for.'

'My heart bleeds,' Bevan commented under her breath.

'What did Parker say?'

'The guy was pretty embarrassed and so was I. He told me that Mr. Moore knew I was 'fooling around with his wife' and I'd better back off or they would both go to Colin Walmsley and tell him exactly what

I'd been up to.'

'How did you react to that?'

'I was angry, but probably not for the reasons you think. I like Gillian, she's actually a nice woman. We didn't expect things to go anywhere – of course, she was heading back to the States that weekend, but the way Parker and Moore were referring to her, it was as if she was a piece of property. You know, like I'd gone for a joy ride in his car or something.'

'Did you argue with Parker?'

'I told him to get lost, but using less polite words, if you know what I mean, and he scuttled off. I reckoned at the time, he'd done what his mate asked him to and he didn't feel like he needed to hang around for any more abuse. Look, Parker was alive and well the next morning, the entire party must have seen him at breakfast.'

'But he was dead by lunchtime, Mr. Shaw. How do we know you didn't arrange to discuss it again the next day, only this time, you made sure he wouldn't be able to make any kind of complaint against you.' Calder maintained steady eye contact with his suspect.

'Because I didn't come back to the Cove until after lunch,' Shaw sounded exasperated. 'Why would I attack Parker? It was *Moore* who was out for my blood. I'm not fool enough to kill the messenger, am I?'

'You may have lost your temper, Mackie, I could understand that. Perhaps you gave Parker a shove, without the intention of killing him.'

Mackie glanced in panic towards the solicitor sat beside him. 'Of course I bloody didn't!'

'Then why are you only telling us about the meeting you had with Parker now. Why did you lie to us when we first questioned you?'

Mackie Shaw suddenly seemed to cotton on to the

seriousness of his predicament. He slumped down in his seat. 'No comment.'

'Okay, that's all for now. But be aware, Mackie, that we've got a warrant to search your cottage in Kilross. The white coats from Glasgow will be going over it with a fine-toothed comb. Right now, our forensic bods are sweeping that headland again for evidence. If we find even the tiniest trace of your presence out there, or on Gordon Parker's body, I'll be filing with the Fiscal to make an arrest for murder.'

Chapter Thirty One

The queues for the checkouts at the supermarket on the outskirts of Fort William were unusually long. Imogen had a trolley full of supplies for Suz and Owen. She judged they should have enough to get them through the weekend.

Whilst she was waiting to reach the till, Imogen considered what she learnt from her trip to Dallanaich. Val Black had drawn a sketchy map to show her where she could find the house in which Sandy and his sister had lived as children. It was such a small place that Imogen discovered the shabby two-up, two-down with ease. She tried to imagine the charismatic father of Harry King spending his youth in this pokey little pebble-dashed, mid-terraced property, but she couldn't quite picture it.

Val also provided Imogen with a list of people. These were the men and women who Val believed would have been contemporaries of Sandy and may well have known him before he left Scotland for Canada. The elderly lady warned that most of these folk would now be dead, but she was trying hard to reach back into the depths of her memory for the names, just the same. By the end of their conversation, Val seemed quite determined that Sandy's 'true' character should be revealed.

If Michael hadn't told her that Julia took a DNA test back in the 90s, she would now be questioning if Alex King really was Sandy Thomson at all. Imogen would be tempted to think it was an elaborate hoax, but devised for what reason, she had no idea. There didn't appear to have been any money to be gained from the Kings claiming a connection to the

Thomsons. It was just that Val was so adamant that Sandy hadn't been the type to abandon his wife and child. But then how many other relatives had been similarly impassioned in their defence of a loved one, even when the evidence of their guilt was completely overwhelming?

The man directly behind her in the queue loudly cleared his throat and Imogen suddenly noticed that she should have been emptying the contents of her trolley onto the conveyor belt. Trying to make up for this breach in check-out etiquette, she smiled sweetly at him and turned her full attention to the task at hand.

Suz hobbled across the room to see what activity Imogen was so engrossed in on her laptop. She perched on the arm of the chair and peered closely at the screen. 'What are you up to?'

'I'm researching the names that Val Black gave me.' She handed Suz the list. 'They were all contemporaries of Sandy Thomson in Dallanaich. I'm hoping one of them might still be alive.'

'Any luck?'

'Not so far. Some I just can't trace, and the ones I have managed to pin down are all deceased. I've put a cross next to their names, see?'

Suz pointed to a name on the list. 'What about Margie McClelland - that's Julia's grandmother, isn't it? Surely she would have known Sandy best of all?'

'Yes,' Imogen ventured unsurely. 'Margie is 94 years old, according to the records, and Michael says she's very on-the-ball. She lives in an annex next to Jeanette and Donald's place, which is somewhere near here. But it's just that if I try to speak with her, Julia will find out what I'm up to and it may lead to a serious diplomatic incident. I'd rather take a more discreet approach first.'

Suz nodded. 'So who are you working on now?'

Imogen twisted the laptop round so that Suz could get a better view. 'I'm looking up a chap called Duncan Lambie. Most of the men mentioned in Val's list were away fighting at the time Sandy left Dallanaich, but Val said that Duncan was lame. He had some kind of birth defect which affected his left leg. She said it had resulted in one limb being slightly shorter than the other, so he walked with a limp. Anyway, that meant Lambie was considered unfit for active service and would have been in the village at the same time as Sandy. In fact, they must have been the *only* two young men in Dallanaich during those early years of the war, what with Sandy not being required to fight either, as he was in a reserved occupation.'

'They had to have known one another then?'

'I would have thought so. I've found Duncan's birth certificate, which indicates he was a couple of years younger than Sandy. There's no marriage or death certificate, though.'

'That's good news, isn't it? It means he might still be alive.'

'It's possible. But he'd be nearly 100 years old by now. I really can't imagine it, especially if he was disabled - back in those days, when the treatments available weren't very sophisticated. I wouldn't expect him to have lived a long life. Let me try a newspaper search. I'll go onto the Mitchell Library website.' Imogen logged on and entered Duncan's details into the search engine. A couple of articles popped up. One was more recent than the other. Imogen reached for her notepad and clicked on the first of the two.

It was a copy of a news column from the Fort William Observer, dated November, 1942. The report was only very brief, but it stated that a Dallanaich man, named by locals as Duncan Ian Lambie, was missing presumed dead after a storm battered the coastline the previous night. Lambie's mother said he'd gone out to the pub earlier in the day, before the weather had worsened. Duncan was seen in the public bar by a group of elderly drinkers until late, but he never returned home. Local police suspected he was washed into the Loch as the waters rose to unprecedented levels during the night. It ended by saying that local police and volunteers were continuing to search for him along the nearby stretch of coast.

Imogen glanced up at Suz. 'I wonder if Val remembers it? She didn't mention anything about the incident to me the other day.'

'It was wartime, Imogen. I expect the local men were being reported missing and dead quite frequently. Val would have been more concerned with the plight of her own menfolk, I'd have thought.'

'That is true.' Imogen clicked on the other article.

This one had appeared in the colour supplement of a national Sunday newspaper, printed in early 1980. There was a photograph of a woman, who looked to be in her sixties. She had shaggy brown hair and was sitting in a conservatory with a black and white collie dog lying passively by her feet. The views through the bank of windows behind them were a wonderful vista of mountains, cloudy skies and heather.

'It looks like a book review of some kind.' Imogen quickly skimmed through the text. She discovered the lady in the photograph was called Maggie Maclure and she'd just had a new book published. It was a murder mystery set in the Great Glen. The first part of the piece discussed the inspirations for her writing. Further through the article, the journalist summarized Maggie's background. It explained how she grew up in the small lochside community of Dallanaich in the 20s and 30s. Maggie was quoted as saying that the tragic death of her disabled older brother during the war had left her with a compulsion to express her grief through writing. The journalist then gave a brief précis of the incident. Duncan Lambie, 31, had gone out drinking one afternoon in 1942. At some point in the evening, an unexpected storm had swept him off the rocks into Loch Linnhe, where it was assumed he'd been taking the route along the shoreline to walk home. His body was never recovered. Maggie commented that Duncan's accident had a profound effect upon the kind of books she decided to write. Maggie always felt she had to create her own ending to the story, because she'd been denied that opportunity in the case of her big brother. Maggie said producing her impressive back catalogue of bestsellers was no substitute for finding out exactly what happened to Duncan that night. But penning her mysteries, with their neat, satisfying conclusions and allowing herself to indulge in the careful meting out of justice, had proved to be good therapy, nonetheless.

'It's a sad story,' Suz said quietly.

'Yes it is. Hugh would agree with Maggie - that it's good therapy to work out your grief through the expression of creativity. I've heard of the woman, but never read any of her books. I'll have to give them a try - if they're still in print.'

'So, there won't be any point in trying to track down Duncan Lambie, then. He's long dead too. It's starting to look as if Margie McClelland is going to be your only source of information about Sandy after all.'

Imogen logged off and pulled the lid of the laptop closed with a sigh. She'd still got a couple more names left to investigate, but she had a funny feeling her sister-in-law was set to be proved right.

Chapter Thirty Two

On the pretext of having forgotten to post a card for Hugh's mother's birthday, Imogen had taken the bus back into Fort William the previous afternoon. She went straight into the largest bookshop in the town centre and skimmed through the extensive crime literature section. Being a Scottish author, Maggie Maclure's books had been given a prominent position on the shelves. Imogen selected a couple that sounded interesting and took them up to the sales counter.

Being aware that this particular chain of book retailers was well-known for having extremely knowledgeable and enthusiastic staff, Imogen asked the young girl behind the counter, who possessed an impressive gelled-up fringe of blue-green hair, her opinion of the author she'd chosen.

'Her books are really good - especially the series about the wee old lady detective who runs the guesthouse in Glencoe.' She flicked over each glossy paperback in turn. 'That's okay. It looks like you've picked a couple of those. Maggie Maclure used to come here a lot to do signings. She lived up in the Highlands somewhere, but this was her nearest branch. Our manager knew her quite well. I think she died about five years back. Her publishers keep churning out new editions though, so the books must really sell well.' The girl smiled, slipping the novels into a small but sturdy carrier bag.

Imogen had expressed her gratitude and gone off to find a nearby coffee shop, where she could have a better look at her new purchases. Imogen could tell the publishers of these books were no longer compelled to consult the author over jacket design.

The covers displayed the generic dark and menacing type of library shot which adorned every bestselling mystery thriller on the market, when in fact, as she carefully read the blurb, it became clear Maclure's books were actually quite quirky and quintessentially reminiscent of another era.

When Imogen returned to Suz's house later that evening, she had placed the books at the bottom of her suitcase, determined to make a start on them when she got back to Garansay the following day. Anyway, she'd finished the pile of holiday paperbacks she'd brought with her within the first week of the break, when the weather had been so awful there wasn't anything else to do but read, so it wasn't really so unusual to be buying some more.

Imogen had her bags packed into the tiny boot of Michael's sports car by first thing the next morning. It gave her the pleasant opportunity of having breakfast with both Suz and Owen before she left to catch the ferry from Gourock. Suz was much more mobile now, but her boyfriend was still fussing around her, insisting she lie on the sofa whilst he prepared bacon rolls for them all.

'If I carry on like this, I'll end up too fat to ever *leave* the sofa,' Suz called through to the kitchen area, where Owen was busily frying several sizzling rashers of bacon and Imogen was preparing a cafétiere of coffee. There was a slightly bitter tone to her voice.

Imogen chuckled as she carried a cup of coffee in to her friend. 'You aren't serious? There's not so much as an inch of excess fat on your entire body, Suz. There never has been.'

The woman gave a thin smile. 'Just give it time. I'm not as young as I used to be.'

Owen rushed into the room with the steaming

butties on two plates, depositing them unceremoniously onto the low table. He had wrapped his own in a piece of clingfilm, the tell-tale blood-red smear of ketchup was oozing out around the edges. Dressed in paint-stained overalls, the tall, handsome man gave Imogen a wide grin. 'It's been great to see you again. Thanks for keeping Suz company these last few days. She won't admit it, but she's been going stir crazy since the fall.' He leant in to kiss her warmly on the cheek. Imogen saw him out of the front door, standing on the threshold and waving as Owen pulled away in his van, windows lowered and radio blaring.

'He's a really great guy,' Imogen stated, as she plonked herself down in the chair opposite Suz, making a start on her delicious looking sandwich.

'He rustles up a half-decent bacon roll and straight-away you become all misty-eyed,' Suz suggested in an accusatory manner.

Imogen laughed. 'You'd certainly never have got that kind of waiter service from Allan.'

Her friend's face became serious for a moment. 'No, I'd have been taken to an upmarket restaurant instead, or swept away for a surprise weekend to Paris – not driven off into the sunset with a greasy fish supper for two in Owen's white van.' She immediately put a hand up to her mouth. 'I'm really sorry, that made me sound like a horrible, ungrateful cow.'

Imogen stopped smiling and leant forward in her seat. She didn't know what prompted her to do so, but she suddenly clasped hold of Suz's hand and said, 'I listened to you telling me the other day how you were glad that Owen still had his own place to go back to. It made it sound as if you weren't really very keen to commit to him. You also said how Allan thinks it's still early days with Penny, intimating that he doesn't know if the relationship is serious yet. Look, Suz, I've never in my life seen a couple happier together than you used to be with Allan. The attraction pretty much crackled between you. The rest of us were all in awe of what you had. Is there any possible way the two of you could get that back? I don't think you're really willing to settle for a future with Owen – lovely as the bloke clearly is.' Imogen edged closer, feeling she should go with it, now that she'd probably burnt her bridges. 'But it *can't* be the same as it used to be with Al. To be honest, my brother has been a total bloody mess without you. It sounds like a major cliché, but you were the love of his life, and I suspect he was for you, too. I might be completely wrong on this. If I am then tell me to mind my own damn business and I promise never to mention it again. But life's too short Suz. If you still love Allan anything like you used to, then for all of our sakes, *please* do something about it before it's too late.'

Chapter Thirty Three

Phil Boag was eating lunch at his desk when Bevan approached their workstation and sat down in the chair opposite. She glanced at the sandwich he was about to put into his mouth and noted that it was of the healthy variety. Two slabs of granary bread held together a thin slither of meat which was padded out with copious amounts of salad. The greenery obviously made it tricky for him to eat, but also considerably more nutritious than the average meal consumed within the Pitt Street Headquarters.

'Did Jane make those for you?' Bevan asked her sergeant in a neutral tone.

'No, I prepare the packed lunches for the family. Jane sorts out our food at the weekend – when we mostly go out to eat or get a takeaway. It's my job to cook during the week.' Phil didn't remove his eyes from the screen whilst he elaborated on the day-to-day routines of the Boag household.

'If all husbands were like you Phil, I might actually consider getting married.'

Phil kept his expression impassive. 'They aren't.'

Bevan chuckled at his deadpan delivery. 'Anything of interest yet in Gordon Parker's computer files?'

Boag leant back in his chair and turned his gaze towards her. 'Nothing that jumps out as unusual, Ma'am. He corresponded a lot with the clients who used his I.T services. It's taken me ages to work through all of that material. A few clients appeared to have been regulars and they always made a point of expressing their appreciation for his work. His web searches are fairly run-of-the-mill too. They simply reflect the interests of a bog-standard, forty-something family man. He was involved in a minor way with his kids' school. It seems he was on the Parent-Teacher Committee. There are a few recent e-mails relating to that. Parker had volunteered to organise a fund-raising event for the school, in order to buy some new sports equipment.'

Bevan reclined in her seat and considered what Phil had told her. 'It's sounding increasingly as if Gordon Parker was Mr. Average and what happened during his holiday on Garansay was as a result of getting dragged into someone else's mess.'

Phil nodded sagely. 'It's certainly looking that way.'

Bevan was just contemplating the bland cheese roll which was sweating within its polythene wrapping on the desk in front of her, when Andy Calder came blustering across the office floor towards them.

'We've got something from forensics, Ma'am,' he called ahead, sounding out of breath. 'It looks really positive.'

'Oh yes? Pull up a chair, Andy.'

The Detective Constable sat down heavily on the nearest swivel seat, his considerable bulk causing it to roll steadily backwards. Andy didn't seem to notice. 'You know we managed to get a warrant to search Shaw's car?'

Bevan nodded.

'Well, the techs have found some fibres in the front passenger seat.'

She raised her eyebrows.

'There were tiny flecks of dark red material stuck to the upholstery. The techies bagged it and took it back to the lab. Apparently, it matches the fibres from the burgundy fleece that Gordon Parker was wearing when he got washed up on the beach.' Calder was beaming from ear to ear.

'So Gordon Parker was in Mackie Shaw's car?'

'It certainly looks that way, although, there's no other evidence of Parker's presence in the vehicle.'

'Could he have been transported to the Cove in the car *after* he was dead?' Phil asked. 'Maybe this means he was killed somewhere else and the body was dumped in the sea. Mackie would have known all about how the tides operated up at that headland. Shaw could even have deposited the body in the water further up the coast and it was just bad luck for him that it ended up back at the beach.'

'There's no evidence Parker's body was in the boot, or even the backseat. The interior of the car hasn't been cleaned recently either, so no attempt has been made to hide anything. Forensically, we can only place Parker in the passenger seat.'

'Which you wouldn't use to transport a dead body,' Bevan chipped in. 'So, Parker was still alive when he was in Shaw's vehicle.' She pulled on her jacket. 'Andy, get onto the station in Kilross again, will you. We need to get Mackie Shaw back in for questioning straight-away.'

'You've been lying to us, Mackie.' Andy made the statement calmly.

The man opposite him had his head hung down low and his hands were gripping the edge of the table. Mackie had now obtained a proper solicitor, one who came from a well-established local firm. But his surly presence at Mackie's side didn't appear to have boosted his confidence in any way.

'No comment,' he muttered.

'We know Gordon Parker was in your car, Mackie. You didn't tell me that before. If you keep quiet now it just doesn't look good. We've got forensic evidence to connect you with Parker and it's enough to file charges. If you don't provide me with an explanation, it's going to make me jump to conclusions.'

Mackie Shaw glanced sideways at his solicitor and then across to Calder. 'Christ, I didn't *kill* him.'

'Then tell me why Parker was in the car.'

Mackie looked up at the ceiling and sighed. 'When I'd had time to cool off, on the Wednesday night, I decided I didn't like how we'd left it.' Shaw shifted about uncomfortably. 'I *was* worried that Parker would tell Murray about my fling with Gillian Moore. I didn't want to lose my job.'

'So what did you do?'

Mackie ran both hands through this thick hair. 'I drove to the Cove early on the Thursday morning. I parked my car beyond the headland, up at the Thorpes' place. I knew they'd gone back to England and there'd be no one around to see it. Then I walked back to the Lodge. I hung about the boat shed and waited until I saw that Parker was alone in the kitchen. I banged on the window and he came outside to speak with me. The conversation lasted no more than a minute. I told him it was crucial we talk again - that I wanted to give him my side of the story. I asked him to meet me at the headland in twenty minutes, then I dashed off. I had no idea if he would actually turn up.'

'So it *was* you that Parker delayed his departure for.'

'I suppose it must have been. We met on the rocks a little later but it had started to rain by then, so I led him down to my car and we sat in the front seats and talked.' Mackie looked Calder straight in the eye. 'We were only in the car to get some shelter. It was nothing more significant than that.'

'What did you talk about?'

'I apologised for losing my temper with him the previous evening. I said I understood that he was just helping out a pal, but I also told him I didn't believe I deserved to lose my job simply because I'd made a stupid mistake.'

'How did Parker respond?'

‘He apologised too. Gordon said it was really none of his business and he wished he’d told Clifford he wanted no part of it all. Parker assured me he had no intention of reporting me to Colin but he couldn’t guarantee that Mr. Moore would not. Parker said he was leaving that day and wouldn’t get a chance to speak with his friend before he left.’

‘So the conversation was entirely amicable?’

‘*Yes*, I swear to you it was. Parker explained that he’d had a lot on his mind recently and he was crazy to have taken on someone else’s problems too. He said it almost like he was talking to himself, you know? I was driving straight back to Kilross, because I wasn’t due to take my group out until mid-afternoon. So I offered Gordon a lift to the ferry port, but he declined. He said he wanted to take a last walk up to the headland first. Parker gave the reason that he’d missed his boat anyway and had to wait for the next one. We shook hands before he got out. I told him to be careful, because the weather looked bad. Parker just smiled and said he’d be fine. Then he shut the car door. I sat and watched him stride off along the rocks. I don’t really know why. But after a short while I turned the car around, switched on the wipers, and headed back towards Kilross.’

Chapter Thirty Four

The police station in Kilross had fewer facilities than Bevan and Calder were used to. It was situated next to the landscaped golf course which ran along the seafront of Garansay's largest town. The building possessed only one storey and while the two Strathclyde officers were discussing the implications of Mackie's new statement, they could see the handsome profile of Murray White, standing at the reception desk.

'What's he doing here?' Bevan asked the duty sergeant, as he proceeded along the corridor next to them. She inclined her head towards the young man standing beyond the toughened glass.

'He's asking to make bail for Mackie Shaw,' the gruff man replied. 'I'm just going to check if he's been charged yet.'

'Well, I can save you a trip. He hasn't. D.C. Calder and I are still in the process of debating it.' Bevan thought for a moment. Turning towards Andy she said, 'I'll go and have a word with him.'

Bevan punched a security code into the pad and pushed open the heavy door. Murray didn't appear particularly surprised to see the detective. Dani gestured towards the seats lining the wall of the entrance lobby and Murray obediently sat down in a chair next to her.

'Is Mackie going to be charged with murder?' He asked, with his usual unguarded candour, 'because if he is, I would like to put up the bail money, so that he can go home as soon as possible.'

Dani didn't know whether she was irritated or touched by the young man's declaration. 'If Mackie *is* charged with murder, Mr. White, he won't get bail, I'm afraid. The crime is too serious for that.'

Murray opened his mouth but no words came out. He looked crestfallen.

'I didn't realise that you and Mackie were such good friends. I got the impression you didn't actually like each other very much.'

Bevan detected a flash of anger in Murray's piercing blue eyes. 'He can be a bit slapdash with his work sometimes and he's got an eye for the ladies, but I don't believe for one second that Mackie could kill anyone.'

'Your boss couldn't be quite so certain.'

Murray hesitated for a moment before replying. 'Colin doesn't work as closely with him as I do. Mackie's got a problem with authority and tends to rub people up the wrong way. But when you're out on the water with somebody day in and day out, when the weather can turn at any moment, you need to be able to trust the person you're out there with - you may have to rely on them to save your life. I trust Mackie, otherwise I wouldn't have him at Cove Lodge.'

Bevan was impressed by the speech. She examined his face carefully. He seemed sincere enough. 'Murray, I'll let Mackie and his solicitor know about your offer. To be honest with you, we haven't decided whether or not to charge Mackie just yet, but I can tell you the evidence against him isn't looking good.'

Murray seemed as if he was working hard to formulate his words, but then he finally blurted out, 'a couple of years ago, when Mackie first came to work for me, his life was in a mess. He'd been engaged to a local lass - who was his girlfriend since school. A month or so before the wedding, she told him she'd met someone else and called the whole thing off. It turned out the chap she'd been seeing was Mackie's older cousin. He's the captain of the Kilross Golf Club.' Murray tipped his head in the direction of the building next door. 'If you went in there right now, you'd find Craig Shaw propping up the bar, keeping all the barmaids enthralled with his exploits on the green. But a year or so after he took up with Kirstie, Craig had moved onto somebody else. He left the lass broken-hearted and begging for Mackie's forgiveness. To his credit, he didn't take her back, but that decision cost him dearly. It was as plain as day to all the world that he still loved her. But quite sensibly, he knew he could never trust Kirstie again after what she'd done.' Murray turned over his hands so that they lay palm up on his lap. 'That's why Mackie's been acting like a Jack-the-lad with the lassies. It's his way of getting over what happened with Kirstie, so I've always cut him a bit of slack over it. For what it's worth, my opinion is that if Mackie were the murdering type then it would have been Craig Shaw who was on the receiving end of it. The fact he took the whole terrible incident on the chin suggests to me that Mackie just isn't a violent person.'

Thinking that this was the most Dani Bevan had ever heard Murray White utter in one breath she replied, 'thank you for that information. It could prove very useful to us. We'll let you know as soon as a decision's been made with regards to Mr. Shaw.' And with that, the detective reached out and shook him firmly by the hand.

But Murray White remained in exactly the same spot for the next few hours. Bevan glanced through the glass partition at him every so often, just to check he was still there, before returning to the tiny, cramped office that she and Calder had commandeered for the afternoon. The stuffy room's only saving grace was the fabulous view of Benn Ardroch which could be seen through a small window set up high in one wall.

Dani had removed her suit jacket and was sitting at the desk in a crisp white shirt which clung to her lean figure. 'How long have we got until we need to make a decision?'

Calder looked at his watch. 'We've got half an hour before we either charge Mackie or release him.'

'I can't help but feel that what Murray told me actually goes against Mackie. Since his fiancé jilted him, Shaw's been carrying around a huge amount of pent up anger and frustration. He didn't take it out on his cousin, sure, but perhaps the consequences would have been too awful if he had done. Instead, when Gordon Parker starts interfering in his relationship with Gillian Moore, Mackie finally flips.'

'It's certainly possible,' Andy put in, 'but all the evidence we have against him is purely circumstantial. The bottom line is that we've no chance of obtaining a conviction on the strength of it.'

'Aye, you're right.' Dani put a hand to her closely cropped hair, sensing this case had already added a couple more dashes of silver to its otherwise dark strands. 'We'll have to let him go while we continue the investigation. But make sure the local plods put a car outside his cottage, at least for tonight. We don't want Mackie booking passage on the first boat out of Kilross Harbour.'

'Okay, Ma'am,' Andy said with a sigh. 'I'll get the duty sergeant to tell Murray White to hang around for another ten minutes, then he can give his friend a lift home.'

Chapter Thirty Five

'Bloody Hell,' said Hugh, puffing out his cheeks dramatically. 'I can't believe you actually said that to her.'

Imogen winced. 'Neither can I. But something in the moment seemed to warrant it.'

'How on earth did she respond?' Hugh padded across the kitchen of the Kilduggan farmhouse to make his wife a cup of tea. Imogen had only been back on Garansay for about half an hour, her bags were still sitting in the hall.

Michael strode into the room, bending down to place a kiss on his sister's cheek. 'I hope I'm not interrupting anything? How was your trip?'

'You're not interrupting at all, Mike. The trip was good. Suz was absolutely fine when I left.'

'Was that despite the fact you'd just insisted she get back together with Allan, after nearly a decade of them living apart.' Hugh took a seat at the table opposite Imogen, while he waited for the kettle to boil.

Michael raised his eyebrows incredulously. '*Really*?'

'Actually, yes I did. But the suggestion was made in the appropriate context. Suz was quite clear this morning that she wasn't entirely happy in her relationship with Owen. Allan has now split up with Abigail after all those years of them being together. I just thought that if there was ever a chance for the two of them to patch things up, it was now. Come on, don't tell me the two of you have never felt that Suz and Allan were meant to be together.'

'What about Penny?' Hugh asked, and Imogen could tell from his expression that he felt genuine concern for her. She wasn't really surprised, as

Hugh and Penny Mills had known each other since childhood.

'I'm sorry about Penny, I really am, but this is Allan's future happiness we're talking about here. We all know he's been a disaster area since his divorce from Suz.'

Michael nodded, 'I have to agree with that. What did Suz say?'

Imogen frowned. 'Not a great deal to be honest. She went very quiet, but she wasn't angry or anything. As I was leaving, Suz gave me a really tight hug, clinging to me for ages. I felt as if she was thanking me for what I'd said. I've no idea what she'll do about it. I certainly don't regret saying something. I should have done it years ago.'

Hugh brought the teas across and placed them down on the table. Then he leant over and planted a kiss on the top of Imogen's head.

'What was that for?'

'Because I love the way you put yourself out for Allan. Plenty of sisters would leave him to wallow in his own mess.'

Michael selected a cup and slipped his hands around its middle, savouring the warmth. 'He's had no one except you and me to look out for him since Mum died. Let's face it, despite Allan's best efforts at playing the fool, we know damn well he'd do the exact same for us.'

Making the most of a quiet couple of hours at the farmhouse, Imogen made a start on one of Maggie Maclure's books. She found it surprisingly gripping. The Highland landscapes the author described were amazingly vivid and although the storyline could be viewed as somewhat dated, the plots were cleverly interwoven with red-herrings and a decent dash of tongue-in-cheek humour. Imogen discovered that she liked Maclure's little old lady amateur sleuth very much. In fact, the character of Mrs. O'Neil reminded Imogen of her own mother, who ran Lower Kilduggan Farm as a guesthouse for many years and possessed the same astuteness and fastidious attention to detail as Maclure's elderly protagonist did.

Imogen had been reading for much of the afternoon when Michael entered the sitting room. The sun slowly lowered itself behind the darkening hills of Kintyre as he settled down in the armchair opposite her. Imogen looked up from the pages and was surprised to note that she had almost finished the book.

'The story must be good,' he commented, nodding towards the thin volume resting in her lap. 'You've been engrossed in it for hours.'

'The woman who wrote it originally came from Dallanaich. It's one of the things I picked up whilst I was on the mainland.'

Michael shot a cautious glance towards the doorway. 'That's what I wanted to ask you about. Julia's upstairs having a bath, so I thought we could discuss what you found out about Sandy Thomson.'

'Certainly, although it's less than I'd hoped for.'

Her brother looked disappointed.

Imogen filled him in on her conversation with Val Black and her subsequent attempt to find someone still alive who might have known Sandy before he left the UK. 'It seems increasingly likely that Julia's grandmother is the only one left who would be able to tell us anything at all about the old Sandy Thomson.'

'Hmm, that could be awkward,' Michael added. 'Julia has always intimated that Margie doesn't really like to be reminded of the fact she was abandoned by her first husband. I can't say I blame her.'

'No, absolutely not. And we'd also have to bring Julia into the picture before we spoke with Margie.' Imogen glanced expectantly at her brother, to see if he was willing to do this.

Michael frowned. 'I'm not sure I want to do that just yet. Tell me again about this Duncan Lambie chap. You say he was swept off the rocks into the loch one night and drowned?'

'That's what the police decided must have happened, because of the stormy weather on the evening he went missing, but his body was never actually recovered.'

'And this occurred in the November before Sandy Thomson left for New York, right?' Michael furrowed his brow even deeper, so that the lines formed a set of deep ridges running across his forehead.

Imogen lowered her voice. 'Are you wondering if Sandy had something to do with Duncan Lambie's disappearance, and that was the reason why he decided to leave Dallanaich for good?'

Michael leaned in closer, answering in a husky whisper, 'well, isn't that what you're thinking too?'

Chapter Thirty Six

Colin Walmsley drove his 4x4 the mile and a half from Loch Crannox Farm to Cove Lodge. He knew that Murray had a group of holidaymakers booked in for a sailing lesson this afternoon and he wanted to show the lad some support. Business had been gradually picking up in the weeks since Gordon Parker's body was found on the shore. Colin was hoping they were over the worst of the fallout from the incident. He just wished Murray could be persuaded to give Mackie Shaw his marching orders, but his young manager seemed determined to keep him on. Colin felt that Shaw had done enough damage through his unprofessional behaviour with one of their female clients to warrant his immediate dismissal. Murray was concerned that this would leave Mackie with nothing. He was keen to give Shaw a second chance. Despite what he told D.I. Bevan the other day, Colin didn't really believe that Mackie killed Gordon Parker. He was still fairly certain the American's death would turn out to simply have been a nasty accident. At least, he hoped that was the case.

Colin believed that Murray's misplaced sentimentality over Mackie Shaw had no place in a successful business. However, he had delegated all the decision-making relating to Cove Lodge to Murray. Colin was reluctant to question his judgment so early on in the venture. Besides, Michael Nichols was also a sleeping partner in the enterprise and Colin had a suspicion that Mike would probably agree with his friend over the issue.

There was no sign of Murray at the guesthouse, so Colin walked down towards the landing stage. He discovered his manager bringing the smaller of the yachts out of the boat shed.

'Hang on. I'll give you a hand!' He called ahead, striding across the shingle and jumping up onto the concrete structure.

Murray turned his head and smiled. 'Could you just steady her at the stern for me?'

Colin took hold of the fibreglass hull and helped to steer the vessel down the slope to the water's edge, where the waves were gently lapping at the foot of the jetty. Murray secured the boat, ready to be launched when his students arrived later in the day.

'Have you got time to stay for a coffee?' Murray asked his boss, wiping his hands down a pair of beige cotton trousers.

'Sure. I came to see if you're managing okay on your own.' Colin fell into step beside the young man, as they made their way back in the direction of the house.

'Actually,' Murray replied casually, 'I could really do with an extra pair of hands this afternoon. Would you mind if I called Mackie and asked him to come over for a couple of hours?'

Colin continued in silence for a few paces before he said, 'don't ring him. I need to head over to Kilross this morning anyway, so I'll drop by his cottage and speak with him myself. It's about time we had a word. I respect your decision to keep Mackie on here at the Cove, but I'd still like to have a talk with him about how I expect my employees to behave. Once I've made my feelings clear to Mackie, I'll feel a lot happier about him returning to work.'

Murray said nothing but his face broke into a broad smile. The young man pushed open the thick wooden door that led into the kitchen of Cove Lodge. Standing back politely, he allowed Colin to step inside.

Colin remained at the Lodge for a quick drink with Murray before setting out for Kilross. He needed to speak with a building contractor who had an office down by the harbour. He could always have rung from the farm, but Colin had learnt over the years that nothing motivated people better than addressing them face-to-face. He hoped this proved to be true for Mackie Shaw too.

Colin decided to make a stop at Shaw's cottage first, as it was situated on the outskirts of the town. It sat in the middle of a quaint little terrace of stone built dwellings which lay at the base of Glen Ardroch. The public footpath which led up to the highest mountain on Garansay passed directly in front of these pretty houses. In fact, Colin could see a group of hillwalkers, with their hiking boots and brightly coloured waterproof jackets, approaching him along the stony track up ahead.

He reached Mackie's front door. The blue paint was peeling slightly on the window frames but other than that the cottage appeared to be well maintained. He rapped hard on the wooden panel, waiting patiently for a response. After a couple of minutes, Colin peered through a downstairs window into the tiny lounge. He could see a sofa and two chairs positioned in front of a small television. A wood-burner was fitted into an alcove in the corner of the room. There was no sign of Mackie.

As he loitered outside, an elderly lady with a head full of wild grey hair emerged from the house next door. 'He's in,' she exclaimed matter-of-factly. 'But sometimes he can't hear very well when he's in the shed out the back. Is it urgent?'

'I'm his boss from the sailing school. I could really do with having a word with him.'

The woman disappeared from view for a minute or

two and then returned, stepping onto the front path and holding her hand out to Colin. 'Here's the key.'

'Thanks very much,' he replied, slipping the key into the lock and passing over the threshold into Mackie's dark hallway.

Colin walked through to the kitchen and switched on a light. He was surprised to see that the modern looking cabinets and appliances had been built into a reasonably sized extension, so there was ample room for a table and chairs. A patio door opened out into the garden. Colin observed how the breakfast dishes had been washed up and left to drain by the sink. The patio area led on to a rectangular lawn which ended at the fence separating this property from the steep incline of the hillside beyond. There was a substantial lean-to in the right hand corner of the plot.

Colin tried the back door and found it to be unlocked. He stepped out into the sunlight and marched straight over to the shed. 'Mackie! Are you in there? Your neighbour let me into the house.' When he reached the entrance, Colin leant in close, to see if he could hear any movement inside. Growing tired of the whole situation, Colin impatiently lifted the sneck which secured the door and roughly shouldered it open.

It took a full half minute for his eyes to adjust to the gloom. When they finally did, he stumbled backwards against a lawnmower, which was hanging up in one corner, nearly losing his footing in the process.

'Mackie?' Colin said in a croaky voice, as if expecting the ghoulish figure before him to offer some kind of explanation.

Colin stared intently at Mackie's body, then, he took a closer look at the interior of the shed. Shaw had obviously set the place up as a workshop. The shelves were lined with several dozen intricate models of wooden sailing ships. In the centre of the space was a workbench where Mackie had clearly been carving his latest creation. Right now, the man was sitting slumped in a chair against the far wall of the outbuilding. His brown eyes were wide open and expressionless. His hands lay palm up on his lap, as if in supplication. But Colin's vision was inexorably drawn to the deep red gash in his neck, which was still slowly leaking a thick, dark liquid down his once white T-shirt. The wound indicated to Colin that Mackie Shaw's throat had been brutally cut from ear-to-ear.

Chapter Thirty Seven

Despite the warmth of the day, Colin was shivering uncontrollably. He could hear his own teeth chattering away inside his head. There had been a scene of frantic activity being played out around him for the past hour and a half, during which time he had done nothing but sit on Mackie Shaw's two-seater sofa in the front room of the man's pokey wee cottage, trying desperately to stop himself from shaking.

Finally, Colin felt a hand gripping his shoulder and heard a question which appeared to be directed at him. 'Would you like a whisky or a cup of tea, Mr. Walmsley?'

'Whisky please,' he managed to mumble.

The hand was temporarily removed but when it returned it placed a heavy glass on the coffee table in front of him. Colin immediately noticed that the tartan blanket which was draped over the back of one of the armchairs had been wrapped around his shoulders.

'Have a sip, Mr. Walmsley, it will help,' the voice said encouragingly. Colin worked out then that it belonged to a woman.

'Okay.' He reached forward and lifted the tumbler, putting it to his lips and allowing the strong liquid to gently burn his mouth and throat. The woman was right. He gradually sensed his body beginning to regain some kind of control over itself.

'I was the same – worse, if I'm honest – when I first witnessed the aftermath of a violent death.'

Colin glanced up to see D.I. Bevan sitting next to him on the sofa. She had her hand resting on his arm. For the first time, he observed how very attractive she was. Her large eyes were a deep chestnut brown and her skin completely clear and unlined. Her lips were full and reddish, formed into a natural heart-shape. He had only seen this physical attribute on one other woman before. Colin wondered what age the detective must be, to have reached the rank of Inspector but to look so very young.

'I have seen a dead body before,' he explained, his voice starting to sound more like his own. 'But the way she had died wasn't quite so gruesome.'

Bevan nodded with understanding. 'You do realise I'll have to take a statement from you. We need to know about everything you saw and touched since arriving here.'

'Of course.' Colin looked the police officer straight in the eye. 'I was actually coming round to give Mackie a bollocking - not because I thought he was a murderer - but because of him fooling around with one of our clients.'

Bevan sighed heavily. 'When the chips were down, I couldn't really see him as a murderer either, more's the pity. If I had, he would still be in a cell at the Kinloch police station right now and the poor man would not be dead.'

*

A couple of hours later, Bevan saw Colin Walmsley into his car herself, being confident by then that he was perfectly able to drive back home. Talking through the event had seemed to help him calm down. Nonetheless, she had given him the number of their NHS trauma counsellor. She sincerely hoped that he used it.

Bevan returned to the police station at Kilross, where they had set up a temporary incident room. After being photographed *in situ,* Mackie Shaw's body had been airlifted to the mainland. His cottage was cordoned off and his immediate neighbours ferried away to stay with friends and relatives for the night. The carefully bagged contents of Mackie's shed had been laid out on several tables in one of the stuffy little offices, where the forensic division had begun the laborious task of labelling them up for analysis.

Dani pulled on a pair of protective gloves and let her eyes pass over the rag-tag of objects which could be observed through their plastic coverings. There was a collection of tiny chisels and knives which Mackie must have used to carve his models. In the centre of the table sat their prime exhibit. A blood stained, burgundy-handled Stanley knife, which at this stage of the inquiry, the white coats had put money on being the murder weapon. It had been dropped in the bushes outside the shed.

Only for the very briefest of moments did the team consider the possibility of suicide. The forensic pathologist explained the impossibility of this explanation as soon as he surveyed the scene. He said that Mackie was most likely attacked from behind and his body later placed in the chair. This was obvious from the blood splatters which resulted when his throat was cut. These were almost all positioned up the back wall of the building. Mackie Shaw very likely never even saw it coming. This thought gave Dani Bevan some comfort. It was also something to tell his family, when they inevitably asked her if he suffered at all.

Dani spent quite some time on the telephone to her Chief Superintendent, trying to persuade him to allow her to keep control of the case, now it was turning into a multiple murder. Mainly because the Glasgow division were heavily involved in an anti-terrorist operation which had been unfolding over the past couple of weeks and were short-handed, the Chief Super agreed to make Bevan an acting D.C.I for the duration of the investigation, appointing her in charge of the Major Incident Team. 'Let's see how you get on,' were his final words to her, before he abruptly ended the call.

Phil Boag had travelled over to the island to join Bevan and Calder. She had gained a couple of keen-looking young D.Cs from the local station to make up her team. As soon as Bevan had surveyed the evidence, she called a meeting in the largest room she could find.

'Andy, do we know when the P.M will take place?' Dani enquired, as soon as her officers were all present.

'Tomorrow morning, Ma'am. The techies are just preparing to take the evidence bags over to the mainland. Shall I put a priority on those?'

'Yes, you'd better.' She addressed her Sergeant, 'Phil, I'm going to need you to write me up a detailed report on Parker's online and phone interactions going back at least three months.'

'Sure. Does that mean we're treating the two deaths as linked?' Phil leaned forward in his seat, with a serious expression on his face.

'Oh aye, I think so,' Bevan responded quickly. 'I was so busy considering Mackie Shaw as a *suspect* that I never thought about him as a potential *witness*. Shaw said Parker wasn't keen to take up his offer of a lift back to Kilross on the morning of his death. I believe the man still had some unfinished business to take care of on Garansay.'

'Like another meeting, you mean?' Phil asked.

'Possibly. Mackie sat in his car and watched Gordon Parker walk away across the headland. Maybe he saw the person that Parker was going to meet.'

'And whoever it was also saw him,' Andy added ominously.

Bevan addressed the rest of the team. 'The uniforms are searching the hillside behind the cottages and checking the ferry manifests. I want you to go over Mackie's interview tapes with a fine-toothed comb - find out if he lets anything slip that we've so far missed.' She turned her head towards Calder. 'Andy, you come with me. It's about time we headed out to notify the parents.'

The man nodded dutifully, lifting up his crumpled suit jacket and solemnly following his superior officer towards the exit door.

Chapter Thirty Eight

Imogen dropped an extra spoonful of sugar into the tea and stirred it around vigorously. She added a generous dash of milk and placed it down with care in front of their visitor.

'Are you sure you don't want anything stronger?'

'Quite sure thanks, I've already had a whisky, if I have any more alcohol I'll be sick. My stomach is already in knots.'

Imogen looked at Colin's face closely. Despite his summer season tan, the colour had almost completely drained from his features. His faithful Irish Setter puppy was lying under the table, gently resting its head upon Colin's feet.

Michael gratefully received a mug of tea and asked, 'does Murray know about it yet?'

'He's still out on the boat. I'll tell him when they come back in.' Colin suddenly appeared utterly exhausted.

'No, you go straight home after this and get some rest,' Michael insisted. 'I'll tell Murray. I wasn't here for him the last time, but now I shall be.'

Colin didn't argue. He was too relieved not to have to deliver the grim facts himself.

'Have the police put you in touch with a counsellor?' Hugh gently inquired.

Colin nodded.

'Make sure you ring them first thing tomorrow morning.'

'Do you think the man who did this could still be on the island?' Imogen shivered.

'Was it not suicide?' Michael said hopefully.

Colin shook his head. 'I couldn't see a weapon close by and there was something about the way the body was positioned. It just didn't look *natural.* I'm no expert, but I really don't think Mackie did that to himself.'

'The police will be monitoring the ferry ports closely and the island will be swarming with officers,' Hugh surmised. 'I'll tell the kids not to venture off alone for the next few days.'

'I hope Bridie isn't too upset by the news, you know how sensitive she is.' Imogen sat down heavily at the table. 'Did Mackie have a big family?'

'Just his mum and dad, they live in Calderburn. I'll leave it a few days and then call round to see them. It's the least I can do.'

'Don't take too much of the responsibility onto your own shoulders, Colin,' Hugh said levelly. 'You know that Mackie had made mistakes. You and Murray were not his protectors, so don't start feeling you're in any way to blame.'

'So what connection did Mackie Shaw have to the American tourist?' Imogen mused out loud. 'Other than the fact the man had warned him off pursuing a relationship with Gillian Moore?'

Colin shrugged. 'I can't really imagine there was one. The only possibility I can suggest is that perhaps he'd offended the wrong person. Mackie had an abrasive personality. He could easily turn folk against him.'

'He'd have to have upset someone pretty badly to warrant that treatment,' Imogen commented dryly.

'A man can get rather put-out when another chap sleeps with his wife,' Michael added.

'That's true,' Imogen conceded. 'We don't know how many other women on Garansay Mackie might have been involved with.'

Hugh glanced across at Colin, noticing how quiet he had become. 'Let's change the subject shall we? Then I suggest we allow Colin to drive home, where he can try to forget about the whole terrible thing for a few hours at least.'

*

'How is he?' Imogen enquired, when Michael returned from the Cove. 'Murray's welcome to come here for dinner tonight if he likes.'

'He had plans to meet some friends in Port na Mara Bay for a drink later on and he's decided to stick to them. The lad is obviously shocked but he's taken it reasonably well. I'll drop in on him again tomorrow. Where is everyone?'

'They've gone over to Kilross to play a round of golf. Julia thought you wouldn't mind her joining them.'

'No, of course I don't. It's a good idea after all the depressing talk of this morning.'

'Listen, Mike.' Imogen led her brother into the kitchen where she had her laptop set up at the table. 'I've been thinking some more about what we were discussing the other night.'

Michael sat down opposite her.

'I've started to write out what we've discovered so far about Sandy Thomson. I've made a kind of timeline.' She turned the screen around so that he could have a look.

'You've started with the disappearance of Duncan Lambie.'

'That's right. At that time, Sandy was teaching at the school in Dallanaich. He'd been married to Margie for about a year. According to Val Black, Sandy was also preaching at the wee Kirk on the outskirts of the town and Reverend Cowan was training him up to be ordained into the Church of Scotland.'

'Val was Sandy's younger cousin, right? She claimed that Sandy would never willingly have left Margie and the baby. She says he was a responsible pillar of the local community.'

'Pretty much. But within six months of this,' Imogen trailed her finger across the line on the screen. 'Sandy had decided to fake his own demise, assume a false identity and start a whole new existence several thousand miles away.'

'So, are we really suggesting that Sandy was involved in the death of Duncan Lambie and he left the country in order to evade responsibility for the murder?'

'Perhaps Sandy felt that if his crime was ever discovered it would drag Margie and the child down with him. In a sense, he left Scotland in order to *protect* his wife and baby, rather than abandon them. It's a theory which fits far better with our knowledge of Sandy's personality. Something I read in Maggie Maclure's book made me think. One of the visitors at Mrs. O'Neil's guesthouse discovers a body buried up the glen. It turns out that he had died thirty years earlier in a kind of duel. Two men from the village had been rival suitors for the same local beauty. Their antipathy reached a point where one of them sent a letter to the other, claiming to be from the girl. It asked him to meet with her up in the hills one starlit night. When the man got there, he found his rival waiting for him. He smashed his head in with a rock and buried the body beneath the heather. The next day, this chap spread the word around the entire village that he'd run the other man out of town. He married the woman and became a successful businessman.' Imogen paused for breath.

'Where on earth are you going with this?'

'Well, what if Duncan Lambie had some kind of connection with Margie? Perhaps he'd forced his attentions on her and Sandy went out to defend her honour and it got out of hand. Maybe Lambie ended up falling into the sea, or cracking his head open on the rocks. I'm sure it was an accident of some sort. But Sandy had to cover it up - get rid of the body and deny he'd ever seen him that night.'

'When you put it like that,' Michael said, with mock excitement, 'it makes this whole theory of ours seem absolutely and totally ridiculous!' Then he started to laugh, folding his arms across his broad chest and rocking gently back and forth in the old wooden chair.

Chapter Thirty Nine

Dani was feeling uncharacteristically reticent as she raised her hand to press on the doorbell of the Loch Crannox Farmhouse.

As Colin Walmsley opened up, with a slightly puzzled expression on his face, Dani observed how much better he looked. His colour had returned and although unshaven and dishevelled, when he began to form a smile, it seemed genuine. Suddenly, Dani heard a feverish barking coming from the corridor behind and a lively, red-haired dog attempted to make a bolt for freedom.

Colin grabbed the puppy's collar firmly, 'calm down Rusty!' he scolded. 'He won't hurt you. He's just a little boisterous, that's all.' He pulled the animal to heel.

'Don't worry, it's not official,' the detective said, as Colin led her through to the kitchen, which appeared to be the heart of the building. Dani tentatively put out a hand to pat the energetic puppy on its head of silky soft fur. 'I've just come to see how you're bearing up.'

The dog settled down quietly in a basket by the back door. Colin busied himself, filling the kettle and placing it onto a double range stove. 'I'll survive,' he responded dryly. 'How did the Shaws take the news?'

Dani sighed. 'As you would expect. It's the very worst part of my job. Once the relatives have partially recovered from the shock of discovering they've lost a loved one, they're gripped by the awareness that certain social norms should be observed, especially with authority figures present in the house. Someone starts offering to make us cups of tea, which we always decline. Mackie's parents seemed like very good people.'

'Oh, aye. The family are well regarded on the island.' Colin fetched down a couple of mugs from a cupboard.

'I wish I'd known that before,' she said quietly.

Colin turned around to address her directly. 'Would it really have made a difference to the way you went about investigating Mackie?'

Bevan considered this for a moment. 'No, it wouldn't,' she finally conceded, before sheepishly adding, 'I grew up on an island myself, you know.'

Colin brought the drinks over and sat down. He said nothing, simply allowing her to continue.

'Well, not for my entire childhood. My father is Welsh. We lived in a wee village in north Wales until I was eight years old. Then my mother died and Dad couldn't seem to get over it whilst we were still in Conwydd. So he took a job on Colonsay, in the Inner Hebrides, within just a few months of Mum's funeral. Dad was the Headmaster of the only primary school on the island for the next twenty five years. He's retired now and he still lives there. I go back over whenever I can to see him, but the job's busy, you know how it is, I'm sure.'

'Did your father ever re-marry?'

'No. He's got plenty of friends in the local community though, and he's always busy. He's the president of the local history society and captain of the island's leading pub quiz team.' Bevan smiled at the thought. 'Did you grow up here at the farm?'

'Aye, that's right. My mother passed away earlier this year. She was staying in a nice wee home over in Gilstone.'

'Oh, I'm sorry to hear that.' Bevan took a sip of coffee.

'She didn't suffer any. My sister, Sandra, and I were with her at the end.'

Bevan nodded. She glanced at her wristwatch and had another swig from her cup. 'I'll need to be getting back to Kilross in a minute.'

Colin smiled and rested his hand briefly on top of hers. 'Of course, I appreciate the fact you've taken time out of the investigation to come up and check on me.'

She smiled back, feeling hot blood rush to her cheeks, making them flush to a rosy hue. Bevan immediately hoped that in the dim light of the kitchen, Colin hadn't noticed.

On the drive over to the east of the island, Bevan looked about her at the precipitous glens which enclosed the little winding road taking her back to Kilross. The landscape here was similar to that which she was used to back home on Colonsay, but it was also reminiscent of the mountainous and rugged beauty of north Wales. Dani experienced mixed emotions when she considered the place of her birth. Because she and her father left their village so abruptly, when the memories she had of her mother were still fresh and sharp in her mind, thinking now about her early childhood sent a stab of immediate pain through her heart. Dani knew that if she spoke to the Strathclyde police psychologist about it, he would say her father took her away too soon - before her grief had had the opportunity to properly heal and scar over. The result being, that she would always associate the time she lived in Conwydd with the image of her mum. Sometimes, when her mind was particularly drawn back to those Welsh hills and valleys, the visions she saw of her mother were so evocative and real, that they haunted her dreams.

Phil Boag had been pacing around the incident

room, waiting for his boss to return. As soon as she placed her jacket on the back of a chair, the sergeant approached with a pile of print-outs cradled in his arms. Fortunately, he didn't press her on where she'd been. 'Andy's out leading the house-to-house inquiries along Shaw's terrace. If you've got time, Ma'am, there's something in Parker's computer records I'd like to run by you.'

'Sure Phil, go ahead.'

'Gordon Parker had been doing some research into his family history. I'd looked through all of the material before, but it didn't seem particularly significant when we still had Mackie Shaw in the frame.'

Bevan pulled the sheets across and laid them out in front of her. 'What I am looking at?'

'He'd made a start on constructing a family tree. Gordon was born in 1972. It appears he was an only child. His father was Franklin Parker, born in New York City in 1944. He died just last year. It seems that Gordon began his research when his father passed away. My sister did the exact same thing after our dad died. It made it easier for her to cope for some reason.'

'Okay, I get that,' Bevan said patiently.

'The Parker section of the tree is largely complete, going back to the turn of the century. From the dates of his internet searches, Gordon had been concentrating more recently on his mother's background. She died in 1979 in a car accident in Connecticut. Gordon had saved a copy of the newspaper reports relating to it. He would only have been six years old when it happened, so it's not really surprising he wanted to find out more about her now.'

Bevan wondered why they were sitting here discussing Gordon Parker's mother, when they were smack bang in the middle of a double murder inquiry, but for some reason, she felt inclined to hear more.

'It looks like he was making some progress. Rosemary Parker had been born in Pittsburgh, on the 25th January 1946. He'd made some notes in the margin which list several addresses in the Pittsburgh area, but that's as far as he'd got. I finally received Parker's bank details today from the Virginia police. I went through it with a fine-toothed comb, like you asked. Everything was fairly well in order. Parker made a decent living from his I.T business and the I.R.S were perfectly happy with his tax situation. But there was something which caught my attention in his statements. For the past year, since his dad died, Gordon Parker had been paying out 1,000 dollars a month to an unnamed source. I called up the Virginia Headquarters and asked them to do a check with the bank. They got back to me pretty fast. The bank had been transferring this money to the account of someone called Lorna Davidson. She lives in downtown Pittsburgh and, according to the U.S police, she works as a private investigator.'

'Ah,' said Bevan, patting her colleague on the back, 'now, that *is* interesting.'

Chapter Forty

Julia Nichols climbed out of the passenger seat of the estate car and headed straight for the house. She felt fully refreshed after a very pleasant afternoon on the golf course. She spotted her sister-in-law, who was stepping out of the kitchen door with a mobile phone gripped in her hand. 'Is Michael back yet?' Julia asked as they passed one another on the gravel path.

'Yes, he's in the sitting room,' Imogen replied. 'Are Hugh and the kids out here?'

'They're just putting the clubs away in the shed.'

'Great, there's a call for Hugh from someone at the university. It sounds like it might be urgent!' she called back over her shoulder.

Julia smiled to herself and continued into the house. She felt the sudden desperate need for a cup of tea. There was a brisk breeze coming in off the bay at Kilross and Julia was a little chilled. She lit the stove and placed the kettle on the hob, padding out across the hallway into the living room. Michael was sitting beneath the tall windows, engrossed in an architectural magazine. 'Would you like a coffee darling?' She asked, leaning down to place a kiss on his cheek.

'Yes please,' he said cheerfully, 'how was the golf?'

'Really great actually, but I need a hot drink to warm me up.'

'You should add a shot of whisky to it. That will do the trick.'

'What a good idea.' Julia returned to the kitchen with the bottle of single malt in her hand. She gazed out of the window and observed Imogen encouraging her boys to place their golf clubs neatly inside one of the outhouses. Hugh was standing to one side of them, speaking absorbedly into his mobile phone. She imagined they would all want a cuppa when they got back into the house, so she lifted several cups and mugs down from the cupboard and lined them up next to the sink.

Whilst she was waiting for the water to boil, Julia glanced around the room for the sugar bowl, which she assumed the kids had tidied away somewhere after breakfast. As she searched, her vision was drawn to a laptop computer which was sitting open on the table. A word on the screen that she recognised encouraged her to take a closer look. After a couple of second's cautious reading, she sat herself down on one of the chairs and pulled the computer towards her. She continued to carefully scan the lines of the document, ignoring the noise of the kettle, which had begun to whistle and rattle violently on top of the stove behind her.

*

'I just wish you'd told me about it,' Julia said despondently. It was the disappointment in her voice that Michael found the most distressing.

'I'm really sorry, darling. I should have told you that Imogen and I had been doing some more research into your grandfather. It's only because we didn't want to upset you with what we might discover.'

Julia had gone straight to her husband, after reading the document on Imogen's laptop. She explained to him what she'd seen and Michael was compelled to tell her that he already knew all about it. They were now sitting opposite one another in the twin armchairs under the window, speaking in hushed voices whilst the rest of the household were noisily preparing dinner in the kitchen.

'We've only been married a few weeks and already you're keeping secrets from me.' Julia looked genuinely hurt.

Michael leant forward and took hold of her hands. 'I promise I'll never do anything like this again. After what we found out in Canada, I have to admit my curiosity was piqued. I had the distinct impression there was more to be uncovered about the man. I don't think you heard her say it at the time, but Mariella Wilson told us that someone else had been asking about the King family in York Bay recently. This was for the first time in maybe forty odd years.'

Julia lifted her gaze towards Michael. 'I didn't hear that, no. What do you think it means?'

'Imogen and I both decided it might be because Sandy Thomson was guilty of more than just deception. Perhaps there was a more sinister reason for him needing to leave Dallanaich.' Michael gripped her hands tighter, watching her reaction to his words. 'Maybe there's a person still out there who knows what that reason is.'

'So that's what Imogen's notes relating to this Duncan Lambie chap were all about?'

'Yes,' Michael said guiltily. 'We tried to find a contemporary of Sandy's who knew him back in 1943, before he left for the United States. That was how Imogen uncovered the disappearance of Lambie. We decided the only individual left alive who really knew your grandfather back then was Margie. But we thought it would be far too presumptuous of us to ask if we could speak with her. *That's* why I never told you.'

Julia was silent for a moment. 'It would certainly seem strange if you or Imogen were to ask my grandmother about Sandy, but it would be perfectly natural if *I* were to do it.'

'Would you be prepared to do that?'

'Well, I'd like to find out what my grandfather was running away from too – if only to clear his name. I need to visit Granny as it is, to thank her for our wedding gift. She wasn't well enough to travel to the ceremony and we didn't have the time to see her when we were in Appin. I really should go anyway.'

Michael tried a tentative smile. 'So, am I forgiven?'

Julia moved forwards into his waiting arms. 'Of course you are, darling. I know you wanted to protect me, but I'm fine. Whatever we uncover, we must do it *together,* and please don't worry, because whatever it is, I'll be perfectly able to deal with it.'

Chapter Forty One

As Imogen carefully tackled a sharp bend in the road which wound itself through the heather dotted hillside towards Kilross Harbour, she thought this must be the most awkward car journey she'd ever made.

Only when they had almost reached their destination did her passenger break the uncomfortable silence.

'I hope it wasn't anything serious,' Julia suddenly said.

'What do you mean?' Imogen replied, trying to sound as bright and amenable as possible.

'Hugh's phone call from the university.'

'Oh, no, that was nothing much. One of Hugh's colleagues had mislaid a set of exam papers. It happens every year. One time, this chap had left them all in a bundle in the front basket of his bicycle. He went into the supermarket for his weekly shop and when he got back outside again the bike had been stolen. One of the students found the bundle dumped in a litter bin a few hours later. It was a huge embarrassment for the university. Apparently, this chap's done it again. If they don't turn up, then Hugh will have to provide his students with a grade based on their essays over the year.'

'I'm amazed he's still got a job – this chap who keeps losing the exam papers, I mean.'

'He's retiring next year. Hugh can't wait.' She paused for a moment, just as the ferry port loomed into view. 'I'm really sorry Julia. I should never have gone behind your back and spoken to Michael about your family. I'm not making excuses, but I have this tendency to stick my nose into stuff that I really shouldn't. I hope we can still be close after this, because I know that Michael loves you to bits and I've waited so long for him to be happy again.'

Julia laughed. 'It's okay, Imogen. I know all about your sleuthing. Michael's told me the details of the cases you and Hugh have solved, they sounded thrilling. I'd love to have your help on this one. I've just been a bit quiet this morning because I'm nervous about the trip. I have absolutely no idea how my Gran will respond to being questioned about Sandy. But that doesn't mean I don't want to know the answers.'

Imogen let out the breath she'd been holding in. 'Thank goodness for that. If you need any help, then give me a call. One of us will be straight up to join you.'

The boat was gliding slowly into harbour as the two ladies strolled along the pier. They joined the end of the queue which was beginning to form. Imogen made sure her sister-in-law got safely aboard and then she stood and watched, as the ferry powered into the still waters of the Clyde, until it became just a tiny black and white dot on the distant horizon.

*

'Right, give me a report before I leave,' Bevan said to her team, perching on the desk next to a whiteboard full of diagrams. Crime scene photos were stuck all around it with blue tack.

Andy Calder took the lead. 'The ferry was very busy on the day of Mackie's death. Several hundred people got off the boat that morning and we've accounted for the majority of them. There are still a few single males and females who we've yet to eliminate from our enquiries, but we're working on it. Our principal theory is that the murderer reached the cottage from the hillside at the back. If he or she was dressed like a walker then they wouldn't have been too conspicuous.'

'But wouldn't they have been blood stained after the attack?' Bevan asked.

'The pathologist says that because Mackie had his throat severed from behind, most of the blood spurted forwards onto the rear wall. However, there would have been some transference of blood when the body was shifted *post mortem* onto the chair,' Calder explained.

'The scenario we're currently working on is that the attacker had a change of clothes in a backpack. He may have swapped the blood stained items for clean ones inside the shed after killing Mackie. I think he was probably in full hiking gear,' Phil suggested.

'So this murder was planned,' Bevan stated decisively, making sure she caught the eye of everyone in the room. 'This person had a good idea of where Mackie might be found *and* they had an escape route worked out. I know what it's like on the Garansay ferry. If you go on as a foot passenger you have to give a name when buying a ticket, but I'm sure no one checks it. We can't even be sure that the attacker arrived in Garansay on the day of the murder. He could have been here for days beforehand.'

'Or, they could be local themselves,' one of the young D.Cs chipped in. 'We don't know who else Mackie Shaw had upset. It might be that this murder has no connection to Gordon Parker's death at all.'

Bevan looked closely at the man. He was lanky, with closely shaved hair. He appeared to have dug out a suit for the purposes of this investigation which usually only got an airing at weddings and funerals. 'Okay. Robertson, isn't it?'

The lad nodded.

'Can you focus on Mackie? Concentrate on where he's been and who he's seen in the last few months. Check out this feud with his cousin, Craig Shaw. Let's see if that rift was still an open sore for the two of them. Get onto the ex-fiancé and find out if they were still in contact. Most importantly, we should clarify that Mackie wasn't knocking off some other bloke's wife, like he did with Gillian Moore.' Bevan was impressed to see the young man was making notes.

'Got that, Ma'am.'

'Andy, keep pressing forensics for some results on the contents of the shed and make sure you personally co-ordinate the stop and searches at the ferry ports. If this guy tries to leave the island, I want to know about it. Phil, I need you to concentrate on finding out what you can about Rosemary Anne Parker, née Taylor, from here. I don't think that Gordon Parker got very far with his inquiries before he was killed.'

'Aye,' said Phil. 'When will you be back, Ma'am?'

'Chief Superintendent Nicolson has given me 48 hours to follow up Phil's lead in the United States. I'll be in constant contact with you all. If anything crops up, even if it seems trivial, let me know straight away. I may be heading off on a wild goose chase with this, so keep the heat on over here. It might well be one of you lot who ends up finding the evidence that breaks this case. If you do, I won't shy away from giving you the credit.'

Chapter Forty Two

Imogen was pacing about the kitchen, feeling at a loose end, when Hugh came in for his morning coffee. He kissed her absentmindedly before seeking out the cafétiere and a bag of ground beans.

'I've only got time to make a quick drink. I promised to drive the boys over to Murray's place. They need to be there by nine.'

'You can have a proper breakfast when you get back then,' she replied. 'Are they sailing today?'

'Murray and Ian are going to try navigating around the island, remember - to get in practise for the regatta? They need to set off early so they can catch the correct tides.'

'So Murray and Colin are still going ahead with the idea of a round island race are they – even after what's happened?'

'It looks like it. They'll need the feel good factor it generates more than ever now, I expect.' Hugh paused after filling the glass contraption with boiling water. He glanced at his wife. 'Are you okay? – you seem a bit distracted.'

'I suppose I'm a little lost – now that Michael and I have passed the investigation into Sandy Thomson back to Julia. It had just felt as if I was getting somewhere.'

'Julia said she'd still like your help. Did she leave you with anything to look into?'

'She gave me a name to do an internet search on, but Michael thinks it's a dead end.' Imogen leant sulkily against the kitchen counter.

Hugh chuckled. 'Those are often the most important leads. Haven't you learnt that fact by now, Mrs. Croft?'

Imogen managed a smile. Hugh had a slurp of coffee and then gathered her up into his arms. He placed his warm, bitter-tasting lips on hers and they shared a lingering kiss. 'I won't be long dropping the lads off. Maybe we could go somewhere nice for lunch?'

'Mmm, that sounds lovely. Bridie may want to come too. It'll give me time to do that research for Julia this morning.'

Hugh was just leaning in towards his wife once more when his advances were interrupted by the noise of exaggerated throat clearing, coming from the doorway.

'Cut it out you two,' said Ian, with obvious disdain. 'You can do all that smoochy stuff when I'm back at uni. It's time to get going now, Dad. We need to have the boat launched before we miss the tide.'

*

The information that Julia left for Imogen had been written on the back of a menu card from the Piazza Hotel, New York City. Imogen was temporarily distracted by the delicious sounding morsels which constituted the hotel's version of High Tea. But the fact there weren't even any prices listed on the card made her quite certain this establishment would be completely out of her league. So she simply concentrated on the name printed there instead.

The Reverend Stewart McLeod was born in Oban on the 21st June 1893. He died in the mid-nineteen sixties, so Michael was correct when he said this line of enquiry might prove to be a dead end. But as it was the only one she'd got, Imogen was determined to pursue it a little further.

Using a genealogy website and some Google searches, Imogen discovered that the Reverend

McLeod became a minister in the Church of Scotland after the end of the First World War. As a young man, he had fought in the trenches and been present at the Battle of the Somme in 1916. Imogen wondered if his experiences in that terrible war encouraged him to follow a career in the service of God. It may have helped him to make sense of the human tragedy. She imagined how for so many others who took part in the conflict, the horrors they had witnessed on the Western Front would have left them seriously doubting the religious faith they had previously held so dear.

McLeod would have undergone several years of study in order to obtain his ordination. Imogen knew how strict the process was, having had an uncle who was a minister in the Scottish Church when she was a girl.

McLeod's ministry was in Ganavan, which was situated a few miles north of Oban Bay. He married in the early 1930s and had three children over the course of that decade. When he set sail for the United States to take Reverend Cowan's place at the convention of Presbyterian Churches which convened in New York City in the March of 1943, McLeod was 50 years old. He must have returned home safely, because the records indicated that he continued to serve his congregation in Ganavan until his retirement in 1955. Imogen was interested to see that McLeod wrote a couple of volumes in the early 1960s which constituted the memoirs of his years in the Church. She found this out because the books were mentioned on the current Church of Scotland website, appearing on a lengthy list of suggested reading material for clerics. Imogen decided to check if they were still in print.

She was just about to type the minister's name into the search engine of a major online bookstore, when the telephone out in the hallway started to ring.

'Hello?' She answered distractedly.

'Hello Mrs. Croft, are you having a good holiday?'

'Oh, hi Allan, yes we are thanks. How are you? Is work okay?'

'You know, busy as usual. Did the new Mr. and Mrs. Nichols enjoy their honeymoon? I hear they took an impromptu tour around Canada.'

'They stayed with Julia's uncle in New Brunswick. It was a good opportunity for her to catch up with that branch of the family.'

'Hmm, lovely part of the world,' Allan commented amiably. There was silence on the line for a moment, before he added, in a steelier tone, 'anything else you might want to tell me about, whilst I'm on the phone, Mrs C?'

Hugh and Imogen drove up the coast to Port na Mara. Hugh turned the car into a winding side road which led up the glen to the main hotel. They served a decent pub lunch in the bar, which had superb views out across the bay. Bridie had decided to join them. She lounged in one of the window seats, closely examining the menu. Although warm, it had been drizzling on and off all morning. In addition to her shorts and t-shirt, Bridie had on a well-worn pair of soft leather hiking boots.

'What do you fancy eating darling?' Her mother asked kindly.

'I'll just have a cheese and tomato toastie, thanks. Will Murray be coming for dinner tonight?'

'Well, he's more than welcome to. I'll be cooking for the boys when they get back from their sail anyway. I'll ask him if you like.'

Bridie smiled triumphantly. Imogen did her best to ignore it, worrying that the fascination her daughter had developed for Murray White was destined to end in tears.

Hugh went up to the bar to order. When he returned, Imogen's husband resurrected the conversation they were having during the journey over. 'So, was Allan very cross with you?' he asked.

'It's hard to tell. He was actually being rather cagey. If I had to put money on it, I would say that Suz was still there at the flat with him.'

'So, she turned up late last night. I suppose we might have expected it, after what you'd said to her.'

'Okay, don't rub it in. Allan says she showed up on his doorstep at about ten. He was totally gobsmacked, because she's never visited him in London before. He always goes up to see her. Luckily, Penny wasn't there. Although, I get the impression she isn't there very often.'

'I don't like Penny all that much,' Bridie chipped in, as she slurped her Irn Bru noisily through a straw. 'She doesn't take any notice of me. I prefer Aunty Suz.'

'Penny isn't the maternal type,' Hugh explained.

Bridie glanced up indignantly, 'but I'm not a *baby*.'

'No, that's right,' Imogen said diplomatically. 'Penny is one of those people who are only really interested in those who have a similar lifestyle to them. She doesn't have a great deal of time for me, either. Because I've been a housewife and a stay at home mum.'

'She doesn't sound very nice,' Bridie added, as the barman set three plates of toasted sandwiches down on their table.

'Penny just has different priorities from us, that's all,' Hugh said in her defence, not sounding entirely convinced by his own argument. 'Not everyone wants the same things out of life.'

'Anyway, Suz arrived at Allan's flat last night and told him she'd ended her relationship with Owen.

Apparently, it had been on the cards for the past few months. He has been pushing for marriage, but Suz knew that wasn't what she wanted. She told Allan that something I said during my visit had compelled her to come and talk to him - in a way they hadn't really done since she moved back to Scotland. Suz said that after all the years they'd spent together, it justified a proper discussion.'

'And was anything resolved?' Hugh enquired.

'Allan didn't say. He'd only called to admonish me. The rest of it trickled out in the course of the conversation. But like I said, I think Suz was still in the flat with him and I didn't get the sense he was particularly unhappy about it.'

'We'll just have to leave them to it now. There's nothing more you can do.'

'Let's be honest, Mum,' Bridie added between mouthfuls, with her eyebrows slightly raised, 'I suspect you've done more than enough already.'

Chapter Forty Three

Imogen knocked on the door of Michael's study. She carried him in a cup of coffee and brought along the notebook where she had recorded the information she gathered about Stewart McLeod. Michael skimmed swiftly through it.

'So his memoirs are out of print?'

'Officially, yes they are. But I called up the headquarters of the Church of Scotland in Edinburgh. The woman there did a check for me. The books are in their library, you can look at them for reference. They're the only copies in existence. The volumes are considered an important record of the Church during the inter-war years.'

'Would it be worth reading them?' Michael appeared sceptical.

'I would only want to look at the section that covers his visit to New York. There might be something in there about Rev. Mackenzie Cowan and Sandy Thomson.'

'Well, I'm not quite sure how we'd manage it, unless we asked Sarah to do the research for us.'

Michael's daughter, Sarah, was a lawyer who lived with her husband in Edinburgh.

'I wouldn't want to bother her if she's busy, but it's certainly an option worth bearing in mind.'

'I'll mention it to her if you want me to. Just say the word.' Michael glanced at the clock. 'It's nearly time to fetch the lads, they should have returned to the Cove by now. Shall I go with Hugh to get them?'

'Yes please, and could you ask Murray if he wants to come back to Lower Kilduggan and have dinner with us? Tell him he doesn't need to bring his motorbike. Hugh will give him a lift back later.'

*

Dani Bevan had managed to tidy herself up before entering the headquarters of the Virginia State Police Department in Richmond. She grabbed a couple of hours sleep after getting off the plane and then took a quick shower. The local detectives sent a car to pick her up from the hotel at nine a.m., by which time she had pulled on a cream coloured linen trouser suit and applied a dash of eyeliner and lipstick.

The office building was modern and spacious. Once she received her security badge, she was led on a short journey by elevator to the serious crime division. Dani was introduced to her opposite number on the case, Detective Sam Sharpe. He appeared to be in his mid-forties, with a craggy but friendly face and a bulky physique which she sensed that at one phase in his early career was pure muscle. He held out a large, callused hand which Dani clasped in a vigorous shake.

'Great to have you back in Virginia again,' he said in a pleasant drawl, leading her towards his workstation. 'I've been assigned to the Gordon Parker investigation. I was sorry to hear there'd been another homicide on your patch.'

'We genuinely thought that Mackie Shaw held the key to solving Gordon Parker's murder. His death has really set us back.' Dani took a seat opposite her new colleague.

'Don't be put off, he may still provide the answer,' the detective responded cryptically.

'Where are you at with your inquiries into Gordon Parker?'

Sharpe hauled across a paper file, sliding out the contents and handing it to her. 'I've been keeping Phil pretty much up-to-date. We've got his bank statements going back five years, all his phone logs and his internet activity. My team are currently going through his wife's mobile phone records too. We only just received the court order to take a look at those. Gabriella Parker was being resistant to releasing them.'

Dani wondered if this was significant.

'I interviewed her again yesterday,' Sharpe continued, as if he could tell what she was thinking, 'after Phil drew our attention to the fact Gordon Parker was using a private investigator.'

'Did she seem surprised to learn what her husband was up to?' Dani watched his expression closely, considering just how good the man was at reading people's emotions.

He leant back leisurely in his seat, folding his thick arms across his chest. 'I'd say it was the first she'd heard about it, but at the same time, she wasn't overly surprised.'

Dani creased her face in puzzlement.

'Parker definitely hadn't told his wife he'd employed a P.I, but she said he'd been acting so weird in the months leading up to his death that it didn't come as a shock. Mrs. Parker thinks it might have had something to do with his mother. Apparently, she died in a car crash when he was very young. Recently, he'd become obsessed with discovering more about the woman's early life.'

'Why didn't she tell us all this when we first spoke to her?' Dani tried to keep the frustration out of her voice.

Sharpe shrugged his shoulders, 'she probably didn't think it had anything to do with his death. Hell, it may very well not have done.'

'And Gabriella Parker might be throwing up a smoke-screen now. It could be *her* that has a boyfriend tucked away somewhere. Maybe Gordon somehow got wind of it, employed a private investigator to uncover the truth, and meanwhile, Gabriella arranged for him to have an 'accident' whilst he was on holiday. That would explain why she's being coy about the mobile phone records.'

'That too is possible. So, what do you wanna start with first, Detective Chief Inspector?' He shifted his weight forward once again and flashed Dani a surprisingly winning smile.

Chapter Forty Four

The lasagne that Imogen had prepared only just managed to provide a decent portion for each of their guests. She placed a loaf of crusty bread and a ramekin filled with butter alongside the bowl of salad on the kitchen table, so that no one felt they had gone without.

'This is lovely, Mrs. Croft,' Murray commented courteously.

'It's nothing special,' she responded with a smile, 'and please call me Imogen.'

'So, what was your time?' Bridie asked eagerly, her cheeks flushed pink by the warmth radiating from the large range cooker.

'9 hours and 48 minutes,' Ian pronounced with some pride. 'Murray says it's the best he's ever achieved.'

Imogen glanced at her two sons, noting how exhausted they both looked. 'I hope you won't need to have too many more practice runs,' she said with concern in her voice.

'That's the last one for me, Mum,' Ewan replied. 'I might go back to Manchester next week. Chloe wants us to go flat hunting.'

'Will you stay with Liz and Howard?' Hugh asked, tearing off a piece of bread and dunking it into the rich tomato sauce.

'Yep, they've got plenty of room in their new place. It's huge.'

'I'll just give Liz a call about it tomorrow, I should really check with her first,' Imogen stated.

'Sure, she'd like to hear from you anyway. Liz is always asking about you all. I get the impression that the holiday we spent with them in Dubai was a really big thing for her,' Ewan said.

'I shouldn't need to take Ian out again,' Murray quickly added, 'as long as we both get plenty of practice on the water in the next couple of months. It will largely come down to the weather and the tides on the day of the race.'

'So you're definitely going ahead with the regatta?' Michael asked, sounding serious.

'If you and Colin would rather I didn't, then I'd be happy to call the whole thing off. The main sponsor is still keen and I would like to have a project to keep me busy. I still believe it will be good for the island.'

Michael sighed in resignation. 'You're probably right. But you'll definitely need another assistant at Cove Lodge, especially now that trade is picking up again. I'll mention it to Colin, so that he can put an advert into the Garansay Recorder next week.'

Murray visibly flinched at the mention of a replacement for Mackie. 'Sure, Michael. I could certainly do with another pair of hands on the boat.' He said this with a valiant attempt at cheeriness, although his face told a different story. As soon as the conversation switched onto a new topic, the young man's expression became blank, and his mind appeared to have removed itself politely from the company present, disappearing off to some other place entirely - one that only Murray White really understood.

*

The internal flight from Richmond to Pittsburgh, Pennsylvania took a couple of hours. Detective Sharpe was squashed up in the seat next to Bevan. She readily agreed to accept his offer of the window position. Her American colleague spent the entire journey reading through the information that Phil

Boag e-mailed them this morning. Dani found herself gazing out of the tiny glass aperture at the tops of the wispy clouds, thinking about what their course of action should be when they arrived.

Sam had drunk a cup of coffee and eaten a Danish pastry in the time it had taken Dani to sip at her weak green tea. 'Do you have a family back in England – kids, I mean?' He asked in an easy-going manner.

'It's Scotland, and no, I don't. I'm not married yet.' She cursed herself for the 'yet', which made it sound as if she was actively on the look-out for a husband.

Her companion, however, didn't appear to have picked up on the implication. 'I've got two boys, they're teenagers now. They both live up in Canada with their Mom. She and I divorced a couple of years ago.'

'Oh, I'm sorry to hear that.'

'I don't think families really fit with a job like ours. My ex and I get on better now than we ever did.' He cracked another of his disarming smiles, and Dani felt suddenly compelled to shift around and face the chair in front, returning swiftly to her plastic cup of hot tea.

When they arrived at the airport, Sharpe hailed them a taxi cab and directed the driver to the first of the addresses listed on the print-outs from Phil. After about thirty minutes, they arrived at a detached house on a long, suburban block. Although the property was large, with pretty dormer windows in the roof, it looked completely run-down, as if no one had lived there in decades. The paintwork was chipped and peeling. Streaks of rusty red damp were cascading from strategic points in the pipework lining the outside walls.

'This was the earliest address that Gordon Parker could find for his mother,' Sharpe explained. 'It came from her school records. Rosemary Taylor attended an elementary school around the block from here. She definitely lived in this house for a while when she was eight years old. Maybe the neighbourhood's gone downhill since then.'

Dani performed some calculations in her head. 'So Rosemary and her parents were living at this place in the mid-1950s. Did Phil find evidence of any brothers or sisters?'

They took a short stroll around the plot.

'No, it seems she was an only child. But Phil has reached a dead-end as far as the parents go. He suggests in the e-mail that Gordon Parker must have done too, and that was why he employed a private investigator.'

A child's bicycle, battered and bent, lay abandoned in a back garden now overgrown with weeds and spiky brambles. Dani shivered in her thin linen jacket. 'Let's go to the next address. There's nothing to see here.'

The taxi driver patiently delivered them to an apartment block closer to the bustling centre of Pittsburgh. Sam handed the man a fistful of notes through the open front window. He informed Dani they should be able to walk to their next destination from here. Sam led the way up a central communal staircase, which was not sealed off from the street by an external door of any kind. They climbed to the third floor, where they stopped at the door of apartment 12a. Sam gave it a brusque knock.

An Afro-Caribbean woman opened the door, with a young child sitting comfortably on her hip.

Sam swiftly produced his police badge. 'Sorry to bother you Ma'am. It's nothing to concern yourself about. We just want to ask a couple of questions about some of the people who used to live here.'

The woman begrudgingly stepped aside and Dani

followed Sam into the large and airy flat. In addition to the little boy being hauled about by his mum, a young girl, who looked to be about 8 or 9, was sitting at a dining table in the living area. She was drawing on a pad of paper, her coloured pencils splayed out all around her.

'Sit down,' the woman said, although she herself remained standing, which Dani felt placed them at a distinct psychological disadvantage.

'What's the little fella called?' Sam asked, treating the lady to that disconcerting smile.

'Aiden,' she replied, 'and this is Alicia. My name is Rhona.'

'Hi there,' he addressed the two children cheerfully, eliciting a big grin from the boy.

'How long have you lived here, Rhona?'

'Since Alicia was born. Nearly ten years.'

'Do you know who lived here before you?'

'They were an older couple. I think they'd come over from Ireland originally. We passed on their mail to them for years. I can't remember the name off the top of my head, but I've got the address somewhere. If you watch Aiden for a minute, I'll go and find it.'

Chapter Forty Five

Sharpe and Bevan were seated in a burger restaurant in downtown Pittsburgh eating their lunch. The American detective made it clear when they were back in Richmond that his department would be picking up the tab for this little excursion. Sam carefully folded up his receipt for the two sets of burgers, fries and cola and tucked it into the top pocket of his checked shirt.

'This is the most my boss would ever allow me to get away with,' he explained apologetically, gesturing towards the cartons of food laid out in front of them.

'What do you mean? This is a veritable feast,' Dani replied in her most broad Glaswegian accent, giving him a wide grin.

'I've got no idea what you just said, but you're smiling, so it must be all good.'

Bevan looked thoughtful again, as she bit into her heavily laden bun. 'So, Rosemary was living in that flat when she met Franklin Parker in the late sixties.'

'Phil says she was working in Pittsburgh Library. Franklin's family lived on the outskirts of town somewhere and whilst Franklin was using the public library to study for his banking exams, he met Rosemary. They must have dated for a year or so because they then got married in 1970.'

'And Gordon would have been aware of what happened to his mother after that time.'

'Yes. He had written it all down in the documents on his computer. When he passed his exams, Franklin went to work for a bank in New York City. The couple lived in an apartment in Queens until they'd saved enough cash to pay the deposit on a house out in Connecticut. Gordon was born towards the end of '72, not long after they'd moved into their new place.'

'Did you read the newspaper accounts of Rosemary's car accident?' Dani took a sip of her diet coke.

'Yeah, I did, and the police reports. It was tragic, but the cops treated it as a fairly clear cut case back when it happened in '79. Gordon was at home with his father when Rosemary went out in the family car to an evening class at the local school hall. On the way home she met a drunk driver approaching from the opposite direction, down the country lane that separated their place from the town. The kid who was driving lost control on a bend and he hit Rosemary head on. She died instantly. The kid was pretty badly injured too but he survived. He went on to serve five years for driving under the influence.'

'It doesn't seem like much of a sentence for ending the life of a young mum.' Bevan shook her head, thinking how Gordon was even younger than she had been when she'd lost her own mother.

Sam squinted his eyes, looking at her quizzically. 'It wasn't bad for those days. But I take your point.' The detective's phone started buzzing insistently in his trouser pocket. 'Excuse me a minute.'

He stepped outside onto the pavement to take the call. Bevan observed him through the glass frontage of the restaurant. He leant against the window pane and wrote something down on a card before pushing open the door and returning to his seat.

'That was someone from headquarters,' he explained, 'I've got a telephone and cell number for the Byrnes, from the address that Rhona Ward gave us.'

'Shall we ring them now?' Bevan scraped back her stool and made to stand up.

'Relax, Chief Inspector, we've still got hours 'till our

flight back to Richmond. Sit down and eat the rest of your burger first.'

Whilst they were finishing their lunch, Bevan received a phone call update from Andy. She listened patiently to his account, whilst polishing off her fries. It seemed that a guesthouse owner in Port na Mara Bay called the Kilross Station yesterday to report the suspicious behaviour of one of her guests. She said he was staying with her during the week of Gordon Parker's murder.

The man was aged between fifty and sixty with thinning grey hair. He had a Scottish accent, was stockily built and generally wore hiking gear to go out. The lady said he had booked in under the name of Tom McLean and took a room for four nights. She recalled the man, because one morning in the middle of his stay, he didn't come down for breakfast as he usually did. She saw him only that lunchtime, as he was coming in through the front door. At the time, she wasn't completely sure whether or not he had actually slept there the previous night. When she read the details of Parker's death in the Recorder, the woman realised that this incident occurred on the day after the tourist's murder took place, a few miles down the road from her at Cove Lodge, and thought she'd better call the police.

'She's a bit late coming forward with this information, don't you think?' Sam said sceptically, after Dani had filled him in.

'Apparently, it was only after the death of Mackie Shaw that the lady really took proper notice of the case. She was shocked by the violent murder of a local lad. I'm afraid she hadn't given much thought to the death of Gordon Parker, she only glanced at the accounts in the paper.'

'It's human nature I suppose,' Sam added, with a

thoughtfulness that Dani found surprising. 'Did this Tom McLean provide an address, or any clue as to where he was headed next?'

'The name and address he gave were false, but Andy is going to check them against the ferry manifests, as he might just have been using the same alias for that purpose too, which will at least give us an idea of when he arrived on the island. He told the guesthouse owner he was visiting Garansay as part of a tour of the Highlands.'

'Just like Gordon Parker,' Sam said quietly.

'The woman is helping to put together an e-fit. Andy is going to get the team to circulate it around all the hotels and guesthouses. To see if this chap stayed anywhere else.'

'He might even still be on the island.'

Dani nodded, feeling a surge of guilt and concern at the thought of her colleagues back in Scotland. 'Right,' she said firmly, gathering up the detritus of their lunch and stuffing it into a litter bin, 'time we got back to work.'

Detective Sharpe used the privacy of a phone box to call the Byrnes. He jotted down their answers to his questions on a pad of paper which he had placed on the tiny metal shelf inside the booth. Dani hovered at his elbow, listening in to as much as she could.

Sam replaced the receiver and looked at what he had written down. 'Nice couple,' he muttered absent-mindedly.

'What did they have to say?'

'The Byrnes moved out of the flat in 2005, when they sold it to Rhona and her husband. They relocated to a residential home in Baltimore, to be nearer to their son. Mr Byrne had been an administrator for one of the big steel companies before he retired. They'd lived in the Pittsburgh flat for 35 years, had their child there. They bought the place in late 1970.'

'Did they buy it from Rosemary?' Dani sounded excited.

'Better than that, they bought it from her *parents*. Apparently, they didn't see very much of Rosemary at all, most of their dealings were with her mum and dad. All they recalled of the young woman was that she was blond, pretty, very quiet, and about to get married.'

'Did they remember the name of Rosemary's parents?'

'Not the surname I'm afraid, but they thought their given names were Mack and Elizabeth, or something similar to that. The main impression they got of the couple was that the husband was older than the wife. They couldn't give me any more.'

Dani thought it was a shame the Byrnes didn't manage to provide them with a surname for Gordon Parker's maternal grandparents, but somehow, she sensed they were very lucky to have received any information about this couple at all.

Chapter Forty Six

Jeanette and Donald Gibb lived in a substantial sandstone house in the heart of Caol, an attractive town which lay at the western mouth of the Caledonian Canal in Lochaber.

Julia was staying in their well-appointed guest bedroom, which had its own en-suite bathroom and a large window with views over 'the narrows', where Loch Linnhe met Loch Eil. She arrived yesterday afternoon and after settling in, spent a very pleasant evening chatting with her aunt and uncle in front of an open fire in their grand sitting room.

'So, you enjoyed your honeymoon in the States, Julia?' Jeanette commenced their conversation, as she prepared the kitchen table for breakfast that morning.

'Oh yes, what a wonderful place. New York is exactly as you would expect from all the movies and television shows.' Julia helped her aunt to set the table by laying out the tea cups carefully in their saucers.

'And married life is treating you well?' Jeanette glanced across at her niece, deliberately catching her eye.

'Yes, Aunty Jean, it is. Michael is lovely. We just thought it would be a good opportunity for me to come and see you and Gran - whilst Michael has his family on Garansay with him. We'll only be apart for a couple of days.'

'What about your dad? Will you be seeing him too whilst you're on the mainland?' Jeanette reached for a packet of Scottish rolled oats from a cupboard. Julia knew she was about to start the elaborate process of preparing the porridge.

‘Of course, I’ll drop in on Mum and Dad on the way home.’

‘Good, because Rob was actually quite put-out when you and Michael went to Canada whilst you were on holiday.’

‘Really? He didn’t sound as if he minded at all.’ Julia was surprised by this news.

‘Well, you and Michael haven’t been to stay with Rob and Jacquie yet have you? But then you spend a week with Harry and Connie. I think they both felt as if the Kings were going to get to know Michael better than they were.’ Jeanette stirred the creamy mixture slowly and rhythmically on the hob.

Julia filled the teapot. She sensed her cheeks beginning to redden. ‘I didn’t even think about it that way.’

‘I know how you feel about your Canadian relatives,’ Jeanette added more cheerfully, ‘they’re very important to you. I find Harry an extremely likeable person too, he’s terribly charismatic. But I’m always aware that Rob’s feelings are very sensitive on this subject. It’s your father’s Achilles heel.’

‘Of course. I of all people know that. When I go to visit them, I’ll do my best to reassure Dad that he and Mum are the most important people in the world to me.’ Julia set down the teapot in the centre of the table and went out into the hallway to call her uncle in to breakfast, quite aware that she’d just been subtly, but very definitely, told off.

Julia carried a tray of tea and cakes through the utility room and along a flagstone corridor that led to her grandmother’s annex. She paused and knocked gently at the door before putting her hand back on the tray, lowering the handle with her hip and pushing her way into the flat. The annexe was in a modern extension which was added to the house about fifteen years ago. It had two rooms and a large, airy kitchen. Julia's grandmother used to live quite independently there. She shopped for herself in the town and prepared her own meals. In the last five years, however, Jeanette had been doing an increasing amount of the chores. She now did all the cooking for her mother and tried to encourage her to come into the main house for her evening meal. The old lady tended to be restricted mainly to the living room during the day, relying on Donald to take her out on excursions or to meet her friends at the community centre.

As usual, Margie McClelland was seated in an armchair next to an electric bar fire. As her granddaughter entered, she took off her reading glasses and placed them on top of a paperback book which was lying face down on the coffee table. Julia deposited the tray next to them.

'How lovely to see you, my dear!' Margie declared, putting out her hands for Julia to hold. 'How was the wedding? Tell me everything!'

The younger woman poured the teas, made herself comfortable in the seat opposite, and then described her wedding day, in as much detail as she could recall.

Margie's face lit up as Julia talked. She was obviously trying to picture the event in her mind.

'Jeanie told me all about it, of course. But I knew you would paint the scene so much more clearly. It was *your* special day after all.'

'Did Aunty Jean tell you we went to New York for our honeymoon?' Julia offered her grandmother a buttered fruit scone.

'Thank you, dear. Oh yes, Jeanie did mention it. That must have been very exciting.'

'Our hotel was right in the centre of the city,' Julia paused to sip her tea. 'And we met up with Harry and Connie King whilst we were there.'

Julia watched her Granny's face closely, as the inevitable dark shadow passed fleetingly across it.

'Oh yes, and how are they both keeping?' She enquired brightly, regaining her composure with a well-practised ease.

'Sally is having another baby at Christmas, so the talk was all about that.'

Margie gave a thin smile.

'Michael and I travelled to New Brunswick actually, to stay with them for a few days. I'd not been to Canada for nearly ten years.'

It pained Julia to see how hard her grandmother was struggling to appear happy about this.

'I hear it's a very beautiful place - much like the Highlands of Scotland.'

Julia was horrified to see that tears were welling up in Margie's clear blue eyes. She clasped at her grandmother's hands. 'Oh, I didn't mean to upset you!'

The old lady shook her head. 'It doesn't take much to set me off these days. I was just thinking about all those poor families who were cleared away from the hills and glens of Scotland and sent to Canada all those years ago. It must have been a terrifying experience for them.'

'But they built decent lives for themselves over there. Many prospered in their new land.'

'It's never the same as the place of your birth, my dear, especially if the decision to go has been taken out of your hands. To be wrenched from your homeland is a wicked thing. You lose that sense of what anchors you in the world. You suddenly become lost and adrift.'

Julia decided to grasp her opportunity. 'Granny, could you tell me about my Grandad? What was Sandy like when he was still living in Dallanaich?'

A silence filled the small, stuffy room, as if Julia had dared to utter the unmentionable. Margie shifted about in the chair, seemingly unable to find a comfortable position. She grimaced, almost like she'd been forced to sit on a set of nails. Finally, the old lady appeared to discover a spot she found bearable and became unnervingly still.

'He was a good man. In looks, Sandy was much like your father, tall and light-haired. I had always known of him when growing up, although he was a few years older than me. We started courting when Sandy was studying for his teaching exams. Then the old schoolmaster retired and Sandy was taken on at the primary school. It was only a small place, with just two or three classes, so he progressed very quickly there.'

'Was Sandy a good teacher?'

'Oh, yes.' Margie's eyes lit up again. 'He was one of those people who have a real gift for it. You'd never have known to speak to him in everyday life, but whenever I saw Sandy stand in front of a class, something very special occurred. All those little faces suddenly turned upwards in rapt interest. He could hold their attention for hours. It's the moment when you realise that person was born to it - it's their calling.'

'What about the Church?' Julia leant forwards.

'I was never quite so sure about Sandy being ordained. We argued about it sometimes. I felt that his place was in the classroom, teaching the kiddies, but Sandy felt a powerful pull towards the ministry. I couldn't have stopped him pursuing it. He had very strong ideas about how things should be changed and made better within the Church.'

Julia took a deep breath. 'What about his trip to New York, how did you feel about that?'

Margie's face hardened. 'He went very much

against my wishes. I didn't like Reverend Cowan much. I'd grown up with that man's interminably downbeat and miserable sermons about *his* God's version of sin and redemption. I was young and it felt as if Sandy was choosing the Church over me and my baby.' Margie unconsciously placed her hand on her stomach, as if she were back there right now, with her husband about to leave on that perilous journey to the United States.

'Did you know a person called Duncan Lambie, when you were growing up in Dallanaich?' Julia asked.

Margie looked utterly taken aback. 'I haven't heard that name mentioned in over sixty years.'

'You knew him then?' Julia persisted.

'We were in the same class at school. Duncan had to walk with a stick, he was lame, you see. He'd been that way since birth. Duncan still played with us just the same, tearing around the playground, almost dragging that useless leg behind him. It never held the boy back.'

'Did Grandad know Duncan?'

'They became friends after the war broke out, what with them both staying on in the village and not going off to fight. They drank together in the pub occasionally. They were a mismatched pair, but pals nonetheless.'

'What happened to Duncan, Gran?' Julia asked innocently.

Margie's features became taut. 'He died, early on in the war. There was a terrible storm and the waves washed him off the rocks into the Loch. It was a tragedy. We all loved him.'

Julia peered closely at her grandmother. She could tell by her plaintive expression and the tears which had escaped onto her cheeks, that the final sentence she had spoken at least, had been totally and completely true.

Chapter Forty Seven

There was one more address to check out before Bevan and Sharpe caught their flight back to Richmond. The police reports indicated that the woman who Gordon Parker was paying on a regular basis in the months leading up to his death lived in an apartment in central Pittsburgh. It was close enough for the detectives to reach on foot. Although, as the streets they walked through became increasingly run down and deserted, Bevan began to consider if maybe they should have called another cab.

'I'm taking it that Lorna Davidson doesn't live in the most upmarket part of town,' Bevan said lightly.

Sam Sharpe chuckled. 'I wonder if this woman is an ex-cop. Plenty of folk who leave the force or retire, go on to become P.Is.'

'It can't be paying that well,' Bevan muttered, as she glanced from left to right at the boarded up shops and graffitied buildings that lined both sides of the block. Dani jumped, as they passed a dark alleyway between two of the tall buildings and heard a shuffling movement within its shadows. Sharpe instinctively rested his right hand on the belt of his trousers. Looking around him, he decided to keep it there.

'Are you carrying a gun?' Bevan said in surprise, as if the thought had never previously occurred to her.

'Of course.'

'Right, yes. I suppose you would be.' Bevan felt immediately foolish.

'It's not my choice. We're required to.'

'Oh, I know. It's just that firearms don't play a major part in my job. I haven't held one since my training days and I only see them when they've been seized from the houses of criminals.'

'Well, count yourself lucky,' Sharpe commented, as they stopped outside the filthy doorway which matched the address they had.

Bevan pressed on a buzzer, but it made no sound. Sam hammered on the door for a few minutes, just for good measure. They stood and waited. Finally, a crackly voice came over an intercom system. 'Who is it?'

'The police. Virginia P.D.' Sam replied.

'Okay.'

Seconds later, a green light flicked on, followed by the noise of a lock releasing. Sharpe swiftly pushed the door inwards. The stairwell was dark and there seemed to be no light switch. Sharpe reached for his holster once again, but this time he took out the gun, holding it steadily in front of him as they climbed the steps. When they reached the first landing, they saw that a large, heavy door was being held open. A woman, who looked to be in her mid-forties, was leaning against it, her arms folded. She watched impassively as they approached.

'Come on, there's no need for that,' she commented evenly, nodding towards Sharpe's weapon.

The detective slowly placed it back into his belt. 'You can't be too careful, Ma'am.'

The woman smiled. 'I'm the only one who lives in this building and I'm harmless enough.' After peering at Sam's badge, she led them inside.

Bevan immediately noted how outward appearances could be deceptive. Lorna Davidson lived in a large converted warehouse with a huge open-plan kitchen area. A bespoke-looking sofa successfully created a separate living space which focussed on a huge wood burning stove. The flue for which disappeared up into the towering roof above their heads.

Lorna herself was dressed in jeans and a sweatshirt bearing the motif for a local football team. She was slim and muscular, but her blondish hair was feathered into a feminine style. Her thin lips were painted a deep red.

'Coffee?' she offered, in a sing-song drawl that made Bevan wonder if she came originally from somewhere in the South.

'Sure,' Sharpe responded, seemingly for the both of them, and then propped himself up on a stool at the impressive central island, which divided the kitchen from the rest of the flat. Bevan joined him.

'Is this about Gordon?' The woman asked, as she filled an industrially sized coffee-maker.

'What makes you say that?' Bevan quickly responded.

'Well, you claim to be from the Virginia Police Department, which is the state where Gordon lives. I happen not to have heard from or been paid by the guy in weeks. The last he told me was that he was off on a trip to the Scottish Highlands. So I'm basing my hunch on that.' She gave a half smile. 'You guys aren't the only detectives around here.'

Bevan nodded. 'What was Gordon Parker employing you to do for him, Ms Davidson?'

'Maybe you could tell me what's happened to him first, before I answer that question.'

'He's dead,' Sharpe snapped back at her, losing his patience. 'Someone killed him while he was on holiday.'

Lorna stopped what she was doing for a moment and looked straight at Bevan. 'Hence the Scottish accent. I should have worked that one out for myself, too.' The woman appeared genuinely saddened by the news. The detectives allowed her to shuffle around the kitchenette, preparing their drinks and taking some time to compose herself. Finally, Lorna was ready to speak. 'He was trying to learn more about his mother. She was called Rosemary Anne Taylor and had died in a motor accident in 1979. Gordon had made pretty good progress with getting information about his mom's childhood and schooling from the age of 8, but anything before that time drew a total blank. He employed me to find out why.'

Bevan sipped the coffee and discovered it was absolutely delicious. 'What did you uncover for him?'

'After I did some digging, it became fairly clear why Gordon had struggled to find out anything about his mother's early life.'

Sam raised his eyebrows quizzically.

Lorna went across to a filing cabinet which sat, unapologetically, in a corner of the vast room. She pulled out a file and brought it back to the island, where she started to flick through the pages.

'Because Taylor wasn't their real surname,' Lorna explained. 'It was changed by court order when Rosemary was eight years old. In some parts of the States and Canada, you don't need to do anything at all in order to change your name. Someone can adopt as many identities as they like. It certainly makes my job a whole lot harder - especially as much of my work involves chasing absentee fathers for child support. Those SOBs just disappear off the face of the earth.'

'Did you manage to find out what their previous surname was?' Bevan placed down her cup and reached for a notebook.

'Because the father actually went to court, there was a record of it. This time I was lucky. Their family name was Cowan. The father was called Mackenzie and the mother was Elizabeth Amelia Cowan, née Parnell. So Gordon's mother had been born

Rosemary Anne Cowan.'

Chapter Forty Eight

Once the plane had taken off, Bevan unclipped her seatbelt and stretched out her legs. She placed her notebook on the pull down table and scanned through the text, barely looking up as Sam rested her cup of green tea in its designated circular recess.

'So Lorna Davidson told Gordon Parker what his mother's real surname had been,' he said, almost to himself.

'It was the last proper communication she had with him. I suppose that once Parker knew what their former name was, he could do the rest of the research independently. But if he *did* find out more, he didn't use his own computer to log what he'd discovered.'

Sam shifted around to face her. 'I think that whatever he unearthed next, it took him to Scotland.'

Bevan nodded, 'I agree. That's why Gordon was so keen to go on this sailing holiday. It makes sense that Rosemary's family must have originally been from there. Her father was called Mackenzie Cowan, for heaven's sake. I mean, you can't get more Scottish than that.'

Sam looked thoughtful again. 'I suppose he could have used internet cafés to complete his research. Then there wouldn't have been a history recorded on his hard drive. The guy worked in I.T, so he would have known all the tricks.'

'But he must have written his findings down somewhere - even if it was simply in a notebook or a paper file. We found absolutely nothing on his body or in his luggage. Parker's mobile was gone, but if he was careful not to leave a trace on his home computer, I doubt he would have left anything on his phone either.'

'Could the killer have taken these notes or notebook? Perhaps that's what they were after in the first place.'

Bevan squeezed her eyes shut and rubbed at her brow. 'Yes, it's possible, I suppose.'

'Look, we're tired now. We can revisit this all again in the morning, when our minds are more fresh.'

Dani sighed. 'You're right. We need to reflect on the evidence for a few hours.'

When the plane touched down in Richmond, it was nearly midnight. The American detective had been very quiet since their discussion during the flight. He directed his colleague towards the taxi rank. As they stood and waited in line, Sam took hold of Dani's hand, but he kept his eyes fixed dead ahead.

'Do you want to come back to my place?'

Bevan did her best to mask her surprise. 'Is it closer than my hotel?'

Sam laughed. 'Not necessarily, but I guarantee the coffee's better.'

She kept her hand in his as their taxi cab pulled up and they slid into the backseat. Sam gave the driver his address.

'I don't make a habit of this,' Bevan said quietly.

'Neither do I. This is my first time since the divorce.'

'Seriously?'

'Well, it's not often that a real life English Rose walks into the office.'

'I'm Scottish,' she gently corrected, but there was a smile on her face.

'Whatever,' he responded dismissively, leaning in closer and ending their exchange by placing his lips over hers.

*

Julia helped her mother to clear away the dishes after dinner. She piled the plates up on the counter next to the dishwasher in the modest kitchen of her parents' house in Oban.

'It's lovely to see you, darling,' Jacquie said as she carried the serving bowls in. 'It would be even better to have Michael here too sometime, perhaps for a weekend?'

Julia stopped what she was doing and turned to face her mum. 'Of course, we'd love to. I'm sorry I didn't bring him along on this trip. His sister and her family are still in Garansay and he didn't want to leave them alone.' She stepped forward and took her hand. 'You do know that it was a last minute decision to visit Canada when we were on honeymoon? I hope Dad wasn't upset about it.'

Jacquie sighed and lowered her voice before answering. 'Well, he was a little bit, darling. You know what he's like when it comes to Harry King. He'll barely hear the man's name mentioned in the house. I really wish you'd brought Michael here to stay with us first. But you're a grown woman and we can't tell you what to do.'

'Oh, Mum, I've been completely thoughtless. Let me go and talk to Dad, I'll try and reassure him.'

'He would appreciate that, just don't mention too much about your trip. As he gets older I swear he's becoming increasingly maudlin about the whole episode with his father. Isn't it incredible what damage folk can do to their children? It really does last a lifetime.'

Julia found her father in his study. She was surprised to observe he had picked out one of his old Bibles from the bookshelf. It sat open on the desk at Corinthians. Julia was aghast to see that his eyes were full of tears.

She immediately put her arms around his shoulders. 'Dad, whatever's wrong? I've never seen you cry before.'

'Only the son of God has the power to return from the dead, Julia. Ordinary men have no business in pretending to be like God. It can only bring wickedness down upon the people around them.'

'I agree,' she said, burying her face into his collar. 'But we can't blame the innocent for the sins of others. Surely we must forgive what Sandy did all those years ago, so that there can be no more suffering now.'

Rob gently lifted his daughter's face, so that he could look her in the eye. A smile flickered across his lined features. '*You* mustn't be upset my dearest, because there's been almost no suffering at all. The only one who was ever hurt by Sandy's actions was me, and that was the cross God wanted me to bear.'

Julia shook her head and the tears escaped down her cheeks. 'But you shouldn't have to bear it. What if there was a reason *why* your father had to leave you? Perhaps he didn't want to and it broke his heart, but he had to go in order to *protect* you – not even Margie, really, but *you,* his unborn child.'

Rob smoothed his daughter's hair away from her face. 'It would be nice to be able to believe that Julia, but one finds in life that people's motives are often far less grand and selfless. Just the fact that you have wished this for me is more than enough to make a sentimental old man feel better.'

Chapter Forty Nine

Michael was very happy to go and fetch his wife from the evening ferry. He'd not felt totally comfortable whilst she'd been away, as if it was a mistake for her to have gone alone.

He held her hand tightly as they entered through the kitchen door of the farmhouse. Imogen had been busily preparing a meal for them all and turned to greet her sister-in-law warmly.

'Sit down while I pour you both a drink,' Imogen suggested. 'How was the crossing?'

'Fine, thank you. It was a little choppy, but I've experienced worse.'

'Sometimes it's better to have a full stomach when the sea is rough. It can often make you feel less sick,' Michael pointed out, giving her the benefit of his long years living by the water.

'But if the nausea has gripped you – then there's no getting rid of it until you're back on dry land,' Imogen countered sagely, looking out of the window at the wind and rain.

'I'm just glad to be home,' Julia stated, slipping off her rain jacket and letting it lie over the back of her chair.

'How were your parents?' Michael asked.

'They're in good health, but Dad's been brooding a lot recently about his father. He was quite upset on the evening I was there.'

'Rob doesn't know we've been looking into Sandy's past, does he?' Imogen joined her at the table, looking worried.

'No, I don't think so. It was our trip to New Brunswick that set him off, and seeing Harry at the wedding too, I expect. I've never known him to be so sad.'

'Maybe we should forget all about Sandy Thomson and lay the whole subject to bed. The last thing I want to do is cause your father distress.' Michael nodded in gratitude as Imogen passed him a glass of red wine.

'Absolutely,' his sister agreed.

'Oh no,' Julia said with determination. 'It only makes me keener to find out the truth. If we discover that Sandy was the morally redundant scoundrel that my father believes he was, then so be it. But if I can provide my dad with a better explanation than that, I'd really like to try and do it.'

'What did your grandmother have to say?' Imogen asked, needing no further encouragement to resurrect their investigation.

'Her description of Sandy was much the same as Val Black's - that he was a good man who was dedicated to his job and the Church. But Margie hinted they'd argued about Sandy's decision to be ordained. Gran gave me the impression they weren't totally contented in their marriage. I'll tell you one thing that struck me though.'

'What?' Imogen leaned in closer.

'Gran was really taken by surprise when I mentioned Duncan Lambie. He'd been a friend of hers at school. I got the distinct impression she'd really liked him, cared for him even. When I asked her about what happened to Duncan, she gave the same story as the newspaper had, about him being swept off the rocks in a storm. But there was something about the way she said it. I know my Gran and I think she was lying.'

'Do you suspect she knows what really became of Duncan Lambie?'

'Yes I do, but I don't believe she'll ever tell us.'

'Then we'll just have to find that out for ourselves,'

Imogen replied.

*

Acting D.C.I Bevan had one more day in Virginia before she flew back to Glasgow. She sat at the spare desk opposite Detective Sharpe and went over her notes once more. Andy Calder had rung her first thing that morning to say they'd identified another B&B in Kilross where the man going by the name of Tom McLean had stayed. He checked out on the day of Mackie Shaw's murder. The team were desperately trying to track down where the man had gone next. Dani praised Andy for his excellent work.

'Sam, did you get anything back from the checks on Gabriella Parker's cell phone?'

The man looked up from his computer screen. 'Yeah, they came back yesterday. Seems pretty much in order. There were a couple of calls to a number in Virginia Beach that Mrs. Parker couldn't totally explain, but they were just to a domestic residence and only for a couple of minutes apiece. I don't think it was her arranging to set up a hit job. Her bank account has shown no large sums going either in or out in the last few months. I'm certain the lady's clean.'

'I believe you're right. I don't think Gabby Parker had her husband killed. But I'd like an excuse to go to the house again. I'm wondering if Gordon left some information there.'

'We've searched his study and the bedroom they shared. Nothing significant came up.'

'I'm not criticising your investigation, Sam. I just have a feeling we're looking for something different now.' Bevan gave him a conciliatory smile.

'We could head over and question Mrs. Parker about those phone calls if you like?'

Dani jumped out of her seat, grabbing her handbag

from where it was hanging over the back of the chair. 'Great, let's go.'

Gabriella Parker seemed resigned to their presence in her house. She stood back from the door and allowed them to walk along a wide, cream carpeted hallway into the main lounge. Bevan noted how they weren't being bundled into a tiny side room this time around. The woman automatically walked into the kitchen next door and began preparing some drinks. She strode back to join them after sticking the kettle on.

'What can I do for you now - any new developments in the case?' The woman's tone made it sound as if she had no hope whatsoever that there would be.

'We're working on a couple of fresh leads,' Sam explained. 'But we'd like to ask you a few more questions too.'

'Sure, fire away,' She lifted her arms up in a gesture of defeat.

Despite the impression of long-suffering detachment that Gabby was attempting to give, Dani noticed how much better she appeared. Her hair was worn loose and carefully styled. There was a hint of lipstick and rouge on her face, which she imagined had not been applied for their benefit.

Sam produced the print out of Gabby's cell phone calls. 'There's just two numbers we couldn't match to the list you gave us of your most frequent contacts, Mrs. Parker. Perhaps you could help to identify them?'

The woman took the sheet from him and broke into a thin smile. She didn't even glance at the digits that had been highlighted in yellow pen. 'His name is Mark Jordan. One of those numbers is for his office and the other is for his home in Virginia Beach. He's married with two children. We've been seeing each other for about three months, ever since we met at a trade fair. We usually keep in contact by work e-mail, the phone is too risky. Do you still want a coffee?'

'Yes please,' Dani responded, 'I'll come and give you a hand.' She followed the woman out into the bright, modern kitchen.

'Just because I'd met someone else, doesn't mean I wanted Gordon dead. Mark hasn't told his wife yet and he may never do. Our relationship hasn't progressed to that stage. My boys have lost their father, I never wished for that.'

'I know. We don't think you were involved in your husband's death, Gabby. But we need to investigate everything.'

The woman poured out their drinks. 'Will Mark's wife have to be told?'

'That's up to Detective Sharpe and his team. However, at this point, I can't see it being necessary.'

When they returned to the living room with the tray, they found that Sharpe had slid open the patio door which led out to the garden. As they gazed across the lawn, Dani saw the detective shooting hoops with one of Gabby's sons, in a paved area in front of the double garage.

'He's got two teenagers himself. He doesn't get to see them very often,' Dani said by way of explanation.

'I don't mind. Cody will enjoy it. It isn't as if Gordon ever used to play out there with him. My husband was a bookish type and latterly he was obsessed with this research into his mother. *We* didn't get a look in.'

'It's starting to appear as if it was your husband's investigation into his mother's past that got him killed.'

Gabby tutted loudly. 'I told him to forget about it,

but he just couldn't let it go. I knew he was set on a course towards self-destruction.' She glanced at Dani. 'I could tell it was going to end badly, almost like when someone is about to have a breakdown. There's a horrible inevitability to it, and all you can do is just stand by and watch.'

Sharpe and the boy had stopped their game. Sam was helping the lad to open the garage door. They disappeared inside for a few minutes and then came out again. Dani spotted the detective slip something into his trouser pocket. She stepped forward, leaning out into the warm air of the late afternoon. 'Detective Sharpe, your coffee's getting cold!'

Sharpe gave her the thumbs up, shot one more hoop with Cody and then made his way back towards the house.

Chapter Fifty

Sam Sharpe shifted awkwardly from one foot to the other. Dani's boarding gate was due to open in precisely five minutes.

'You really don't need to stay,' she said coolly.

'I realise that. But I'd actually like to. I thought you Brits were pretty big on good manners.' He appeared genuinely cross.

Dani took his hand. 'You're quite right. I'm just not sure what I'm supposed to be saying to you, that's all.'

They stood next to one another in silence for a minute or so. 'I wish we'd had the time to read through that notebook together before you had to leave,' he finally commented.

'Take a look at your copy when you return to the department. I'll read mine on the plane and then we can e-mail each other with our thoughts.'

'It just suddenly struck me, when we were in the house, that Parker might have entrusted his findings to his son. I knew he'd never have told his wife, not with the state of their marriage, so the kids were probably the only ones left that he trusted.'

'You've got good instincts, Detective Sharpe.'

A voice over the tannoy system announced Dani's flight. She lifted up a small soft bag and leaned her face towards Sam's, placing a light kiss on his cheek.

'Is that all I'm getting?' He managed a half smile.

She squeezed his hand, 'I still need your help to solve this case.'

'Well, you've got my number Detective Chief Inspector.'

'And you've got mine.'

With that, she turned on her heels and was gone.

*

Imogen gave a cursory knock and then entered the downstairs room that her brother used as his study.

'Have you got a minute?' She said tentatively.

Michael turned to face her. 'Of course, what's up?'

Imogen perched on the desk in front of him. 'I wondered if you could ask Sarah to take a look at Reverend McLeod's memoirs for us, just the section that covers his trip to New York in 1943. Now that Julia is so determined to find out why Sandy left Scotland, I think it's time to make sure we've followed up every lead.'

Michael nodded, 'I'll call her tonight. I believe she's just finished a case, so we may be in luck.'

'Good. Thank you - and Mike, let's be certain to tell Julia all about it.'

Imogen passed back across the hallway, and as she did so, the telephone started to ring. Lifting the receiver, she was surprised to hear Penny Mills' voice on the other end of the line.

'Hi Penny, how are you?'

The woman gave a noncommittal grunt. 'Could I possibly borrow your husband for a moment, Imogen? Don't worry. I'll be sure to give him back.'

'I'll just go and call him.' Imogen jogged up the stairs to get Hugh and then she left them to it, diplomatically withdrawing to the kitchen to make a pot of tea.

Her husband came into the room to join her about 20 minutes later. She poured him out a cup. Hugh ran a hand through his thick, silvery hair, his expression one of sadness.

'How is she?' Imogen asked, experiencing a feeling of commiseration followed by a surge of guilt.

'Penny says that Allan and Suz have decided to take a holiday together for a couple of weeks. So they can talk things through on neutral territory and come to some kind of decision about the future. Allan told Penny he's very sorry, but he can't continue to pursue a relationship with her, not when he isn't totally clear about his feelings for Suz.'

'Poor Penny,' Imogen said quietly. 'Is she very upset?'

'Her pride has taken a knock, but I think she'll be okay. Penny admits that their relationship hadn't really progressed very far. She knew Allan had a complicated history.'

'It doesn't make it hurt any less though, does it?'

'No,' Hugh replied. 'But this is what you wanted, Imogen.'

She stepped forward and placed her arms around her husband. 'Yes it was, although it doesn't feel quite so good in reality. I'd not properly realised that people were going to have to suffer in order to achieve it.'

Hugh held her tight. 'Penny will be alright. She wasn't that serious about Allan anyway.'

'Is that what she said?'

Hugh nodded.

'Oh, poor Penny,' Imogen lamented once again.

Chapter Fifty One

The incident room at Kilross Police Station was bustling with activity. Dani Bevan pushed through the doors and was immediately heartened to observe that as she entered, the officers present began to gather themselves respectfully around the flip-chart at the front of the room. Andy Calder stepped forward to greet her.

'Ma'am, how was the trip?'

'Good, Andy, thank you. I'll give you all a précis in a moment, but first, I'd like to hear how the investigation's going from this end.' Dani stood back and allowed the D.C to take the floor.

'Okay. Our main lead continues to be the man who is referring to himself as Tom McLean. He travelled to Garansay under that name four weeks ago. McLean stayed at Mrs. Gilmore's guesthouse in Port-na-Mara Bay for the four days covering the murder of Gordon Parker. He then stayed at a B&B in Kilross in the week before Mackie Shaw was killed, checking out on the day of the murder. We are working on the assumption that the suspect is staying in places for a few days at a time and possibly using a different alias at each one.'

'So now we've circulated his particulars, he'll be lying low. Do we think he might have left the island?' Dani asked.

Andy turned to address his superior. 'He's definitely not left by either of the two ferries. We've had uniforms checking everyone leaving Garansay since Shaw's death. However, we cannot guarantee that someone hasn't taken him off the island by boat. He may have an accomplice, or he could have paid somebody.'

Dani nodded. 'Right. Carry on.'

'Forensics says that all the blood in Mackie's shed was his, which we were expecting. There were no other prints on the door or the articles on the workbench. Disappointingly, we got nothing from the Stanley knife either. So we assume that McLean wore gloves, which again, is not a surprise, as we know the murder was planned. We have a group of fell walkers who saw a man hiking alone on the hillside behind the row of cottages on the day of Shaw's death. They give a similar description to the one we have from Mrs. Gilmore, but all they could tell us was that this man was striding off into the hills above Kilross. They assumed he was about to climb Benn Ardroch, as the path in front of Shaw's cottage leads up there. They say the mountain path was very busy that day.'

D.C Robertson chipped in. 'It appears as if Mackie Shaw had a string of brief relationships over the past year. They were all conducted with young women living in Kilross or thereabouts. None of the girls were married or had serious boyfriends. He met them in the local pubs and hotels, where he was known as a bit of a womaniser. The ex-girlfriend, Kirstie Bell, is in a new relationship and expecting a bairn. His cousin, Craig Shaw, seems pretty devastated by Mackie's murder. He showed real remorse for stealing his fiancé. For what it's worth, I believed him Ma'am.'

'I think you're probably right,' Dani responded. 'So what are your current lines of enquiry?'

'Neil and Chris are checking out all the retailers in Scotland that supply the Stanley knife. We're working on the assumption the killer brought it with him. The attack happened so quickly that there wasn't really a chance for the assailant to risk looking around for something suitable.'

‘Good. It may have been a mistake for him to drop it.’

‘We’ve got this Tom McLean’s e-fit plastered all over the west of Scotland. It’s just a matter of time before we flush him out, Ma’am.’ Andy hauled his bulky form up straight and looked determined.

‘Well done, all of you,’ Dani said to the team, moving forward so that she was level with the flip chart. Bevan turned it over so there was a clean sheet and then outlined the information she and Sharpe had discovered about Gordon Parker’s mother.

Dani produced a small battered A5 pad from the pocket of her suit jacket. ‘Inside this notebook, is the reason why Gordon Parker was in Scotland in the first place. I believe it will also lead us to his killer, and the killer of Mackie Shaw. Gordon Parker’s research into his mother’s family disturbed a secret that somebody out there is desperate to protect. I think he stumbled into this unwittingly, but, as a result of Gordon’s obsessive need to find out about his mother, two innocent men have wound up dead.’

Chapter Fifty Two

Imogen decided to print out the e-mail she received this morning from her niece in Edinburgh. Sarah spent an afternoon in the Church of Scotland library, reading and taking notes from the Reverend Stewart McLeod's memoirs.

When Michael's old machine had churned out the papers, she took them into the sitting room, settling in one of the battered armchairs beneath the window to examine Sarah's findings.

Reverend McLeod spent his long career as a minister in the town of Ganavan, on the western coast of Scotland. Imogen knew there was a lovely sandy beach there. Friends of theirs had visited the holiday park that was situated in the bay several times. McLeod chronicled the many trials and tribulations of his congregation in this two volume tome and those of the nearby town of Oban. The section which referred to McLeod's trip to the Convention of Presbyterian Churches in New York City, Sarah had transcribed word-for-word into the e-mail for her:

I received a phone call late on a Sunday night. Tired after a long day in which I was called upon to counsel a local woman who had recently lost her son in action, the call took me somewhat by surprise. It was from the Moderator himself, a man whom I greatly respected and had had the good fortune of many positive encounters with.

His first purpose was to inform me of the death of the Reverend Mackenzie Cowan of Dallanaich in Appin. I knew Mackenzie a little, having met him on a handful of occasions and although I respected his many years of service to the Church, I had never fully taken to the man. I acknowledged the tragedy of the news, particularly as a young school teacher who had been accompanying him on the journey was also presumed drowned.

I had an inkling of what the Moderator was going to say next, although it still came as something of a shock to hear the words. He wanted me to take Cowan's place in New York, representing the Church of Scotland on his behalf. Of course I was flattered. But I also knew the dangers of the task being asked of me. I was immediately aware that my wife and children would be greatly distressed by the idea of the hazardous voyage over to America. The request proved to be a significant test of both my faith and my calling.

Within a few days, I had decided I must go. Arrangements were swiftly made to put in place a young minister during my absence. A man called Reverend Robert Innes took on the role and many years later, he became a key member of the General Assembly, contributing a considerable amount to the development of the Church during the succeeding decade. I prepared for my trip in prayer and contemplation. I wished to know what God's purpose would be for me in America and what I could usefully share with my colleagues during that terrible time of war. I also reflected upon the fate of Reverend Cowan. I had experienced some guilt over my lack of grief for his death. Somehow, I felt that his drowning had been a kind of judgment upon Cowan, although I couldn't imagine why God had allowed an innocent young man to die alongside him, leaving a young baby without its father. However, it meant the internal investigation which had recently been launched into the ministry in Dallanaich would now be halted, and the wider Church saved from the shame of what it may have unearthed. For this reason alone, I felt more relieved than saddened by Cowan's death. My reaction to the news of the Reverend's passing caused me much soul-searching in the months which followed.

According to Sarah's postscript, the chapter went on to describe McLeod's voyage and the conference itself, which she thought contained nothing of any relevance for their investigation. Imogen's niece concluded her communication with a list of lawyerly style questions. Sarah suggested they should look more closely at Reverend Cowan, to find out what the nature of the internal investigation into his ministry might have been. Sarah said she could find no more reference to it in McLeod's memoirs.

Imogen laid the sheets of paper down on her lap and gazed out of the window. Dark clouds were billowing in across the Sound, but the wind was so brisk that they weren't hanging around long enough to deposit their load. Hugh entered the sitting room and placed a mug of coffee on the table in front of her. 'Everything okay?' He asked.

'I've just been reading the e-mail that Sarah sent.'

Hugh sat down in the chair opposite.

'It looks as if Mackenzie Cowan was about to be investigated by the Church, before he was drowned on the Minerva.'

'Really? I wonder what for. Was the investigation official?'

'No, it was purely internal and then it was closed when Cowan died. I don't think there's going to be any kind of record of it now.' Imogen looked downhearted.

'So perhaps it was Cowan who was running away from something. But what does the investigation into the Church have to do with Sandy Thomson. Do you believe he may have been involved in some way?'

Imogen sighed heavily. 'I'm not sure. Just when I was beginning to get a good idea of what Sandy was fleeing from, we suddenly get this information about Cowan. Maybe the reason Sandy left Dallanaich had nothing to do with Duncan Lambie at all.'

'I suspect that's very possible Im, as this seems a much stronger lead. Are you going to tell Michael and Julia this new information?'

'Of course, and I shall leave it entirely up to them what they would like to do about it.'

Chapter Fifty Three

Bevan had allowed Phil to return to Glasgow and work from the Pitt Street office. As the primary carer of his two teenage daughters, it didn't seem fair to require him to remain away from home for too long.

Dani and Andy Calder were staying in a pleasant little B&B in Kilross, with a view up the glen. When she finally returned to her room, the detective laid her laptop on the bed and checked her e-mails. She smiled to see the subject line of a message from Sam Sharpe in her inbox. He wanted to share his thoughts on the content of Parker's notebook. Dani flicked back through the pages of the dog-eared pad herself, before reading what Sam had to say.

Gordon Parker had noted down the real names of his mother and grandparents. From this information, he was able to find out the dates and locations of their birth. His mother had been born in Pittsburgh in 1946, as he was already aware. His grandmother had been born Elizabeth Amelia Parnell, in the same city, twenty five years earlier. Dani felt an inward shiver of surprise, as unsettling as it was when she first experienced it, when examining the details recorded about Mackenzie Cowan. It appeared the man was born in Fort William, Scotland on the 19th February, 1895. So he was 51 years of age when his daughter was born and his wife just 25. No wonder the Byrnes had remembered the age difference between Rosemary's parents. Cowan would have been well into his seventies at the time they sold the flat to the couple and his wife in her early fifties.

Gordon wasn't able to locate any death records for his grandparents. He made a specific note of this.

Their passing was not recorded under either of the names they had used during their lifetime – Cowan or Taylor. Gordon still only had the details of his mother's traffic accident to go on. He added a postscript here, pointing out that his father always insisted Rosemary's parents were dead by the time of the accident. He claimed there was no one from Rosemary's side of the family at her funeral, and very few friends had attended either.

From this point onwards, Gordon had concentrated on the Scottish connection. He had discovered that Mackenzie Cowan became a minister in the Church of Scotland, spending many years in the small town of Dallanaich, on the banks of Loch Linnhe. Then, in early 1943, Cowan had set sail for Canada, on the S.S Minerva. The liner was sunk by a torpedo and Cowan presumed dead. This was where Parker's Scottish research had hit a brick wall.

'But Cowan wasn't dead after all. The old dog managed to get himself to America and start a new life,' Dani muttered under her breath. She lay back against the covers and considered her own Scottish childhood. The tale of Cowan's ill-fated voyage had reminded her of something. On the rugged, exposed western cliffs of Colonsay, there was a memorial to commemorate the deaths of the 800 souls who were lost with the sinking of the S.S. Arandora Star on 2nd July, 1940. The ship was transporting German and Italian prisoners of war bound for St John's, Newfoundland, Canada where they were being taken to internment camps. Many of the bodies were washed up on the coast of Colonsay and laid to rest there. It was one of the worst atrocities of the war at sea and was a significant part of her adopted island's collective history. She knew that eyewitnesses saw hundreds of men clinging to the sides of the ship as it went down, with others breaking their necks as a result of jumping or diving into the water. It made Dani burn with anger that somebody might use such a tragedy for their own ends.

She returned to Parker's notebook. Having no luck finding out any more about Cowan, Parker had decided to re-examine every item he possessed that was associated with his mother. Parker's dad had passed away the previous year and his house was still in probate. So, one weekend, Gordon had driven to the property, on the outskirts of Washington D.C. He pulled out all of the boxes which contained those articles of his late mother's that Franklin Parker had decided to keep. There wasn't very much, but a paperback book at the bottom of an old tea-chest had caught his attention. It was one of those 1970s historical mysteries. The front cover displayed a ruined Scottish castle, surrounded by a sea of wild purple heather. He picked it up and began to flick through the thin, yellowed pages. Out of the centre of the book fell an envelope, kept surprisingly crisp by its placement within the thick tome. Quickly, he had slid out the letter inside and begun to read.

It immediately became clear the letter had been sent to Mackenzie Cowan and not Parker's mother. Gordon assumed she must have kept it as something to remember him by, a keepsake perhaps. The content of the correspondence had been innocuous enough, just a cataloguing of the day-to-day activities of an old woman living in a Scottish Highland town. But it had been the sender's address that seized Gordon's interest. The letter was sent from a lady called Annie Gibson who, at the time of writing, was living in Glengarry Cottage, Drumnadrochit.

The Morgans had claimed that was where Gordon Parker was headed on the day he was killed. He must have thought he'd uncovered a person who had known his grandfather whilst the man was still living in Scotland. This lady was a direct link to the two lives of Mackenzie Cowan. Gordon would have been very excited by the discovery. Bevan's team had already ascertained that Annie Gibson died in the mid-70s. She didn't appear to have had any children. There was nothing further in Gordon's notebook, but he *must* have identified somebody in Drumnadrochit who would be able to tell him more about Annie and her connection to his grandfather. Bevan was convinced there was a person out there determined to prevent Gordon from finding that information out. Perhaps it was this Tom McLean chap.

Dani clicked on Sam's message and skimmed through the lines. His interpretations were very similar to her own, but he did provide some interesting fresh insights. Sam wondered if the Cowans had used any other aliases during their time living in America. He suggested maybe that was why Parker couldn't come up with their death certificates. The detective had a hunch Rosemary's parents adopted another surname during the 1970s which may have kept them under the radar during those years. He added that he would look into the possibility from his end.

Bevan felt exhaustion sweep over her as she shut down the screen. Kicking off her shoes, she lay back once again, slipping into unconsciousness without even removing the rest of her clothes. As she dropped off, Dani's mind was picturing the memorial on the clifftops of Colonsay, where she often walked with her father as a child. He would always make her stop for a moment. They would stand facing the pearly grey waters of the ocean and remember. Her father said the most important thing they could do for those poor people who lost their lives on that terrible night was to make sure they were never forgotten.

Chapter Fifty Four

Julia held the hair back from her face as a sharp wind swept across them from the west. Imogen hoped there would be more shelter when they reached the King's Caves. The strong gusts were making it difficult to hold a conversation, so they walked along in companionable silence. Thirty minutes later, they'd reached the larger rocks which populated the headland lying at the base of a huge system of underground caverns.

Hugh led the group into the biggest of the caves. It was damp and dark, but provided some much needed relief from the elements. Bridie strode on ahead into the gloom, intending to investigate the set of tiny tunnels which led off the central cave, stretching far into the depths of the hillside.

'Don't get yourself stuck!' Imogen shouted after her. 'I don't fancy having to call out mountain rescue,' she muttered under her breath.

Julia sat down on one of the smoother boulders. 'I don't like the idea that my grandfather was trying to protect Mackenzie Cowan, especially if he'd been doing something illegal whilst running the ministry in Dallanaich.'

'We've got no evidence that Sandy Thomson knew about the investigation into Cowan,' Michael said.

'Is there any way we could find out if he did know?' Julia asked.

'I've spent the last 24 hours thinking about it, but I can't for the life of me imagine how we could. The only option would be to interview Margie again, to see if we can get something else out of her. However, there's no guarantee she knows anymore and it could permanently damage your relationship with her.'

'I agree,' Julia replied with feeling. 'I don't want to bother Gran about it for a second time.'

'Then we've reached a dead-end,' Hugh stated, not sounding particularly unhappy about the prospect.

'Maybe Harry or Jim know more than they're saying about their father? I've always felt that Harry King was holding something back.' Michael creased up his face in concentration.

'I could certainly ask Jim about his dad,' Julia said. 'But my gut instinct is that Alex King would have confided in his eldest child, if anyone at all. I also can't imagine Harry breaking ranks with his father, they were very close. I don't think he'd tell us a thing.'

Michael nodded in agreement.

Imogen stepped away from the protection of the hillside and onto the shore. Immediately, she noticed that the wind had died down. The sun was coming out once more and she decided this would be a good time to begin heading back. Just as Imogen turned to re-enter the cave and fetch the others, she was stopped in her tracks by the sound of a faint, but blood-curdling scream.

Hugh jumped to his feet and jogged straight to the hole that his daughter had vanished through. He stuck his head into the recess and hollered, 'Bridie, where are you?'

'I'm in here dad, but I can't find my way out!' came the distant reply.

'Don't panic, I'm coming in to get you!' he called back.

Michael instinctively moved towards one of the other entrances to the tunnel system. 'I'll take this one. Between us, we should be able to locate her.'

As the two men disappeared inside, the terrible scream could be heard once again. This time, it was slightly louder.

'Bridie, are you okay? Just try to stay calm, sweetheart. Dad and Uncle Michael are on their way!' Imogen kept her tone even and confident. But the answer her daughter gave chilled her to the bone.

'I'm trying to Mum, honestly I am. But I'm really frightened, because I think there might be someone in here with me.'

*

It didn't take Hugh long to reach her. Bridie was already crawling towards him when he spotted his daughter's dark brown hair trailing along the rusty-red sandstone tunnel. Hugh hooked her under the armpits and pulled her through the narrow space until they finally emerged together into the main cave. Hugh collapsed onto the wet pebbles and sand in exhaustion whilst Imogen dragged Bridie into her embrace.

'Is Michael still in there?' Julia asked in alarm.

Hugh started to pick himself up. 'Don't worry. I'll go back for him.'

This didn't prove to be necessary, as Michael abruptly appeared at the entrance to one of the other tunnels. He uncomfortably squeezed his long body out through the small aperture. 'Sorry, I ended up in a whole other section. There's another large cave in there, like a central hallway, with several corridors leading off it. The entire structure is quite labyrinthine.'

'Bridie said she thought there was someone in the tunnel with her,' Imogen declared.

The girl lifted her head up from her mother's shoulder. 'I came out into the larger cave too. There was a little bit of light filtering in from all the passageways, but it was still pretty dark. Suddenly, I felt something brush against my arm. I'm sure I heard breathing too.' Bridie shivered and her mother held her tight.

'I didn't see anyone else down there,' Michael commented. 'I'm afraid it could have been a large rat, or an otter or something. These tunnels provide a great burrow for wild animals.'

Imogen looked at her daughter, who didn't appear totally convinced. 'I think we should call the incident room in Kilross. The police are still trying to find that man who they think killed Mackie Shaw. It's probably nothing, but we need to report it just the same.'

Hugh nodded. 'Let's head back to the farmhouse. As soon as I can pick up a signal on my phone, I'll call the station.'

Chapter Fifty Five

At least the wind had died down a little, Bevan thought to herself, as she gazed up at the vertical sandstone stacks of the cliff housing Garansay's famous King's Caves. She was mightily pleased to have some local officers with her. Dani didn't know the geography of this area at all well. The headland had been completely cordoned off. But even the Strathclyde police could not hold back the tide, which was slowly edging its way up the shore.

'We've got about forty minutes until the cave is totally underwater,' D.C Robertson said, as if Bevan had spoken her concerns aloud.

'Shit. It's not long enough to search that tunnel system.'

'We haven't got the equipment to do it properly either, not until mountain rescue get here and they're on a call out down at Glen Ardroch.'

'How far does the sea water reach when the tide is at its highest? Could a man actually hide out in there for any significant length of time?'

'I honestly couldn't say for certain. Most of the caves, tunnels and cavities will be flooded. You'd have to know the inside of that hillside pretty damned well to be aware of a spot that wasn't.'

'Do the tunnels actually lead out anywhere, beyond the shoreline?'

Robertson shrugged his shoulders.

Dani sighed in exasperation and looked carefully around her, trying to identify any objects amongst the rocks that might have been dropped by their man. As she did so, Dani made out a broad figure in the distance, with a dog on a lead, standing quite still on the other side of the police tape. She strode over to confront him. Drawing nearer, she saw it was Colin Walmsley, with Rusty leaping about restlessly by his side.

'My friends at the neighbouring farm were the ones that called in the siting. They told me about it soon after, as the caves are so close to my land,' Colin explained.

'It was hardly what I'd call a siting. The girl could simply have had a close encounter with a family of bunny rabbits.'

Colin smiled. 'I know Bridie Croft very well. She's a level-headed kind of lass. Her parents wouldn't have bothered you if it wasn't something credible.'

'I know,' Bevan said apologetically. 'I'm just frustrated because we can't make a start on searching the caves. The tide's coming in.'

'I thought that might be a problem. You can't even access the tunnels by boat at high tide. The entrance is completely submerged.'

'Do you know if the tunnel system comes out anywhere else? On the clifftop perhaps?'

'That's why I'm here. I wanted to show you something.'

Bevan called her team on the walkie-talkie and told them she was going to examine the wider area. She informed Robertson and Calder to stay put and wait for mountain rescue to arrive.

Dani swung her legs over the barrier and joined Colin as he paced across the field towards the roadside. Rusty was pulling hard at his lead, desperate to be allowed to run free. But his master kept a firm grip on the excitable pup. 'We're just entering old Joe McAndrew's land. He's got a flock of sheep who roam about up by the cliff path. There's no way I could let Rusty loose around here.'

Colin took them along the roadside for a few hundred yards and then mounted a stile in the barbed wire fence which led them into another field. 'My sister and I used to play in those caves, although our mother didn't like it. It's incredibly dangerous. If you get trapped anywhere below sea-level at high tide, you would certainly drown.'

They walked on a path which circumnavigated the farmer's field and took them towards a place where the gradient began to steepen. Their course had delivered them back to the shoreline once again. Bevan decided they must now be on the other side of the headland. At the point where the cliffs rose up sharply to their left, lay a smaller collection of caves and inlets carved into the rock face, set further back from the beach.

Colin stopped by the entrance to one of them. He finally let Rusty off the lead to have a run on the sand. 'A couple of the tunnels come out here. Even when the tide is at its maximum, these caves are dry. The land on the western side of Garansay is rising fractionally each year, you see. These caves would have been created centuries ago, when the sea level was marginally higher. Sandra and I always made sure we came out of the caves this way. It was definitely the safest route.'

'So if our man really was hiding in these caves, he would have escaped out of here and be long gone by now.' Bevan kicked the point of her low-heeled court shoe against a rock, scuffing the soft leather. 'Damn it!'

'Sorry to be the bearer of bad news.' Colin laid a hand on her arm.

Bevan withdrew from him slightly, having the sudden, ludicrous idea that she should tell Colin about meeting Detective Sharpe when she was in the States. She shook this crazy notion out of her head. 'No, it's fine. If we find any evidence of this chap having set up camp in there then at least we know where he's been. The man will eventually run out of options and we'll find him.' She glanced about her at the stunning pastoral landscape, surrounded by the dark backdrop of various mountain ranges. 'Where could he have gone to from here?'

'If he's got hiking gear, the man may have headed up into the hills. He'd need some decent outdoor skills, but the weather's no' bad, he could easily survive out there for a couple of weeks.'

'Well, he can't manage in the open forever, and when he slips up, I'll be there to tap on his shoulder.'

Abruptly, the sky was filled with the noise of spinning rotor blades, battling against the stiffening westerly breeze. Rusty raced back towards his owner, frightened by the unexpected sound. Colin and Dani looked up towards the flatter area of land which created a plateau at the top of the cliff, just as the mountain rescue helicopter lowered itself to the ground. Bevan shook the farmer firmly by the hand and proceeded to climb the steep slope, gearing herself up to take charge of the search.

Chapter Fifty Six

First thing the following morning, Bevan noticed how tired the team looked. There was nothing like disappointment to sap a police officer's energy levels. The adrenaline that they'd been running on seemed to have left their system overnight. She determined to do her best to raise their spirits.

Dani strode straight to the front of the room, a wide smile on her face. 'Okay, everyone. We now know for sure that McLean had been hiding out in those caves. He wasn't expecting to get spotted and in his haste to get away he left some of his stuff behind. We have a sleeping bag and some items of clothing, all of which will need to be checked and traced. Just like the Stanley knife, it's a mistake, and we need to capitalise on it.' She placed her hands down flat on the table in front of her and leant in towards the men. 'McLean is still on this island and we're closing in on him. He wasn't prepared to have to find a new hiding place so quickly. There are uniforms all over the hills and glens of Garansay. It's just a matter of time before we get him.' Bevan struck her fist hard on the tabletop, just hoping the speech was rousing enough to have boosted the lads' morale.

When she returned to her desk, Andy came over to join her. 'Ma'am, I've been thinking about something.'

'What is it?' Bevan asked with genuine interest, knowing that Calder's instincts were good.

'It's just that our guy seems more than averagely adept at survival skills, especially for someone reputed to be in their late fifties or early sixties.'

'Okay,' Bevan said slowly. 'Are you considering the likelihood he's ex-army?'

'Maybe,' Calder sat down in a chair and dragged it closer. 'But what really strikes me, is how well he knows the topography of the island. Not only does he hike, but he must also be reasonably proficient at caving. We've all but eliminated the possibility of him being local to Garansay. Now, no army training has ever taken place on the island, I've checked. But outward bound courses are a different matter. Those types of expeditions have been coming to Garansay for donkey's years.'

'You believe that McLean may have been some kind of outward bound instructor, perhaps before he retired? That would certainly explain his knowledge of the local landscape.'

'Apparently, the King's Caves and the climb up to Ben Ardroch are the two most popular destinations for these outdoor adventure parties. Groups flock from all over the world to experience them.'

Bevan nodded her head. 'Then we should concentrate our search on those parts of Garansay which would be most familiar to him. Which are the really well-trodden paths, Andy - the route up to Ben Mhor via Aoife's Chariot, perhaps?'

'Aye, that and a few more besides. I'll get the uniforms to concentrate their search on those areas. Otherwise, they're having to cover tens of square miles.'

'Great. Get the uniforms fully briefed on that Andy, will you?' She slapped him on the back. 'And bloody well done.'

Bevan reclined in her seat and pulled forward a sheet of paper. She jotted down the name Tom McLean in the centre and put a question mark next to it. Then she drew a line coming off his name and wrote *outward bound instructor?* She thought for a moment, considering how many schools had brought groups to Garansay over the years. Dani was aware there was a field centre in Port na Mara Bay that accommodated school parties, so she also added *P.E Teacher?* to the list. Her mind then drifted to Annie Gibson, living in Glengarry Cottage, Drunmnadrochit, and Dani wrote the name of the Highland town on another part of the sheet. She drummed her fingers on the page. 'What's the connection?' Dani murmured to herself. The D.C.I had given Phil Boag the job of investigating the lady who wrote the letter to Mackenzie Cowan all those years ago and decided to call him for an update.

'Hi, Phil? How's it going?'

'Morning, Ma'am. Let me just grab the file and I'll fill you in.' There was a moment's delay before he returned to the line. 'Okay. Annie Gibson and her husband lived in Drumnadrochit for the majority of their married life. The husband was called Douglas and ran a couple of local businesses in the town.'

'Such as?' Dani prompted.

'An auto repair place and a sort of hardware store. Douglas Gibson died in 1974 at the age of 85. His wife lived on in the cottage until she died in '79, when the lady was 81.'

'Do we know much about her background?'

'She was born Anne Thomson in Oban hospital on the 30th January 1908. Her parents were Hugh and Eliza. They had both passed away by the late 30s. Annie had a younger brother called Alexander, but that's it.'

Dani noted all of this information down.

'Annie and Douglas Gibson had no children together. I'm still waiting to hear back from the CRO, but I can't imagine either of them having a record.'

'Well, let's keep an open mind on that until we find out for certain. Look, I'm calling because we may have a new lead. Andy thinks this guy we're hunting must have some kind of outward bound expertise. Perhaps he had a career as an instructor. I've had a thought. Maybe McLean was a *teacher* and he'd taken school groups to Garansay in the past. Could you do a check on all the P.E. staff who have recently retired or are reaching retirement age in the Drumnadrochit schools? I've just got a hunch that our man comes from the area. Do some ringing around if you have to. You've got the man's description.'

'Sure, Ma'am, will do.'

'Thanks Phil, and keep me posted.'

Bevan sat in silence for a moment. So Annie Gibson, née Thomson, was born and presumably grew up in the Oban area. Mackenzie Cowan was a minister in Dallanaich, which Dani knew was about 30 miles along the coast from there. It wasn't on the doorstep, but it was certainly within shooting distance. Could this be the connection, she wondered? Did Annie and Mackenzie know each other from childhood? She shook her head. The age difference was too great. It was more likely Annie was a member of his congregation. But it could well be that Dallanaich was the factor which linked these two people. Dani reached for her sheet of paper once again. She carefully wrote the name of this village, which lay on the banks of the lovely Loch Linnhe, in capital letters at the bottom of the page.

Chapter Fifty Seven

She wasn't sure why, but Imogen decided to dig the two paperback novels by Maggie Maclure out of her suitcase. She took them downstairs and positioned the books in a pile on the kitchen table. Imogen smiled to herself as she placed the old kettle onto the hob of the range cooker, thinking how silly she was to imagine that these dog-eared novels might actually provide her with the inspiration to solve this mystery. But somehow, she felt a need to keep them close by.

Her sister-in-law came down to join her a few minutes later. Wrapped in a long, silk dressing gown, Imogen was struck by how elegant the woman looked. Julia filled a bowl with cereal and sat down at the oak table, eating in silence for a while.

The kettle began to whistle intrusively so Imogen swiftly removed it from the heat and set about preparing a *cafétiere* of coffee. She laid a selection of her mother's hand thrown mugs on the table and sat down herself, to finish her slice of toast. Imogen noticed then that Julia had begun reading one of the books.

'You can borrow it if you like,' she said cheerfully, 'I've already finished them both. They're really good.'

Julia put it down. 'Oh, that's okay, thanks. I've read them too. She's one of my favourite authors.'

'Really? Did you know that Maggie Maclure was Duncan Lambie's little sister?' Imogen leant in closer.

The other woman's mouth fell open in surprise. 'No, I didn't. Just to think, I've been reading her stuff since childhood.'

Imogen poured the coffee and took a sip in quiet

contemplation.

'Do you know what's funny?' Julia suddenly exclaimed. 'My Uncle Harry said that his father was a fan of her books too. You see, she writes under several pen names. Her Maggie Maclure books are the ones about the old lady running the guest house in the Highlands, but then she also writes under the name of Catriona Gregory, and those mysteries are historical - you know, very Victoria Holt – all about governesses discovering terrible secrets in windswept Scottish castles. When we met Harry and Connie in New York, I really pressed him as to whether my grandfather showed any interest in his Scottish heritage. And that was when he said that Alex King had enjoyed the books of Catriona Gregory. I got very excited about it, because I had loved them too. I felt it gave me some kind of connection to my grandad.'

Imogen sat back in the chair, holding the warm cup to her lips. 'So, Sandy Thomson read the novels of Duncan Lambie's sister, *after* he'd started a new life in Ontario. He may even have closely followed her career.'

'Why would he do that? If he'd been involved in Duncan's death, it surely doesn't make any sense, unless he was just torturing himself and he read the books out of guilt.'

'No, I think Harry was correct, and he read those books in order to maintain some kind of link with his homeland. Perhaps through Maggie's books, he could connect not only with the landscape of his youth, but also with his long lost friends.'

'So was Maggie his friend?'

'I don't know. But by reading the books, it made him feel close to her. You develop a kind of intimacy with an author when you read their novels – it gives you a window into their thoughts and dreams.'

'But Sandy never once tried to correspond with my

dad in all those years,' Julia added, almost plaintively.

Imogen laid a hand over hers. 'I know, but this connection with Maggie Maclure was safe for Sandy. Thousands of other people were reading her mystery books all over the world. It wasn't like a letter, which could easily be traced.'

Julia nodded. 'I think I understand.'

Imogen smiled wistfully, wishing that she did too. Why on earth did Sandy want to maintain a link with Duncan's sister? Imogen was beginning to believe there might be a whole other side to this puzzle that they knew nothing about.

At first, Dani Bevan wasn't sure why she had woken. Then, the persistent trilling of a mobile phone broke into her consciousness. She reached across to the bedside table in an attempt to silence it. 'Hello?'

'Hi, Dani? Sorry to wake you.'

'What time is it?'

'The middle of the night – for you, anyway.'

She hoisted herself up so that she was leaning against the pillows and rubbed vigorously at her eyes, absent-mindedly flattening down her short-hair, as if Sam Sharpe could see her on the other end of the line. 'Have you got something?'

'Sure have. Otherwise, I promise that I wouldn't have disturbed you at this hour.'

'Okay. Fire away.'

'I got to thinking, after you replied to my e-mail. I'd been through Gordon's notes with a fine-toothed comb, but for some reason, I felt it was important for me to see the actual letter from Annie Gibson itself. I know that Parker had said the contents were run-of-the-mill, but I just had a hunch there might be something in there which could throw up a line of inquiry. I mean, the whole reason for Parker's murder was related to this Drumnadrochit connection after all.'

The American detective had Dani's interest now. 'Go on.'

'So I went back to the Parker's place. Gabriella was very cooperative. She's much more relaxed now I've told her that her affair isn't playing a part in our investigation. She let me search the place top to bottom. I found it. The envelope was still tucked inside that old mystery book. Gordon had simply slotted it onto a bookshelf in the living room. Can you believe it?' He chuckled.

'Hidden in plain sight,' Dani responded, feeling her heart begin to beat faster.

'There were several pages of it, written in an almost indecipherable kind of joined up handwriting. I got to wondering if the old bird had arthritis or something when she wrote the damn thing. I've copied it and I'll scan it through to you in the morning.'

'What did you find Sam?'

'Well, the old lady was describing to Cowan about how she had a problem with damp in the cottage. The story being relayed was pretty mundane, but she mentions how she couldn't really afford to get a builder in to fix it, so Dougie's son had applied a damp course for her.'

'Phil said the Gibsons didn't have any children.' Dani's mind was ticking over fast.

'No, not together. But perhaps Douglas Gibson had a child from a previous marriage.'

Dani sighed, 'Gordon Parker was one step ahead of us. After he made this discovery, he didn't write anything down. When he read the letter from Annie and looked at the date it was sent, Gordon must have known the old woman would be long dead. But he'd picked up on this reference to a step-son.

Gordon tracked him down, thinking that this man might be the only one left alive who could tell him more about his grandfather.'

'That's what I figured too. Perhaps Gordon had been in contact with him. This step-child invited Parker to Scotland in order to meet up. Maybe he enticed him there with the promise he would explain all about Cowan's life in Scotland and the reason why he left. With Parker's obsessive need to discover more about his mother's family, it would have been very hard for him to resist the offer.'

'Little did Gordon Parker know that this man was actually luring him to his death.'

'If only Parker had confided in someone about what he was doing. They might have been able to point out the dangers.'

'Gabriella tried, remember? She begged her husband not to go on the trip to Garansay. But by that stage Gordon *had* to know, it had all gone too far. Gabriella said it was like watching somebody you love heading for a nervous breakdown. There was an awful inevitability about it, but all you could do was stand by and watch, as they slid towards self-destruction.'

'But Parker didn't self-destruct. This man murdered him. Dani, I'm relying on you to make sure the bastard pays for it.'

Chapter Fifty Eight

Phil Boag was extremely apologetic. Bevan could tell he was really kicking himself for the oversight. Unfortunately, she didn't have the time to massage his bruised ego.

'Dougie Gibson was married for a couple of years in the 1930s. They'd divorced by the time the war began. They had one son, named Thomas, but when Dougie's first wife re-married a few years later, Thomas pops up on the census as a member of the new household. He'd taken on his step-father's surname, which was Erskine.' Phil paused for a moment. 'I hate to break this to you Ma'am, but Thomas Erskine passed away in October 2011.'

Dani nodded on the other end of the line. 'He was going to be too old to be our suspect anyway. So Thomas Erskine was Annie Gibson's step-son. He must have kept in contact with his real father over the years, then.'

'The Erskines lived in Inverness, which wasn't very far away from the Gibsons. I have found out something else, Ma'am. Thomas Erskine got married in 1956 and his wife had a baby boy a year later.'

Dani did the calculations in her head. 'Which would make him 57 years old now. Could you find out any more about him?'

'Richard Erskine has lived in Inverness for most of his life. He's unmarried and doesn't have a long-term partner that I could identify. Erskine took early retirement at the end of last year and get this – he'd completed 35 years of service as a Geography teacher in one of the big secondary schools in Inverness.'

'Yes!' Dani banged her fist on the desk. 'Have you

spoken to his previous employers?'

'Yep, according to the Headmistress, Erskine was a quiet sort of chap. Very knowledgeable about his subject, although perhaps a little slow to take on new ideas regarding teaching methods. She says he took early retirement by mutual consent. The way that education was moving just didn't quite suit him. What she really praised Richard Erskine for was his contribution to extra-curricular activities. She says he was a Duke of Edinburgh expedition leader and a keen walker and climber in his spare time.'

'Had be ever taken school parties to Garansay?' Dani tried hard to mask the eagerness in her voice.

'Only every spring break for the past twenty-five years.'

Dani quickly gathered her team together in the cramped incident room. She dropped her heavy files on the desk to gain everyone's attention and began. 'The suspect we are looking for, out there in the hills, is most likely a retired Geography teacher by the name of Richard Erskine. He's 57 years old, but he knows the terrain of Garansay extremely well. This chap's been bringing school groups to the island for the last 25 years. He lives in Inverness and the local plods are currently ripping his house apart.'

Robertson raised his hand. 'One of the major retailers which stock the type of Stanley knife identical to the murder weapon used on Shaw has a big out of town store in Inverness.'

'Great, we'll have to get onto them and see if Erskine was stupid enough to use his credit card to purchase it. Even if we catch this man, we'll still need plenty of evidence to tie him into the murders of Mackie Shaw and Gordon Parker. We need to secure a conviction.'

'But *why* did he do it, Ma'am. He'd just retired from a respectable career where he served others for decades. Why kill someone?'

Dani took a step forward. 'He killed Gordon Parker to protect his family. What he was protecting them from we just don't know and we might never find out. But it's our job to bring Erskine to justice. It doesn't matter if this chap was a bloody saint before now. We all saw the state of Mackie's body. Erskine killed that young man in cold blood because he believed he'd witnessed him murdering Parker. He's a very dangerous person who needs to be stopped.'

'Will headquarters send us any more bodies to assist in the search, Ma'am?' Andy Calder asked, with an expression of pure frustration on his face.

'No, Glasgow are still tied up with these anti-terrorist raids. But I agree, Andy. Our efforts should be directed towards tracking down this man. I want you all to put aside your current lines of enquiry and get yourselves along to the outward bound shop on the pier in order to get kitted out. Don't worry lads, I'll be joining you.' She glanced at her watch. 'We rendezvous with the mountain rescue team on the Glen Ardroch path at midday and I swear to you, we're going to catch this bastard.'

Chapter Fifty Nine

Imogen rushed out through the front door of the farmhouse. She stood in the garden, watching silently, as the mountain rescue helicopter approached along the Kilbrannan Sound from its base on Tarbert, before swooping in low over the roof of the building and heading away up the glen. The dust and gravel in the courtyard made swirling patterns on the ground in its wake. Imogen turned to see that Julia had emerged from the house to join her.

'Do you think there's been an accident?' The younger woman enquired.

'No, I expect they're still searching for that man.' Imogen shuddered. 'Let's go back inside.'

For some reason, she felt the need for a wee dram to warm her up and went straight to her mother's old drinks cabinet in the sitting room. 'Shall I pour you one, too?'

'Go on then,' Julia replied.

'You know, the only avenue we haven't explored yet is your grandfather's sister. Val Black said Anne Thomson moved away from Dallanaich before Sandy left on the Minerva. Did you meet her at all while you were growing up?'

'Great Aunt Annie lived with her husband in Drumnadrochit. I probably only met her twice before she died and it was when I was just a toddler. I got the impression Dad didn't like her very much, it was a duty rather than a pleasure for him to take me up to visit. But I suppose she was the only one left from the Thomson side of the family.'

'Val used a strange word to describe her. She said Anne was a 'bluestocking.'

Julia laughed. 'Actually, that's quite a good description. The house they lived in was called something cottage, but in reality, it was more like a big old manor house. After her husband died, she rattled around in it all on her own, probably living in just one or two freezing rooms. She wore her hair very short, but not in an old person's kind of style – you know, all sort of blow-dried and sculpted – it was tufty and spiky, like she cut it herself with the kitchen scissors.'

'Do you think she could have been in contact with your grandfather after he absconded to Canada?' Imogen finished off the last dregs of her whisky and poured them both a little more.

'According to my dad, Annie hated her brother for what he'd done. The news that he had been alive all along came as a terrible shock. Annie spent the last five years of her life railing about it. She was particularly angry about Sandy abandoning his unborn infant. Annie used to say that she'd been cursed with not being able to bear a child, yet Sandy had blithely left his behind, without giving it a second thought. In Annie's mind, it was unforgivable. In that sense, she and my dad had a lot in common.' Julia sipped at the strong liquid. 'Although she'd moaned about not being able to have babies, my mum always said the woman didn't have a maternal bone in her body. She claimed, rather unkindly, that if you saw Annie Gibson from behind, in her tattered old trousers and shirt, and with that awful cropped hair, you'd think she was a man.'

Imogen was quiet for a moment. Both ladies stared out at the still waters of the Sound, as the white clouds scudded rapidly across the sky to the south.

'My mother used to have a favourite saying. It originally came from Hamlet, but mum had messed about with the wording, I'm sure,' Imogen explained evenly. 'She used to say: 'the lady doth protest too much, me thinks'.'

*

Dani looked up at the sky and prayed that the weather would hold. It had been a typical Scottish summer, with intermittent sunshine and showers which meant that one minute you were bathed in beams of brilliant, hot sunshine and the next you were running for cover under a heavy downpour. The clouds were moving so fast above them right now that Dani simply couldn't predict what it was going to do.

She fell into step with Andy Calder as they climbed towards the peak of Ben Aonach, which was not as high as Ben Ardroch, but was arguably a more strenuous ascent. When they reached the top they were both breathless, but Dani was the one who recovered the fastest. 'We've got a great view from up here.' She put the binoculars to her eyes and scanned the glaciated valleys which ran between these central mountain ranges. 'Where the hell is he?'

'Lying low during daylight hours I expect, when he knows we're out in force looking for him.'

'And at night he's raiding farms and scavenging for food. Have any of the local operations noticed anything going missing?'

'They're all starting to bring in the harvest. Most places wouldn't notice the odd scrap that's amiss.'

'I suppose not.'

Dani led the way across the narrow track which passed between Ben Aonach and Ben Dubh. They had the benefit of a fabulous vista provided by the Clyde coastline on one side of them and the rugged beauty of Glen Keir on the other, with the burn twisting and turning through the centre of it. Andy had the job of surveying the eastern side of the hill and Dani the west.

Twenty minutes later, Dani heard the crackle of her walkie-talkie. After a short exchange, she tapped her colleague on the shoulder and gestured for him to cut down the mountainside with her, towards the foot of the glen. 'One of the guys has spotted something moving by the burn - he thinks it might be Erskine,' she explained in a lowered voice.

Andy nodded and Dani noted how pale and sweaty he was looking. She desperately hoped he was able to pass his next medical. The man was a great cop.

The two officers kept low as they sidestepped down the hill. Apparently, the figure on the path by the burn was heading due north, so, as soon as the gradient had flattened out, they followed the contours of the rocky stream at a slow jog. The level of the burn was reasonably high and Dani hoped the sound of water rushing over rocks would mask their approach.

Just as the D.C.I was seriously beginning to tire, she spotted something lumbering amongst the larger boulders up ahead. She immediately dropped down below a thick gorse bush and glanced behind in order to signal to Andy. At first she couldn't see him. Then she looked again. The D.C appeared to be lying on his back, in the centre of the path along which she just came. He didn't seem to be moving. Dani kept herself low and practically crawled along the ground until she reached his prone form.

'Andy,' she rasped urgently, 'what's happened?' Looking at his contorted face, the answer was quite obvious. 'Oh shit,' she said under her breath.

Andy was clutching at his arm and gritting his teeth against the pain. His cheeks were bright red but an ice cold sweat was saturating his entire body, creating dark circles underneath his armpits. Dani grasped for the walkie-talkie and fought to keep it steady in her hands. She looked frantically around her, stating in a loud whisper, 'we need the air ambulance right now. Police officer down. Immediate assistance required. I'm about two miles north of Ben Aonach, down by the burnside in Glen Keir.'

Andy's hand tugged at her sleeve, she leant in close. 'Carol,' he murmured.

'Don't exert yourself. Whatever happens, we'll look after her.' Dani felt the tears begin to prickle at her eyes. 'Hold on in there. The paramedics will be here soon, they'll give you something for the pain.'

Within five minutes, the mountain rescue lads arrived. Thankfully, they'd come bearing a stretcher. As soon as the men were within hearing distance Dani stood up. 'He's having a massive heart attack. He needs the correct drugs, like, yesterday.' She grabbed one of the men by the arm. 'He's only 34 years old - his wife's about to have a baby for Christ's sake.'

The volunteer nodded tolerantly. 'We'll do everything we can, I promise. You go after your suspect.'

Dani looked surprised.

'We've been listening in to all of your communications, in case someone gets injured. We're in charge of your officer, he's in safe hands. The best thing you can do for him now is to go after your man.'

Bevan didn't need any further encouragement. She turned on her heels and sprinted. If Andy didn't make it, she was damned if it was going to be for nothing. It took just a matter of seconds to reach the gorse bush she'd been hiding behind, but when she scrutinised the route ahead, she could no longer see anyone amongst the rocks. Dani shifted into a crouching position and continued to move forwards.

The burn was beginning to climb more steeply by this point so that she could observe its course much farther into the distance. That's when she spotted him. The man was wearing dark clothing and boots but his silver hair was really quite noticeable against the nearly black slate of the hillside. Dani got on the walkie-talkie and informed her colleagues of his position.

Dani Bevan was fully aware she needed to wait for back-up. That was basic procedure. Erskine could be armed and he was certainly dangerous. But Dani didn't think there would be any harm in tracking him, so she kept pushing forwards, following the winding progression of the burn, as it regularly tacked back and forth up the hillside. The adrenaline must have been driving her faster than she'd realised because suddenly Dani was only metres behind him. She was close enough to make out the brand of his walking boots. She was also close enough for him to hear her. A loose stone under her left boot made a clunking sound as she inadvertently kicked it into the water. The man up ahead of her froze momentarily and then began to turn. Dani braced herself by placing her feet a little further apart and grabbing the nearby heather with both fists. Figuring it didn't matter much if she made a noise now.

What struck Dani immediately was how old he looked. A few days' worth of stubble covered the lower half of his face and the eyes which were currently boring holes into her were bloodshot, with dark circles beneath. Erskine was obviously physically fit but several nights sleeping out in the open had taken its toll upon him.

'It's Richard. Is that correct?' Dani tried to keep her voice as level as possible.

'Ricky, actually,' the man almost snarled.

‘Well, we need you to come into the station and answer some questions for us, Mr. Erskine. You can’t stay out here in the wilderness forever. I can see how tired you are.’

‘Oh, is that right?’ He retorted and in a flash he swung back towards the hillside and started to climb steadily upwards, making scarily good headway.

‘Bloody hell,’ Dani muttered, falling into step behind him and trying to match the man, stride for stride.

By the time they reached the top of the ridge, Dani was exhausted. For a brief moment, she couldn’t see Erskine at all, but when she scrambled onto the summit, she found him sitting further along the mountain path, his legs dangling over the edge of a sheer drop which shelved down abruptly on the opposite side of the ridge.

‘Looks like we’ve reached the end of the road,’ he said quietly.

‘Not necessarily. You haven’t had the chance to give your side of things Mr. Erskine. *I* want to hear your explanation. I know you’re a good man. You taught all those children, Ricky, and introduced them to wonderful landscapes like this. Any jury would take that into account.’ Dani discovered she could hardly get out the words as she was breathing so heavily after her recent exertion.

But Richard Erskine seemed to respond to something she had said. He twisted around to look her squarely in the face. In his eyes she saw a terrible sadness. ‘Well, it was all for the children. That’s why they did it. We needed to protect them. They made a huge sacrifice but no one ever knew. I had to help them to keep it that way.’

Dani tried to maintain steady eye contact with Erskine, as she had just spotted D.C Robertson approaching him stealthily from along the mountain path to the east. She refused to succumb to the almost overwhelming urge to shift her vision in the young detective's direction. Just when she believed she could fight the urge no longer, Robertson grappled Erskine into an arm lock, twisting the suspect so that he was face down on the ground and firmly securing his wrists in cuffs behind his back.

Chapter Sixty

D.C.I Bevan strode purposefully through the corridors of the Strathclyde Police Headquarters in Glasgow. When she reached the interview suite, she joined a group of officers who were gathered around the bank of monitors.

'Is he talking?' She demanded, of no one in particular.

'Oh, yes,' said Detective Sergeant Phil Boag, who was resting his weight on the edge of a desk, with his arms folded. 'What's the news on Andy?'

'He's stable. They think the drugs were administered in time, but he's got a bloody long convalescence ahead of him.'

'When is Carol due to give birth?'

'Next month.'

Phil whistled. 'Poor lass.'

'We'll look after her,' Dani added with determination. 'Now, what's Ricky got to say for himself? I just wish Andy could have conducted the interview.'

'Actually, D.S Corthine is doing a really good job. I've got a hunch that Erskine responds better to women than men.'

One of the other officers present turned towards Dani and said, 'you'll need to review the last ten minutes of the tape Guv, then we'll require your authorisation to send a search team out.'

'And what will they be looking for exactly, Detective?'

'A body Ma'am.'

*

The sun was slowly rising over the Kilbrannan Sound on what was supposed to be the last day of the Crofts' holiday. Ewan had headed back to his student digs in Manchester over a week ago and Hugh needed to return to their home in Essex in order to prepare for the new university year. But as Imogen was considering what they should do on this bright, crisp morning, the phone in the hallway suddenly rang and all their plans were overturned.

It was Julia who lifted the antiquated receiver. She immediately became engrossed in a conversation which was conducted for the most part in hushed tones. After a while, Michael joined his wife and spoke intermittently to the caller himself. When the exchange was finally over, Michael and Julia entered the kitchen together, with expressions on their faces which were quite unreadable.

'Good grief, what on earth's the matter?' Imogen exclaimed.

'You'd better make some sweet tea,' Michael suggested, guiding his wife gently towards a seat.

Hugh came into the room. Sensing the charged atmosphere, he leant against the counter top and said nothing.

'That was Mum,' Julia explained, in a quiet voice. 'She told us that Dad is with the police. They've been telling him something about his father. Mum didn't know much more than that. But she wants us to go over to the mainland and be with her. The police have been digging up almost all of the hillsides in Dallanaich. Mum said they're searching for a body. Well, the remains of a body more like.'

'Whose body are they looking for?' Imogen asked levelly.

'I don't know yet,' Julia continued, 'but I'd be really grateful if you'd come with us, Imogen. If we're going to find out the truth, then I need you to be there.'

Imogen glanced over at Hugh, who shrugged his shoulders. 'You could go with Julia and Michael if you like. I'll drive Ian and Bridie home tomorrow. I really must get back, darling. Term begins in a few days.'

'Oh, of course. I'll get the train home later in the week. Kath and Gerry can pick me up from the station.'

Julia smiled with relief, almost collapsing forward onto the table. 'Thank goodness. I feel a terrible knot forming in my stomach whenever I think about what I'm going to hear, but with you and Michael by my side, I'll have the strength to face it.'

Imogen volunteered to drive Michael's car to Dallanaich. She had pretty much got used to the vehicle's idiosyncrasies after her trip to Fort William. Imogen's brother was sitting next to her in the front seat and Julia was curled up silently in the back. Her slender legs were tucked towards her chest and her eyes closed.

'The police have set up their operation in the primary school hall. Rob and Jacquie are staying in a room above the pub. It's the only accommodation in the town, but they say the place is perfectly comfortable. I've booked us in there for tonight, if you don't mind?'

'No, that sounds good. We want to be close to Julia's parents. Did they tell you any more information?'

'Not really, Rob wants to explain things to Julia face-to-face. He made it clear that none of them are in any trouble, but that we would all have to endure hearing some uncomfortable truths. Rob said he needs to be in Dallanaich to help heal the wounds of the police investigation. The village doesn't have a minister of its own any longer and he feels it's his duty to take on the job.'

'Julia's father is a good man,' Imogen commented.

Michael nodded his agreement and they spent the remainder of the journey in quiet contemplation. Imogen tried to savour the views of Loch Linnhe from the coastal road but all too soon, she made out the profile of Balnagowan Island and knew they had arrived at their destination.

As they entered the lounge bar of Dallanaich's only hostelry, they found Rob and Jacquie Thomson sitting at a small circular table near the fire. The older couple immediately sprang to their feet, embracing Julia warmly. Imogen offered to get the drinks. It surprised her to observe that Rob and Jacquie both had tumblers of neat Scotch whisky in front of them. She decided to order her companions the same. Returning a few minutes later, Imogen set down the drams and took her seat. Imogen had expected Rob to appear bleak and depressed but he didn't. To her, he actually looked relieved.

'Thank you all for coming,' Rob began and he raised the heavy glass. 'It isn't the best of circumstances, but it's genuinely lovely to see you.'

'And you,' added Michael with feeling.

'Now, I'm going to explain what the police told me. In many ways I was a step ahead of them, knowing more about certain elements of the story than they did. But the crux of the tale I had no idea about and neither do you, so brace yourselves for something of a shock.'

Everyone around the table nodded.

'The police contacted me yesterday because the story involves my late aunt, Annie Gibson, and the details will undoubtedly end up in the national press. I am the last surviving Thomson and they took it upon themselves to inform me first. So what I shall convey to you is the whole story as I understand it. Right from the very beginning.'

Imogen glanced at Julia and watched her take a large swig of whisky.

'It all began in the wild autumn of 1942. The weather had been unsettled here in Dallanaich for several months. There'd been heavy rain and strong winds battering this part of the coastline on and off for days. At the time, my father was the young Headmaster of the local Primary School. He'd not long been married to my mother and they'd just found out she was expecting a baby the following spring. Sandy Thomson was very settled in his existence but was keen to pursue what he believed was his calling to be ordained in the church. So Sandy was regularly taking services as a lay preacher in Reverend Cowan's chapel. Sandy didn't have a great liking for the man, but respected his knowledge and experience. Cowan had also invited him to attend an important church convention in New York City the following March, which Sandy knew was a wonderful opportunity. He would have been back in plenty of time for the birth of the baby.

Then, a twist of fate changed their fortunes forever. Sandy's elder sister Annie came to stay with them for a week. She had moved away from her childhood home to live with her husband in Drumnadrochit. She didn't often come back to Dallanaich, a place which she professed to despise. However, the death of their parents necessitated that she should visit her little brother every so often. But this trip was a difficult one. When Margie informed her sister-in-law that she was expecting a baby, Annie was very upset. She explained to Margie how she and Dougie had been trying for years to have a child but nothing had happened. Annie hinted to Margie that she'd been *damaged* in some way and that was why she couldn't conceive. My mother didn't really understand at the time what the woman was talking about and dismissed it as one of Annie's eccentricities.

For the next few days, Annie caught up with her old friends in the village, people like my father and Duncan Lambie, who had not left the place to go and fight in the war. Annie had always enjoyed what would then have been considered typically *male* pursuits, such as hillwalking and fishing. In the exercise of these activities she had a companion in Duncan Lambie, a lame young man who didn't have a great deal of purpose in his life and was able to spend his free time with Annie Gibson.

It was as the pair were returning from a fishing trip up at the headland that Annie caught sight of the Reverend Mackenzie Cowan. He was striding through the centre of the town, apparently on his way back to the chapel. When Annie laid eyes upon him, she immediately went hot with anger. This was a new reaction for her, as previously, the man had invoked in Annie, and all the other young girls in his congregation, nothing but fear.

For some reason, the fear which had previously enveloped and overwhelmed Annie Gibson, whenever she was in the vicinity of Reverend Cowan, had somehow evaporated - now that she was older and a married woman, perhaps. But the emotion had been neatly replaced by a gradually mounting and equally all-consuming sense of hatred. Annie barely said another word to her fishing companion but returned with haste to her brother's little terraced house on the edge of the town.'

'What had the Reverend Cowan done to Great Aunt Anne to make her hate him so much?' Julia said quietly.

Rob simply raised his hand, in a gesture which

suggested she should wait and see. 'Sandy and Margie couldn't really comprehend Annie's odd behaviour that evening. She was monosyllabic throughout dinner and before my mother had a chance to brew the tea, Annie pulled on her thick overcoat and announced she was going out. It was wet and windy once again, but Annie simply turned her collar up against the cold and marched through the centre of Dallanaich, heading purposefully for the tiny chapel on the shore. Lights were flickering inside when she got there. Annie stood in front of the battered and scratched wooden door for a long time and then she pushed it open.

Mackenzie Cowan was moving about in his shirt sleeves and dog-collar at the far end of the chapel. The churchman was calmly collecting together the hymn books and placing them in a pile on the book shelf. The man stopped what he was doing and glanced across as she entered. It seemed to take several minutes for him to work out who she was.

'Why, if it isn't wee Annie Thomson. How is married life treating you?'

'Not all aspects of it were a mystery to me Reverend.'

The man feigned to be puzzled by her response.

So Annie continued, 'are you still doing it, Reverend? Taking the wee girls into your vestry for Bible study? And you're helping out at the school now I hear.'

'Your brother finds me of great assistance to him. Under my tutelage those wee girls aren't quite as wayward as you used to be. I had to teach you a lesson Annie and show you how real ladies ought to behave. Just look at you now, a fine figure of a woman.'

Annie began to stride down the aisle in his direction, tears blurring her vision. Cowan shrank back into the shadows. 'Now, now,' he said. 'I suggest you go back to your brother's place, Mrs. Gibson. Who would ever believe someone like you – a mannish aberration – over a respectable pillar of the community like me?'

Annie discovered that she was standing by the entrance to the cramped vestry. She was practically holding herself upright against the frame. Glancing inside, her eyes alighted upon an ornate metal letter-opener. Annie had no specific thought in mind, but made a grab for it, probably because she wished to see fear on Reverend Cowan's face, not that self-satisfied smirk he had adopted. The metal object felt heavy in her palm. When she turned back towards the altar, Cowan had disappeared. Then she spotted him, cowering in a dusty corner, with a look of pure horror on his face.

"Forgive me," the man cried out and Annie wasn't sure to whom he was addressing the plea. But she didn't much care, as she repeatedly stabbed the sharpest point of the letter-opener into his arms and chest.'

Chapter Sixty One

The lounge bar was so eerily quiet, that the occasional crackle of the logs in the grate was all Imogen could hear. Michael had taken it upon himself to buy another round of drinks.

'Was he dead?' Julia asked.

'Oh yes,' her father replied.

When Michael returned with the topped up glasses, Rob continued. 'Annie threw down the weapon and fled from the scene. Her light blue shift dress was smeared with blood and it dripped from her outstretched hands. Her coat flapping open, she walked all the way back to the village in that state, oblivious to the wind and rain.

As she paraded through the centre of the town, a handful of people came out of their houses. Some of them tried to take hold of her and asked what had happened, but she simply shrugged them off. Finally, she reached the pub, where she knew most of the remaining menfolk would be - her brother and Duncan and those too old to fight. They gathered around as she entered, finding her a seat and fetching a brandy.

Once Annie had composed herself, and the violent shivering had subsided, she informed them of what she'd done. Annie told them everything about Reverend Cowan, what he had inflicted on her and probably countless other young girls over the years. Some of the men around her nodded their heads, muttering that they'd known, or at least suspected something. A couple had even written letters to the Moderator, when their daughters had come home from Bible study in tears. But no action had ever been taken. Not until now.

They sat around in this very bar, talking until the sun came up. All the elders of the village were called to the pub and a good number of the womenfolk too. For a while, the situation seemed hopeless. Cowan was dead, murdered in cold blood. They had a body to dispose of and the man's sudden disappearance to explain. In the end, it was Sandy who had the idea. My father couldn't allow his sister to be hanged for murder. At first, he offered to take the blame. But Annie and Duncan wouldn't allow him to do that, so he came up with a different plan instead.

Sandy and Reverend Cowan were due to travel to America in just over three months from then. Sandy's plan was that they would keep Cowan's absence a secret until the day of the trip. It would be the depths of winter, Dallanaich often got cut off for a couple of weeks during that period and Cowan had no family to speak of, so it wouldn't be too hard to achieve.

Then, when Sandy set off on the ocean liner in February, on that treacherous transatlantic journey, he could claim that Cowan became ill during the voyage, or fell overboard in stormy seas. It wouldn't have been ideal, but when Cowan's disappearance was finally noticed, Sandy would take the blame for his murder. By that time he would be long gone, starting a new life thousands of miles away. It was a terrible sacrifice, but at least no one would be hanged for the crime.

It was Duncan Lambie who pointed out the flaws in Sandy's scheme. There would need to be *two* men getting onto that ship if they were to get Mackenzie Cowan officially declared dead, he argued. That way, they might actually be able to cover up his murder entirely. Duncan explained that someone would have to *impersonate* Cowan if the plan were to work. Duncan immediately volunteered for the job. Life held nothing for him in this isolated town. He had always longed to go to America. Duncan was actually willing to take on the role. He saw it as the beginning of an adventure.

So, by dawn, they seemed to have a strategy. The first element of which, was to bury the body. Three men from the village were designated that unpleasant task. Their wives had the job of scrubbing clean the Chapel's flagstone floor. But the most important element of the plan was that the children of the town would never know what happened. *They* would be protected from the burden that their elders had to bear. The womenfolk were content to keep the secret, relieved that their daughters were now safe from the risk of abuse. Many of them never told their husbands when they returned home on leave, either. Why should they encumber those brave men with the knowledge of yet more death and depravity?'

'We discovered that Duncan Lambie went missing, in the November of 1942, does that mean the plan failed?' Imogen enquired.

'Oh, no, that was *part* of the plan. If Duncan had vanished at exactly the same time as Sandy went off on the Minerva, it would have been perfectly obvious it was he who'd taken Cowan's place. The villagers of Dallanaich were cleverer than that. A few days after Cowan's murder, they staged Duncan's disappearance. They chose a particularly stormy night and gave the impression he'd been washed off the cliffs.'

'So where did he go between November and February, when they set sail on the Minerva?'

'Duncan spent quite a few weeks hiding out in the chapel. He responded to Cowan's correspondence and made sure he had plenty of the clergyman's clothes to take with him on the voyage. Duncan also needed to gather together Cowan's papers and passport. All of that took several weeks of preparation. Between times, he hid out at Annie's place. She had told Dougie everything as soon as she returned home.'

'Did Duncan Lambie's sister know anything about the plan? She seemed to genuinely believe her brother was drowned in November '42. It's what she claimed in a magazine interview, although she could have been lying I suppose,' Imogen stated.

'Maggie Maclure the mystery writer? She would have been too young to be told the truth, along with folk like Val Black. Val's mother, on the other hand, would have known about it all.'

'And Kenneth Garvie would have been away fighting in the war during all of this, so he didn't know anything about the plan either,' Michael suggested. 'So when he spotted Sandy in Toronto in '73, he didn't realise that the man's existence needed to be kept a secret.'

'They couldn't have predicted the Minerva would be sunk, that must have been unexpected.'

'It was always going to be a dangerous journey,' Rob pointed out. 'But you are correct. It did complicate things. In the days before they left for America, Sandy and Duncan were busy making preparations. Duncan was going to dress in Cowan's dog-collar and dark woollen coat. He'd grown a half-decent beard by that time which he hoped would help mask his age. Duncan was a lot younger than Mackenzie Cowan. Sandy only had to play himself, although in many ways his was the harder job. There was so much he was leaving behind.'

'Did Granny know about Cowan's murder? Did she agree to Sandy leaving for good? Why couldn't he simply have come back after Cowan was declared dead?' Julia appeared exasperated.

'Apparently, Mother knew all about it. She'd been party to every single discussion. The aspect of this episode that you really need to grasp, Julia, is that they never expected to be able to cover up Mackenzie Cowan's murder. The villagers simply thought they might be able to hold off the authorities just long enough for Sandy and Duncan to flee the country and disappear somewhere. Then they could take the blame but would never be caught. As it turned out, the police didn't work out what they'd actually done for another 70 years. But Sandy was willing to make the sacrifice of never returning to Dallanaich, in order to save his sister from the noose.'

'And to protect the children of the village,' Imogen added, 'including his unborn child.'

'Do you think that Sandy and Duncan were also driven by a sense of duty to defend their youngsters and womenfolk? They must have felt some guilt at being exempt from active service. Perhaps this was their opportunity to show how they could act with selfless bravery.' Michael took a healthy swig of his single malt.

'That may very well be true,' Rob said. 'I spoke to my mother this morning. She said the last words Sandy exchanged with her were to implore Mum to find herself a good man - someone who would be a wonderful father to me.' Julia's dad paused to put a hand up to his face and rubbed vigorously at his eyes. Imogen thought for a moment he may need to stop, but Rob took a deep breath and carried on. 'Sandy and Duncan boarded the S.S Minerva with very little fuss. It was wartime and the ship was full of military personnel. The two men had the correct documentation so they didn't warrant much attention. The first part of the journey was very rough and just as Sandy told us; he was suffering from sea-sickness. But it wasn't just him up on deck unable to sleep that night, Duncan was there as well.

As the ship was torpedoed, the two friends were together. In all the panic there wasn't much time for them to think, but Sandy realised the situation could be used to their advantage. In the pandemonium of the evacuation they could both disappear. Sandy Thomson and Mackenzie Cowan would be presumed dead.

In these few precious moments, the conspirators divided out the money the villagers had scraped together for them. Sandy said that wherever they ended up, each of them should use their cash and documents to get to America and start a new life. It would have been too risky for either of them to try and contact the other, so they vowed not to. Then they shook hands on the agreement, climbed into separate lifeboats, and as far as I'm aware, they never set eyes on one another again.'

Chapter Sixty Two

Imogen encouraged the others to order some food. All this whisky on an empty stomach felt like a mistake, especially as the image of Mackenzie Cowan, lying prostrate on that chapel floor, kept flashing periodically across her mind's eye. Julia insisted she wasn't hungry, but Michael persuaded her to at least order a sandwich.

Imogen was desperate to find out how Rob knew all these details. She could not understand how the police had uncovered the conspiracy after all these years had passed. It must have meant there was a connection to some crime committed in the present day. Then she experienced another flash, this time it was an idea. 'Rob, does the death of Mackenzie Cowan have anything to do with the murders on Garansay this summer?'

Rob gave a wistful smile. 'Julia told us you were very clever. Yes, it does. The police finally apprehended the man who was hiding out in the hills of Garansay. His name is Richard Erskine and he killed Gordon Parker and Mackie Shaw. It was he who recounted this story.'

'So how did this Richard Erskine know about it?' Imogen sat back as the barman set down their plates of food. 'I think we discovered pretty much everything there was to know about the life Sandy Thomson led as Alex King, but we had no idea that Duncan Lambie had started a new life too. Does the murder of Gordon Parker have a connection to this other side of the puzzle? Was he linked to Duncan Lambie?'

Rob nodded. 'Duncan's lifeboat took him to the outer isles, from where he made his way back to

Glasgow. The money he had was just enough to secure passage on another liner bound for the Americas. Duncan travelled to New York City on Mackenzie Cowan's passport and he remained there for several months. He took on numerous jobs in hotels and bars and on station platforms. Duncan had always been able to overcome his physical disability. He never allowed it to hold him back. America was a place where new opportunities were opened up to him. As long as he worked hard, his lameness wasn't considered a problem.'

'That's what Granny said too, that Duncan didn't allow his disability to hold him back,' Julia added.

'At this stage of the war, America was experiencing something of a manufacturing boom. One of Duncan's workmates told him about the flourishing steel industry in Pittsburgh, Pennsylvania. So the young man headed down to Grand Central Station one day and got on a train to the city. He became an apprentice welder for one of the big corporations and that's where he stayed. Duncan was still living as Mackenzie Cowan when he met the woman he wanted to marry. She was called Elizabeth Parnell. The difference between Sandy and Duncan was that Sandy never told another living soul about his previous existence – not until he bumped into Kenneth Garvie in 1973 and was forced to. Duncan, on the other hand, told his new wife everything. She was a few years younger than him and happy to keep Duncan's secret. They had a daughter just after the war who they called Rosemary. But Duncan was always nervous about keeping Cowan's name. He worried that the clergyman's body would be found and the police would be led straight to him. So a few years later, the whole family changed their surname to Taylor. In the late 1960s, Rosemary Taylor started dating a local man called Franklin Parker. They married in the early 70s. Their son, Gordon, was born in 1972.'

'Ah, so Gordon Parker was Duncan Lambie's grandson,' Imogen chipped in.

'Yes, but he'd never known it. His mother was tragically killed in a car accident in 1979, when Gordon was just a young lad. He was brought up by Franklin and his family. It was only after his father died that Gordon began to dig into his mother's past. Her whole existence had always been a mystery to him and Gordon became obsessed with finding out about her.'

'And that brought the entire edifice tumbling down.'

'Aye, something like that. Gordon found out about the name change and discovered how his grandfather had been receiving letters from a lady in Drumnadrochit in the Highlands of Scotland. As I said, Duncan wasn't quite as good at cutting his ties as Sandy was. He and Annie had been writing to each other for decades. From the letter he read, Gordon ascertained that Annie had a step-son whom he believed might still be alive. Dougie Gibson had been married before and remained close to the son he had by his first wife. Because Annie was never able to have a child of her own, she became close to the boy too. Dougie's son had taken on his step-father's surname and was called Thomas Erskine. In the fifties, Thomas's wife had a wee boy called Richard. From the minute that wean was born, Annie adored him.'

'So Gordon Parker managed to track down the whereabouts of Thomas and Richard Erskine. Is Thomas still alive now?' Imogen asked.

'No he isn't. But Gordon struck up a correspondence with Richard instead. *He* was the reason that Gordon Parker came to Scotland.'

'Had Annie told her grandson all the gory details of

Cowan's murder? It seems a little peculiar.'

'I think we have to accept that Aunt Anne *was* a little peculiar. Although I suppose we can't blame her for that. Richard used to visit his Granny and Grandad at Glengarry Cottage from a young age. I vaguely recall Annie mentioning Doug's previous offspring but I never met them. In fact, I had very few dealings with her over the years – she reminded me of things I'd wanted to forget. So she focussed all of her attention on this wee boy. I don't know what age he must have been when she told him the full story, but I expect he was still quite young. Annie introduced it to him as a special secret, one that he had to promise to help his grandmother to keep.'

'Hugh would say that Annie was unburdening herself on the child. It would have been like a form of therapy for her. People do it all the time and hardly realise the damage they're inflicting. Children can be the most remarkably good listeners.'

'When Gordon Parker got in contact with Richard it must have seemed to him that the secret was about to come out. Parker was absolutely determined to keep digging into his family's past. Unfortunately, he confided his discoveries to the wrong person. Erskine fed Gordon bits and pieces of the story. He told him about Sandy and Duncan adopting new identities, but he had omitted to mention Cowan's murder. Richard informed Gordon that Sandy had changed his name to Alex King and settled in York Bay, Ontario.'

'Was it Gordon Parker who'd been to York Bay asking about the Kings?' Michael suddenly asked.

Rob looked a little surprised that his son-in-law knew this. 'He did do that, yes. Parker had even employed a private investigator at one stage. When Erskine got to hear all of this, he panicked. It was obvious that Gordon wasn't going to stop until he'd uncovered everything. So he enticed the man over to Scotland. Erskine said he possessed letters and documents which would reveal everything about Gordon's grandfather and his childhood in Scotland. But Erskine explained that he wasn't happy to post or scan them, and felt Parker needed to come over from America and read them himself.'

'It would have seemed perfectly natural, I suppose. Gordon can't have imagined he had anything to fear from Richard Erskine,' Julia said matter-of-factly.

'So when Gordon's Sailing Club organised a week's holiday at Cove Lodge on Garansay, he saw his chance. It provided him with a cover to visit Scotland and he would be able to meet up with Richard whilst he was there.'

'On the day Gordon was killed, he hung around the Cove for several hours, sending his luggage on ahead and missing his ferry,' Imogen supplied. 'Was it Erskine he had arranged to meet?'

'Yes. Gordon had decided to travel to Drumnadrochit to rendezvous with Erskine at Annie's old cottage, but Richard never had any intention that Gordon would get that far. Erskine didn't want anyone to spot them together. So he called Parker on his mobile on the Thursday morning, saying he'd travelled to Garansay and wanted to give him the letters straight away. Gordon was very keen to get his hands on the documents, so he was happy let the taxi go on ahead with his luggage and wait for the time they'd agreed to meet.

But a few minutes later, Mackie Shaw showed up at the kitchen window of Cove Lodge. He wanted to discuss his affair with Gillian Moore and ensure that Parker wasn't going to report him. This entire situation was a huge irritant to Parker. By this point he must have been wishing he'd never got involved with it. But he had an hour to kill, so he went out to join Mackie at the headland. It was raining heavily and they talked in Shaw's car. They sat in the vehicle, where it was parked at the Thorpe's holiday cottage. After smoothing things over, Gordon climbed out of the passenger seat and set off towards the planned meeting place at the point of the headland.

But Mackie didn't leave immediately. He stared out of the windscreen at Parker's retreating form. The young man watched, as if in a trance, right up until the moment when Parker reached Erskine and they shook hands. Richard quickly realised they had an audience and took a mental note of the car's registration number. Although, Erskine had been observing the Cove ever since he'd arrived on the island - he already knew who Mackie was.'

'What did Erskine do to Parker?'

'He led him right down into the shelter of the larger boulders. The man produced some plausible looking documents and handed them over. Gordon sat himself on a smooth rock and began eagerly flicking through them. Before he had time to realise he'd been duped, Erskine picked up a sharp, heavy stone and brought it down on Gordon's skull. He pocketed the American's mobile and the phoney papers. Then, he hauled Parker's unconscious form to the tip of the headland and tossed it into the waves. Erskine didn't much care if it washed up again later, he was fairly sure the body would get pounded by the rocks, making a cause of death difficult to identify.

Erskine was pleased that the disposal of Parker had been so straightforward, but he was concerned about Mackie Shaw. He didn't know how much the man had witnessed. So Erskine remained on the island. His accommodation was at a local B&B where he'd used a false name. No one had any reason to suspect him. Some nights he stayed out and watched Mackie's cottage from the hillside at the back. He formed a good picture of the man's movements. Erskine shifted to a guesthouse in Kilross so he could be closer to his quarry. He kept abreast of developments in the case by religiously reading the Garansay Recorder. The ladies who ran the guesthouses he stayed in were also an absolute goldmine of local gossip. It was from his landlady in Kilross that he discovered Mackie spent a solid twenty four hours being interviewed by the police. Then, suddenly, they let him go. This worried Erskine. He suspected that Mackie had told them something about what he'd seen on the morning of Parker's death, or he was about to. Either way, he had to get rid of him. He couldn't risk having Mackie identifying him in a line up and testifying against him in court.

Richard Erskine is a retired teacher and an expert in outdoor survival pursuits. His cover for being on Garansay was that he was on a hiking holiday, so he had a reasonable amount of kit with him. Richard knew that if he killed Mackie Shaw, it would have to be a cold-blooded attack and the police would be swarming the island within hours. He would need to lie low for at least a few weeks afterwards. So he planned this murder very carefully. Richard placed a change of clothes in his rucksack and left the rest of his luggage hidden under rocks on the hillside, where he could recover them later. He had a small tent and some essential equipment with him, including a Stanley knife. This is what he used to kill Mackie. Richard said it was surprisingly easy. He came down the hillside, slipped in through the gate in the fence and crept straight into Mackie's workshop. The poor man didn't stand a chance.'

'I'm amazed that Erskine provided the police with so much detail. The whole reason for him murdering

Parker was to stop the secret of Mackenzie Cowan's murder being revealed.'

'The police had got cast-iron evidence against him. He'd bought the Stanley knife from a hardware store in Inverness on his credit card and the implement has a serial number. They'd also found the letters from Gordon Parker in Erskine's flat. The D.C.I who I spoke to said they persuaded Richard Erskine to confess by explaining that his motive would actually garner some sympathy from a jury. It was his only hope for mitigation, particularly with the brutality of Mackie's murder. Erskine's solicitor agreed, although, the defence will be able to muddy the jury's opinion of Mackie in the courtroom. The man was no angel and he won't be there to defend himself. '

'I'm really glad we got the full story in the end, aren't you, Dad?' Julia enquired tentatively.

'Oh yes, darling,' Rob replied. 'In many ways, it explains everything.'

Chapter Sixty Three

The view from the sash window, of the perfectly calm Loch Linnhe with the hills of Lochaber in the distance, should have been having the effect of soothing Imogen's frayed nerves. It didn't appear to be working, so she had a long soak in the bath instead, nearly missing breakfast down in the residents' dining room.

By the time she entered, Rob and Jacquie had already finished their food. Plates bearing the smeared remains of sausage, bacon and eggs sat in front of them and they were now reclining in their seats, sipping tea.

'Do you mind if I join you?' Imogen asked.

'Not at all,' Jacquie smiled, shuffling along just a fraction so that Imogen could fit a chair at the table. 'Julia and Michael aren't down yet.'

'Yesterday's revelations must have taken it out of them. It took me a while to get off to sleep myself last night.'

'Jacquie and I are always early risers, regardless of whether or not the world is collapsing around our ears.' Rob smiled, to take the sting out of his words.

'Do you feel as if it is? I don't think you should.' Imogen accepted Jacquie's offer of a cup of tea from the pot.

'It will simply require a period of reflection in order to adjust. I've spent the last forty years believing my father to be guilty of the crime of abandonment. I now have to accept that his misdemeanour was of a different nature entirely. At my age, such a mind shift isn't easy to achieve. It's going to take some time.'

'But he never wanted to leave you. That must be

very important to know,' Imogen ventured to say, before she ordered a bowl of porridge from the waitress.

'Yes, it's very significant indeed.'

'Will Jim and Harry King have to be told the whole tale?'

'I expect it will be all over the internet when the news story breaks. They're bound to find out somehow,' Jacquie said.

'It would be better if they heard it from me. Perhaps Jacquie and I will make the trip to Canada in order to inform the family over there. It's going to come as a terrible shock. I feel it should be done face-to-face,' Rob added.

'I think that's a very good idea.' Imogen beamed broadly.

Imogen re-packed her overnight bag. Michael was going to give her a lift to Fort William so she could catch the train to Glasgow. She was just securing the zip when there was a knock at the door. Imogen paced across the room to open it.

'Hi Michael, sorry, I'm not quite ready yet.'

'A Detective Chief Inspector has just arrived in the bar downstairs. She's speaking with the proprietor. It seems her team have found something - the remains of a body.'

They walked down the carpeted staircase together. Julia and her parents were already sitting up at the bar. The detective and the manager were standing with them.

'Is it alright if we join you?' Michael asked politely, slipping an arm around his wife's shoulders.

'Of course,' the detective replied in a business-like voice, before introducing herself. 'My name is D.C.I Bevan and I'm in charge of the Gordon Parker and Mackie Shaw murder case.'

Imogen eyed the woman carefully. Bevan was strikingly attractive, with a short crop of dark brown hair. The policewoman appeared to be in her early thirties but Imogen knew she must be older than that to have reached the rank of D.C.I.

'At 9.30 this morning, a unit from the search team discovered a shallow grave lying roughly 500 feet up the hillside from the old chapel. We are currently in the process of bagging the contents, but at this stage we are fairly confident it contains the remains of Reverend Mackenzie Cowan. I have requested that a forensic anthropologist perform the tests on the skeleton, when we get it back to the lab in Glasgow.'

'Is there any chance you'll be able to *prove* it is Cowan?' Imogen asked.

Bevan sighed. 'We don't have any record of Cowan's D.N.A. However, a search will commence for surviving descendants of the man. We will also see if there are any dental records which remain extant. Sadly, I don't hold out much hope of that. But finding a living relative is definitely a possibility. We'll do our best. The circumstantial evidence, however, is absolutely compelling. Amongst the fragments of bone and clothing, we also found a metal object. It is totally intact.'

'The letter-opener,' Imogen supplied.

'Correct. This provides physical corroboration of the story that Richard Erskine gave us. I have to admit that before we spoke to you, Mr. Thomson, and started cross-checking the facts, we thought the man was spinning us one heck of a line. Now we've got the body, we know for certain that it was all completely true.'

Chapter Sixty Four

Bevan had often thought that the cry of a newborn baby was quite unique. It was impossible for anyone within hearing distance to ignore it. The noise emitting from the tiny bundle in her arms was no different. 'I'm not sure she likes me very much, Andy.'

The man chuckled. 'Amy's just not used to you, that's all. She does the exact same thing to me and Carol between the hours of midnight and two a.m.'

Bevan grinned unsurely, jiggling the baby up and down. 'It sounds a bit of a nightmare.'

'It gets easier. Or so I'm told.'

Andy retrieved the bottle from its carrier and leant forward to take Amy back into his arms. The little girl instantly settled as she locked her tiny mouth onto the teat and guzzled noisily.

'Just like me, she enjoys a drink,' Andy said with the raise of an eyebrow.

Bevan laughed. 'Not any longer, so I hear.' She looked the Detective Constable up and down. He must have lost at least a stone since they'd last worked together. Apparently, he now spent an hour in the gym each day and was sticking to a strict diet which only allowed for the occasional bottle of beer. 'When are you coming back?'

Andy gave a noncommittal shrug. 'In a month from now and I'll be cuffed to a desk for the foreseeable future.'

'You'll have to take it slowly, Andy, you know that. There's too much at stake.' Bevan placed her hand gently on the soft fluff which covered Amy's head.

'You're right.' He made an effort to look cheerful. 'And how about you, *Detective Chief Inspector*, any interesting cases in the pipeline?'

'We're still tying up loose ends from the Gordon Parker investigation. We need the evidence against Erskine to be watertight. There's also a possibility that we've found a relative of Mackenzie Cowan. Well, Phil has, anyway. She's called Megan McCrory and believe it or not she lives in Wisconsin, U.S.A.'

'Does that mean another trip to the States for you, Ma'am?'

Bevan looked immediately awkward, shifting from one foot to the other. 'I think it should be me that goes. The woman will really need the situation explaining very sensitively to her, before we take a D.N.A. sample.'

'Of course Ma'am. Just make sure it's not all work and no play when you get there. Take it from me, life's too short not to make the bloody most of it.'

*

Imogen couldn't believe that she was back on Garansay again so soon. The summer had now settled into a mild but windswept autumn. She drove Ian up to the island a couple of days ago and since then had barely set eyes upon him. He and Murray had been putting the final touches to the boat they would be taking out on the water for the round island race which commenced tomorrow morning.

Garansay was absolutely buzzing with excitement about the event. Coaches from all over Scotland were clogging up the narrow mountain roads and most of the hotels and guesthouses were full. Cove Lodge was providing the accommodation for a crew from Denmark who were competing in the race. Imogen knew the boys would be busy, but she couldn't resist making the short journey along the coast to the tiny bay where Ian and Murray were hard at work in the boat shed.

Imogen pulled the car up onto the grass verge at the top of the beach and strolled towards the house, recalling the day that the body of poor Gordon Parker was washed onto the shore. Richard Erskine was currently on remand awaiting trial. Imogen had been impressed by how few details about the case had leaked out to the press. Regardless of this, Rob and Jacquie took it upon themselves to fly to New Brunswick in order to explain the turn of events to Harry and Connie. She hoped this would mark the beginning of some kind of relationship between the three brothers. They were all keeping their fingers crossed.

Colin Walmsley was out in the yard, fixing a loose join in the guttering of the house as Imogen approached. He rose from his squatting position and kissed her on both cheeks. 'Are you looking forward to the race?' He enquired with a friendly smile.

'Oh yes, I'm very excited. Where will be the best place to watch?'

'I'm going to the Port na Mara Sailing Club. They've got an elevated lounge with superb views out over the Kilbrannan Sound. I should be able to see the boats go over the finish line from there. Would you, Julia and Michael like to join me? I can get you in as my guests.'

'We'd love to Colin. Thank you.'

'How are Hugh and Bridie?'

'Absolutely fine, thanks, but their terms started a couple of weeks ago and sadly couldn't come. Bridie is gutted, poor girl. I think she would have enjoyed the opportunity to see Murray again.'

Colin smiled ruefully, 'perhaps it's for the best she couldn't make it then. The lad seems to have that effect on women but I don't think he's particularly interested in finding a girlfriend at the moment.'

'No, he's young and wants to make something of his business. There's plenty of time for all that later on. Bridie's too young for him anyway. I'm pleased he's never taken advantage of her crush on him.'

Colin led his visitor towards the boat sheds, 'you should see what they've done to the yacht. It's really impressive.'

Imogen climbed up onto the jetty and the two of them entered the large shed, the smell of newly applied paint and varnish immediately assaulting their senses. Ian and Murray were working away at opposite ends of the hull, carefully touching up the bands of colour that they had added to the body of the boat.

'It's looking fantastic,' Imogen called out. 'I can't wait to see it in the water.'

'Hi Mum.' Ian put his brush down and came over. 'I'm glad you're here because Murray wanted to show you something.'

The shy young man emerged from the depths of the workshop and greeted the visitors warmly. 'Good. You're both together. I wanted to check if you approved of what Ian and I have done.'

Colin adopted a puzzled expression but allowed Murray to lead them around the underside of the impressive vessel to the bow, where a sticky sheet of transfer paper covered some freshly applied lettering. 'I've changed the name of the boat,' he said quietly. 'I hope I did the right thing. Somehow, it seemed appropriate.' He took hold of a corner and gently pulled back the strip, revealing the new name, which had been rendered in striking white: Mackie.

'I think it's very appropriate,' Imogen said, laying a hand on the lad's shoulder. 'You know, I've got a funny feeling you boys are going to win this race, and what a fitting memorial that would be.'

†

Acknowledgments:

My gratitude goes, as always, to my design and editorial team. Their hard work makes the production of my books possible.

If you enjoyed this book, please take a few moments to write a brief review. Reviews really help to introduce new readers to my novels and this allows me to keep on writing.

Many thanks

Katherine.

To find out more about Katherine Pathak's books, including special offers and new releases go to:

www.wordpress.KatherinePathak.com

or follow me on Twitter: @KatherinePathak

© Katherine Pathak, all rights reserved, 2014.

The Garansay Press

Made in the USA
Las Vegas, NV
24 February 2022

44498147R00160